Cox &
Shoppers

Julie Shorter

For Renny, Zoe and Chloe

Acknowledgements

This book wouldn't have been written without the help of countless generous people. Sincere thanks to …

Jane Reed, for letting me in on the world of Cabin Crew.

Anne-Marie Larkin, the loveliest Regatta Landlady in Henley-on-Thames, for her stories on sharing her home with international oarsmen.

Ben Needham, for an oarsman's (and an American's) view on the Royal Regatta and rowing in general. Any mistakes are mine.

Helen Pattinson, for invaluable advice and the rear cover image.

Special thanks to Lesley and Pete Lawes, for providing encouragement, technical support and for always seeing the funny side.

Alison Biddle, for endless patience and proof-reading.

Tim Ruddock and Pete Randolph from Agar Studios, Henley-on-Thames, for the front cover image.

Annabel Eyres, for the delightful illustration of the Henley Royal Regatta course.

Di Binley, at Rock the Boat, for putting me in touch with Annabel.

Sheena Oliver, Nina Randall and Kevin Thomas, a.k.a Tom.

Mum and Noel, for delicious dinners, hours of childcare and a comfortable chair.

Dad, for all those reminders that I had to crack on with it.

Everyone at YouWriteOn.com and Legend Press, for believing in new writers and giving them a chance.

As always, thanks to my beloved Renny, Zoe and Chloe for everything, above and beyond.

HENLEY ~ the Regatta course

START

Temple Island

Copas Enclosures

N / E / W / S

1/4 Mile

THE BARRIER — Cattle grid

the BUCKs station

The Bushes

Remenham Church

Remenham Farm

DOWNSTREAM

Women's Henley Enclosures

the BERKs station

Fawley Court

Fawley Boat House

FAWLEY (halfway)

3/4 Mile

Upper Thames R.C.

Green's Field
(car parks and picnics)

Remenham Club

Remenham Club Enclosure

Fawley Meadows

Women's Henley FINISH

Barn cottage

REMENHAM LANE

Selwyn's Field

1 Mile

General Enclosure

Lion Meadow

1⅛ Mile

Fawley Bar

Stewards' Enclosure

Phyllis Court

Progress Boards

Poplar Point

Butler's Field

Phyllis Court Stand

Bridge Bar

Press Box

Judge's Box — HRR FINISH 1 mile 550 yds

Boating Area

Little White Hart

Leander Club

The Little Angel

St Mary's Church

Red Lion

Henley Bridge

Regatta Headquarters

Angel on the Bridge

© Annabel Eyres

River & Rowing Museum

7

Chapter 1

With the sensitivity of a lover, Purser Rachel Ryder found the cabin temperature control's 'G-Spot', lulling the majority of passengers into a dry-mouthed slumber. The rest, a hard core of red eyed insomniacs, remained glued to their rear seat videos, not bothering the crew with air rage, premature labour or the sudden desire to open an emergency exit at 37,000 feet, let alone a request for a packet of cheesy biscuits or a G & T. Yet despite the pliant cargo Rachel was exhausted - still jet-lagged from her last trip: a back to back, London - New York - London, twice in under a week.

Slipping into one of the toilets she unbuttoned her waistband and with relief, rubbed the pink criss-cross impressions on her stomach. Something the on board 'How to have a Healthy Flight' tips page didn't mention, was that flying long-haul plays havoc with your guts, filling them with painful gas. Rachel had never quite figured out how the gas got in, but she knew only too well how it got out. Her passengers could squeeze out their unwanted wind into their seats, carefully adjusting each buttock to allow a discreet and controlled volume of air to escape. Rachel wasn't so lucky.

She concentrated instead on her face, removing her stale make-up and, to combat the aeroplane's arid recycled air, slathering on a heavy duty moisturiser. A generous layer of foundation, eye-shadow and lipstick, and several squirts of *Eau de Lancôme* later, she was once again ready to face her public. Closing the door behind her, she noticed that the other toilets were occupied and a queue had formed. 'Sorry to have kept you,' she smiled and re-opened the door. 'Here you go.'

At the front of the queue was an elderly Indian woman. A look of alarm passed over her face and Rachel assumed she was afraid of using the toilet, in case she got stuck inside. 'It's OK, I'll stay right here,' she said ushering the woman inside. 'You just knock when you're ready and I'll have you out in a jiffy.'

'Toilet I do not need. You come to help my husband, very sick,' said the woman, pushing past Rachel and scuttling back through the dimly lit cabin. Oblivious to the other passengers snoring, dribbling and farting, their dignity undone by communal travelling, Rachel followed.

'Here is my husband Ravinder Singh. You see, I can't wake him,' said the woman, grabbing a fist full of her husband's thinning hair and banging his head back against the headrest.

Turning on the overhead light Rachel cast herself in an unwelcome spotlight and several passengers turned to stare. Mr. Singh, no doubt expecting to feel the cold in the fickle temperatures of a British summer, wore a heavy anorak over his clothes and rivulets of sweat dripped off his ashen cheeks, leaving dark splashes on his collar.

'Mr. Singh! Mr. Singh, wake up!' Rachel said, brusquely tapping his shoulders.

Nothing. No flicker of life. Pressing the overhead call bell Rachel beckoned frantically to Steve, the Cabin Service Director, as he stuck his head through the galley curtains. Desperately, Rachel tried to remember her aviation medical training, was it 'Breathing, Airway, Circulation, Defibrillator' or was it 'Airway, Breathing, Circulation, Defibrillator?' More to the point, did it matter? It was obvious by now that the poor old sod didn't give a damn any which way. Rachel yanked off the old man's coat followed by his jumper and taking a firm grip on his shirt, ripped it open, shedding buttons like confetti. Underneath Mr. Singh wore a thick cotton vest.

At last, Steve appeared, carrying the on board medical kit.

'The guy's wrapped up like a pass the bloody parcel,' hissed Rachel under her breath, and grabbing a pair of scissors from the medical kit, hacked at the Indian's vest, exposing a mass of grey chest hair.

Steve wiped the sweat from his upper lip and passed Rachel a razor. 'That lot will have to come off or the pads won't stick.'

Quickly, she drew the blade across Mr. Singh's chest, making shiny nature trails amongst the forest of hair, and whipping off the protective backing, smacked the Defibrillator's sticky pads into position.

'Too high!' Steve said, his voice rising with hysteria.

Rachel yanked the pads off again, ripping out several stray hairs in the process. She flicked her tongue over her upper lip, now beaded with perspiration and slapped the pads on again, an inch lower than before and stared anxiously at Steve, as he read the Defibrillator's readout.

'No Shock Advised!' he said, grabbing the old man under the armpits. 'We're going to have to do CPR. Quick get him into the aisle!'

Rachel took hold of Mr. Singh's ankles and together they lifted his lifeless body onto the floor. The plane shuddered suddenly, hit by turbulence and an empty lager can rolled down the aisle and landed with a hollow ting against Mr. Singh's ear. Batting it away, Rachel pulled a face shield from the medical kit and fixed it to her mouth. She paused momentarily to glance at the old man's eyes, paper thin and clamped shut, before tilting his chin, so that his mouth fell open and she could cover it with her own. She breathed out deeply, willing the oxygen downwards, when suddenly she became aware that she was being watched, and turning her head ever so slightly, stared directly into Mr. Singh's eyes - wide open and terrified. Instinctively, her head snapped backwards, and rocking on her heels she tore the mask from her face.

Watching her, Mr. Singh shook his head disapprovingly. 'Why were you trying to kiss me?' he asked, before looking down at his shredded vest in amazement. 'And who has destroyed my underclothes?'

'I did Mr. Singh. I was trying to resuscitate you!' Rachel said, blushing.

Mr. Singh sighed and trying to sit up he said, 'This is most extraordinary.'

Trembling as her adrenaline levels began to drop, Rachel offered him her hand and when she spoke her voice was shrill. 'You can say that again Mr. Singh! You've had your clothes ripped off, you've been shaved, your wife's been rattling your head like a cocktail shaker and you slept through it all!'

Steve placed a restraining hand on her shoulder. 'Rachel, you're in shock, try to stay calm please.' He turned his attention to Mr. Singh who smiled beatifically, as if determined to see the bright side. 'Right, Mr. Singh let's make you a little more comfortable shall we?' Steve said, helping the old man back into his seat. 'The Captain will radio ahead for paramedics to meet us at Heathrow. We'll be given a priority landing slot and get you properly checked out, OK?'

Steve offered Rachel a hand getting up. 'I'll take over from here Rachel, go and get a hot drink and half an hour's kip. Well done.'

Rachel nodded and still shaking, made her way to the rear galley where a concerned colleague handed her a mug of tea.

'Thanks, I'm going to get my head down for a bit,' she said, disappearing into the crew bunk room.

The cramped communal couchette, hidden in the aeroplane's tail section, with four pairs of bunks stacked one above the other, reminded Rachel of an aristocratic family crypt; creepy and exclusive. Rachel sipped her tea and wishing that the rules allowed her something stronger, peeled off her uniform, damp with sweat, and slid into one of the lower bunks. She left the short, pleated curtain at the foot end which was meant for privacy, open, and shuddered at the thought of drawing it closed, knowing it would make her feel like a spectator at her own funeral. She lay watching the curtain twitch back and forth and feeling the whole bunk room shudder, fastened her seat belt over her blanket. Eventually, ignoring the cross winds buffeting the tail end of the plane, lurching and bouncing like an over excited puppy, she slipped into a fitful sleep and was relieved when at last, Steve came to tell her to take her seat for landing.

Several hours later at the crew report building, First Officer Josh Stewart wrapped his arms around Rachel's waist and kissed the back of her neck. 'Ughh, stale air-con and reheated chicken casserole. What's it called babe, Eau d'

Economy?' he said, wrinkling his perfect Roman nose.

Rachel laughed and shoved him off. 'Get lost you. You're not exactly fragrant yourself!'

Josh sniffed unimpressed. 'Neither would you be, if you'd been stuck in a space no bigger than an en-suite for the last seven hours!' he said, picking an imaginary hair from the silver striped cuff of his blazer. As the youngest First Officer on the fleet he was still in the habit of admiring the way light tripped off the silver thread.

'Who are you trying to kid?' Rachel said, suddenly in no mood to pander to his ego. 'You were in your bunk for two hours and don't try to deny it because we could all hear you snoring!'

Josh scowled. 'At least I didn't carry out CPR on a heavy sleeper!'

'Nobody could sleep through what I did to that guy. I swear Josh, I thought he was dead!' said Rachel, blushing at the memory.

Josh shook his golden head in disbelief. 'There's no way I'm dropping off on the way home, you might start thumping my chest and sticking your finger down my throat!' And smirking, he asked. 'How was your de-brief?'

Rachel shrugged and sat down on the corner of her suitcase. 'You know what it's like when you've had a medical case on board. Suddenly all the managers start acting like they're in an episode of *E.R.* I'd like to see them try C.P.R with 300 people watching.' She looked up scanning the airport's perimeter track, saying crossly, 'And where the hell is the crew bus? They're supposed to come every ten minutes.'

Moments later, a bus pulled onto the forecourt in front of them and pulling Rachel onto her feet, Josh said, 'Here it is my sweet. You jump on and I'll load the cases.'

Numb with exhaustion, they sat in silence as the bus delivered them to the staff car park. Home to hundreds of cars, each bus-stop was identified with a letter and a number, designed to act as an aide memoir for jet-lagged crew. The bus did a full circuit, offloading its passengers at regular intervals until only Rachel and Josh remained on board. The driver sniffed loud enough for them to hear before swinging the bus around in an exaggerated arc and beginning another tour of the car park.

'Shit! We're going round again,' said Josh, suddenly ducking down. 'And there's the Skipper. Don't let him see me or I'll never live this down. How many black Golfs can there be in this damn car park?'

Rachel stared out of the window at the milky blue of an English summer morning. 'I've counted at least nine,' she said. 'Maybe I should have tied a giant red luggage strap round the car, like people do with their suitcases.'

Suddenly Josh jumped up, frantically pointing. 'Look! There it is in D2. Thank you Driver, you can let us down here,' he said, tugging Rachel's arm. 'Get a move on or I'll be late for my match.'

As Josh loaded the Golf's generous boot with their suitcases, Rachel felt a familiar twist of frustration. On joint trips they were forced to take her car rather than Josh's Porsche, with its miniscule and therefore useless boot, and somehow he always managed to persuade her to drive home, while he slept peacefully in the passenger seat beside her. True to form he settled down for a snooze, before she had a chance to pull onto the airport's perimeter track.

The track ran parallel with the airfield and for a short distance, before her turn off for the M4 motorway, Rachel fought the urge to race an Air Portugal Airbus, taking off on the eastern runway. Overtaking a cargo truck instead, she slipped into the fast lane of the west bound carriage way, clicking on the air-conditioning to keep her awake and turning the radio on low for company. She looked across at the east bound traffic, where thousands of cars sat nose to tail in the early morning rush hour and felt lucky by comparison. The pain of a red eye flight was a breeze compared to a daily commute to London.

Josh mumbled in his sleep and Rachel stole a brief glance, before turning her attention to the road ahead, marvelling how he managed to look so attractive, even after a long-haul flight. Often, she would try to catch him with crusty eyes or a dribble trail on his chin, as he emerged from the Flight Crew rest bunk which was squeezed like Dr. Who's Tardis in a space behind the cockpit, but she was always disappointed. With his aquiline profile and his blond hair softly curling onto his face, he reminded her of an emperor embossed on a Roman coin.

Glancing at the green hedgerows she realised that they were nearly home, but disconcertingly she had no recollection of coming off the motorway onto the scenic A-road, that led to the riverside town of Henley-on-Thames.

'Perils of the job,' she said to herself, struggling to recall a time when she'd felt totally awake.

'What?' slurred Josh, suddenly re-surfacing.

Rachel sighed. 'Nothing, I was talking to myself as usual.'

Josh stared out of the window and shrugged. 'Sorry, I was knackered.'

Instantly Rachel saw red. 'You're knackered! I served dinner and breakfast to sixty snotty business men, cleaned up two lots of puke and had to bring someone back from the dead and what did you do? Flick the bird onto autopilot and play Sudoku!'

Josh opened his mouth to protest but Rachel was on a roll. 'And I've driven us home ... as usual!'

'Look, we're both knackered ... OK?' He sighed as if placating a small child and closed his eyes again.

They crossed the bridge over the Thames and, deciding to take a leaf out of Mrs. Singh's book, Rachel accelerated hard so that Josh's head banged sharply against the headrest. On the town side the traffic lights changed to red, and rather than make eye contact with Josh and risk starting another argument, she stared out of the driver's side window. The café opposite advertised 'Full English Breakfast or Tea and Buttered Crumpets', and the pavement was awash from the dripping hanging baskets above. Further up the road, in the town square, were bright bedding plants in tidy rows and shiny green black benches hallmarked with a bold 'H', topped with a golden crown. The ancient river town was comfortingly English and Rachel found its predictability reassuring; it meant home - no time zones, no playing Russian roulette with malaria pills and no foul smelling insect repellent but also, unfortunately, it meant no room service. The lights changed and momentarily she was tempted to pull over and pick up some croissants; a French market was coming to life in the square and she could smell the sweet, candy-floss scent of crêpes, but she drove on; she daren't risk putting Josh in a worse mood.

With a sigh of relief she found a parking space just two doors along from 'Cygnets' Nest', the elegant white town house they'd been thrilled to call their own for the last two years. Dumping their suitcases in the hall Josh disappeared upstairs and Rachel made for the basement; her favourite part of the house. Having spent several hours, miles above the earth's surface she found the subterranean kitchen, with its mellow oak cabinets and low ceiling, a comfort. Kicking off her flight shoes, she pressed her sore feet into the refreshing coolness of the slate floor and as she filled the kettle, ran her hand along the work surface, re-connecting with home. The cat flap opened with a pop and a dishevelled grey face glared at her through the gap.

Rachel looked up and beckoning the cat forward, she said, 'Don't be such a grump, Biggles. You can't have the house to yourself all the time, mummy and daddy have to come home sometime.'

The cat remained motionless, considering his options, before sliding the rest of his body into the room. Knowing that she would have to make the first move, she scooped him up and sniffed. He smelt of the garden, having recently swapped his spring bed of burnt out bonfires for lush piles of freshly cut grass. Her dark blue uniform was a magnet to his fur, so with a final delicious sniff of his outdoor scent; she let him down and made tea; *English Breakfast* for her and *Redbush* for Josh.

Next she checked the post; three bills, a flyer for a new pizza delivery service and a *Betterware* catalogue with a flowery handwritten note attached from 'Your friendly, local distributor - Linda', requesting to be left outside for collection on Thursday. Rachel glanced at the calendar on the fridge. Shit! Today was Friday. The last time she'd apologised to *Betterware Linda* for the late return of her catalogue, she'd been forced to listen to a doorstep rant about how difficult it was to run a small business and how people like Rachel made it more so. This time, Rachel resolved to tell her that she had better things to do with her precious days off than search for a new sink tidy and no, she couldn't return the catalogue as it was now perfectly at home in Biggle's litter tray!

The red flashing light on the answer phone indicated that they had two messages. She pressed the replay button and smiled as she heard a familiar voice.

'Hi, it's Sarah. Hope you had a great time in NY or was it Jo'burg? I can't keep up with you sometimes. Biggles is fine... but then you know that if you are listening to this don't you? ... Did you manage to get the B...a...r...b...i...e for Millie? She's been driving me potty about it. I think that's it... oh, and I made extra cassoulet so there's a pot of it in your fridge ... you just have to reheat it on the hob, OK? TTFN.'

Click

'Hi, it's Andrew, Sarah's brother. Thanks for your message. I'll come round as soon as I can, maybe Saturday.'

Click

Josh appeared at the door dressed in chinos and a navy polo shirt, embroidered with 'Isis Golf Club' in curly white script, an inch above his left nipple.

'Was that the gardening guy?' he asked, taking a carton of milk from the fridge and sniffing it suspiciously. 'Man of few words isn't he?'

'I guess he's busy. Could you finish the teas while I jump in the shower?' On her way out she glanced at the kitchen clock. She had precisely twenty-seven minutes to do the test and manoeuvre Josh into position.

She showered quickly and as she towelled dry, pondered the wisdom of dating a guy ten years her junior.

Between the sheets they were a match made in heaven but they were hardly what she would call a meeting of minds. Right now she reminded herself, it wasn't his mind she was interested in.

With a heavy sigh, she lifted the lid off the Ali-Baba laundry basket and reached into its depths until her fingers curled around a thin, cellophane wrapped box. Removing the contents she threw the instruction leaflet in the bin. She didn't care to remember the number of times she'd squatted over the toilet and aimed at the 'paddle,' and she had the two minute waiting routine timed to the last second; remove eye-make up, brush and floss teeth, and comb in two squirts of leave-in conditioner for 'fly-away' hair (which always made her laugh). By which time, the two blue lines may or may not, have miraculously appeared in their tiny windows of opportunity.

'Any plans for your days off?' Josh asked, tapping the space next to him on the sofa as she reappeared in the kitchen, wrapped in a silk dressing gown.

Rachel nodded and sat down. 'I thought I'd make a start on the garden. Sarah's brother is coming round to give me a quote but I'm not sure he'll be interested in our little postage stamp. You could cut our lawn with nail clippers.'

'I wouldn't know. It's not my bag, flowers and horse shit!' he laughed and having lost interest in the conversation already, turned to his latest copy of *Flight International*.

Rachel glanced at her watch. Fourteen minutes left, that was really pushing it but guys were always up for a quickie – weren't they? Pretending to stretch, she lifted her feet onto the coffee table making sure that her dressing gown slipped open, exposing what she hoped was a tantalizing flash of thigh. Nuzzling his neck she said, 'Babe …'

'Umm,' he said, not taking his eyes off an article discussing the pros and cons of scramjet technology.

Undeterred she continued. 'The timing's just right you know.'

'Hardly Rachel, I'm due to tee off in ten minutes,' Josh said, not looking up from the page.

Rachel tried to hide her frustration. 'But we've got two blue lines on the ovulation predictor, by the time you get back from golf it might have changed to one.'

'For Christ sake not that again!' he said, hurling his magazine onto the coffee table.

Rachel stared at him open-mouthed. 'What do you mean, not that again? It's the only way I can tell what my body's doing. You know my periods are all over the place. My ovaries don't know what time zone they're in, let alone the time of the month!'

Josh jumped up, knocking her feet off the coffee table onto the stone floor. 'So what?' he spat, saliva fizzing at the corners of his mouth as if he were literally bubbling over with rage. 'Isn't it the same for all crew? Perils of the job, you're always telling me.'

In her confusion, she forgot the searing pains that were now shooting up her legs. Why was he so angry all of a sudden? Hadn't he shared her disappointment every month, when once again she'd had to pack a box of tampons in her cabin bag?

'It only matters when you're trying to conceive,' she said quietly. 'I thought it's what you wanted too.'

Still irritated, Josh glanced at his watch. 'I really don't have time for this. I think we should forget the baby thing for a while, maybe you should go back on the pill and give us both a breathing space.'

Rachel felt the room tip sideways. 'I don't have time for a breathing space,' she pleaded. 'I'll be forty next year!'

Frantically she searched his face and at last saw what she was looking for; a flicker of compassion in his eyes. Maybe he did care after all, she thought; maybe she'd just pushed too hard or maybe it had finally dawned on him that he was shacked up with a peri-menopausal old nag?

But then he looked away and picking up his car keys, tipped them from one palm to the other, as if physically weighing up the advantages and disadvantages of his decision. 'I'm sorry Rachel. I've been meaning to say something for a while now. I'm not ready to play happy families. I want to concentrate on my career, have a bit of fun … like we used to. I've made up my mind and you need to make up yours, it's me or baby, not both. I'll ask Jerry if I can stay over at his for a few days, to give you time to think.'

In an effort to stop herself begging him to stay, Rachel sipped her tea. The signs, she realized, had been there for months but Josh's excuses of jet-lag or a sore back from all the hours he spent hunched up in a cockpit not much bigger than bathtub, had seemed reasonable at the time. But how could she ever forgive him for asking her to choose?

He left the room without looking back and she listened to his footsteps on the floor above, mentally tracing his journey from wardrobe to drawers, as he pushed spare clothes into his suitcase still packed from their trip. She listened to the clunk-clunk thud of its hard plastic wheels on the stairs, leaving tell-tell tracks on the carpet for her to rub out later with furious fingers and, finally, the reproachful click of the front door closing. Slowly, wincing from the pain in her legs, she got up and poured her tea down the sink. In the absence of the longed for croissants or anything else resembling breakfast, she tipped Sarah's cassoulet into a saucepan and reheated it on the hob.

Noticing the lining in Biggle's dirt tray was past its best, she tipped the repugnant contents into a bin liner and relined it with great care, ensuring the torn pages of *Flight International* sat snug inside the grey plastic. Satisfied that the cat now had somewhere clean and interesting to crap, she took a bottle of wine and the steaming stew up to her bedroom.

All visible male signs were gone, only the scent of Josh's after-shave lingered. Placing her tray on the bedside table she pushed open the large sash window, allowing a breath of summer drizzle to blow into the room. Below, she could see a dry grey rectangle on the road where Josh's Porsche had been and she watched, forgetting the casserole congealing in its bowl, until the pale grey merged with the black tarmac, swallowed by the rain.

Chapter 2

Naked and sweating, Rupert Fotheringham-Allen stepped out of the summer house into the brilliant afternoon sunshine and feeling a dull ache in his lower back, bent to touch his toes and perform several squats. Lucy was such an athletic girl that sometimes he found it difficult to keep up with her sexual demands. As usual though, he'd pulled out all the stops and they'd both fallen into a contented post coital snooze. Then, awakened by a noise from the garden, he'd decided to go in search of champagne and cigarettes. He walked barefoot across the immaculate lawn, still damp from the morning's rain, and as he rounded a mature Buddleia, smashed headlong into a wheelbarrow coming in the opposite direction.

'Christ almighty!' he yelled, hopping on one leg, clutching at one shin then the other. 'What the hell are you doing here?'

'It's Friday. I always do your garden on a Friday,' said the gardener, concentrating hard on the contents of his wheelbarrow, to avoid getting an eye full of his employer's floppy cock. 'If it's not convenient I've got a turfing job over in Hambleden I can be getting on with.'

Suddenly, remembering that he was stark bollock naked, Rup forgot his bruised shins and pulled a branch over his exposed manhood. 'Might be a good idea Andrew old chap and I can carry on with the nuddy sunbathing, eh?'

Rup had to get rid of him before Lucy emerged from the summer house demanding to know where her champagne had got to. The trouble was he couldn't be sure exactly what Andrew had seen, or just as damning, what the blasted gardener had heard! The summer house doors had been wide open and Andrew came and went as he pleased; he could have been dead heading the roses, just feet away from Lucy, screaming in orgasmic bliss.

'I'll be off then Mr. Fotheringham-Allen,' said Andrew, turning his wheelbarrow round and heading off in the direction of his van, which he'd parked at the front of the house.

Rup sprinted after him, grabbing the nearest thing to hand from the washing line. Could he count on Andrew's discretion? He wasn't sure. He would have to do what he always did when the going got tough; he would buy his way out. Paying for Andrew's silence would cost him a lot less than a messy divorce from Carolyn.

Andrew was packing up his tools and only his legs could be seen underneath the back door of the van. Barefoot, Rup appeared soundlessly. 'How are things in the gardening business these days?' he asked, making Andrew jump and crack his head on the roof of the van.

'Shit that hurt! … err, fine thanks Mr. Fothering …'

'Rupert, please.'

'Fine thanks … Rupert.'

'Got any large contracts lined up? I know lots of wealthy business people, perhaps I could …'

Andrew cut him off. 'I'm always pleased to have recommendations Mr. Fother … Rupert, but I wouldn't want any special favours. I've got friends in the business and we like to play fair, win work by our own labours. If word got round that I was involved in something dodgy…'

Christ, thought Rup, this was going to be harder than he'd imagined. The gardener was so straight it was turning his stomach. 'No, of course not, nothing dodgy, far from it old chap but a helping hand never hurt anybody.'

'Agreed,' nodded Andrew reluctantly. 'But as my grandfather always said, "hard graft never hurt anybody and there's nothing like an honest pound in your pocket".'

Rup had to swallow his disgust, at what he considered sentimental bullshit, and he interrupted before Andrew had the chance to continue. 'Yes, yes fine virtues but did they get your grandfather very far?'

Andrew bristled at the dig at his recently deceased grandfather, a man he'd looked up to all his life. 'Yes, they did.' He glanced over Rup's shoulder to the palatial pile that was the Fotheringham-Allen residence, 'Perhaps not by some people's standards but he did well enough to leave me a generous amount in his will.'

'Enough to change your life?' pressed Rup, finding it hard to believe that the naïve little twerp would still be cutting his lawn if he'd come into a serious amount of cash.

Andrew pulled himself up to his full height, which at six foot four was significantly taller than Rup and glowered at his boss. 'Enough to buy another van and maybe employ someone, expand the business.'

'Yes, yes I can see that,' said Rup, suddenly feeling defenceless, clothed only in a temporary loincloth honed from his wife's 'Hot Stuff!' gym vest. He stepped back so that the van door stood between them. 'Yes, you could do that of course and it would be splendid but invested in the right place, say the Bulgarian property market, your windfall could bring you huge dividends and you could buy hundreds of vans! In fact, I can personally guarantee it!' he said, gesturing at his property with a wide sweep of his arm. 'After all, how do you think I paid for all of this?' He saw a brief, wistful look sweep across Andrew's face and knew that he'd hooked him; it was like taking sweets from a baby. 'I would be delighted to invest the money on your behalf,' he continued, 'and I give you my word that you will be more than happy with the result.'

Andrew's head was spinning. Less than five minutes ago he'd been trying to avoid going eyeball to eyeball with his boss's penis and now Rup was offering to invest his grandfather's money in a place he'd barely heard of. As he looked into Rup's eager face his strongest urge was to tell him to get knotted; but the guy did have a point. Rup was obviously a man who knew how to make serious money and if his dreams of running an organic gardening business were ever going to take off it was going to take a large amount of cash. Since the reading of the will, the weight of responsibility of spending his grandfather's hard earned money had been weighing on his mind, and suddenly the thought of handing it over to a successful business man such as Rupert felt like a blessed relief.

'It's a tempting offer Mr. Fother ... Rupert, but it's come out of the blue. I think I'd like to sleep on it.'

Rup shrugged. 'Sleep away but you won't find a better

offer. The proof's right in front of you.'

Andrew hesitated. His eyes flicked over the house – there had to be at least ten bedrooms.

Seizing his moment, Rup grabbed Andrew's hand, pumping it firmly. 'You know a good opportunity when you see one. I can see it in your face. You know it makes sense. Who needs sleep eh? Sleep is for wimps, not men like us. And by the way, the little incident of my sunbathing in the buff ... would rather that didn't go any further. Mrs. F-A thinks I'm a little old for that sort of a lark and we don't want to upset her do we?'

Railroaded Andrew gaped, his head caught somewhere between a nod and a shake.

'Excellent. Will keep you posted on the Bulgarian front. Remember not a word to anyone.' Rup tapped his nose with one perfectly manicured finger and walked back to the house. Feeling a familiar stirring under the baby pink gym vest, he wondered if Lucy was awake.

Chapter 3

With the weekend papers squeezed under her arm, Rachel dragged the steamer chair into the sun and was delighted to see dirty grey tracks appear on the pristine patio. Then, dumping the papers she placed a mug of coffee on one of the arm rests and a packet of Marlborough cigarettes on the other and sat, hugging her knees. For the last six months she'd given up all of her favourite treats; wine, soft cheese, coffee and cigarettes, but now that a baby was no longer on the agenda she could see no further reason to deny herself. She took a cigarette from the packet, lit it and settled back to enjoy but winced as something sharp stabbed her left buttock, and pushing her fingers down the back of the plump seat cushion, she found a tube of factor 50 sunscreen. 'And you can get lost too,' she said, lobbing it through the French windows. 'You can stick your UVA micro-bloody filters. I'll bake myself as brown as a camel's arse if I want to!'

Even if she did overdo the sunbathing, she was confident that she had a miracle cream on her dressing table that would return her skin to its golden best. At the airline's 'Grooming Rooms' the world's top beauty products were always available at cut price and the Cabin Crew encouraged to avail themselves of the latest beauty treatments. Seven days a week crew of both sexes were waxed, exfoliated, plucked, buffed, massaged and polished to perfection by a legion of hairdressers and therapists.

Like the *Stepford Wives* of the air, the crew were told what to do, when to do it and how to dress, from the height of their heels and the diameter of their stud earrings, to what shade of lipstick to wear. Any plans of a personal nature, from a family wedding to elective surgery required an application for annual leave, months in advance. Spontaneity was not an option. To the thousands of young hopefuls, who every year completed their application forms to become Cabin Crew, this was a small price to pay for a year round tan, and the opportunity to buy all the fake Gucci they could get their hands on.

Drawing deeply on her duty-free cigarette and shuddering with pleasure as the nicotine filled her lungs, Rachel wondered, and not for the first time, whether the airline was her employer, or her pimp. Exhaling slowly, she watched a delicate blue butterfly rest briefly on the end of her chair and then take off on a meandering course up the garden, before disappearing into the pink froth of her neighbour's climbing rose. 'That's it, bugger off why don't you,' she shouted after it. 'You won't find any pollen in this garden. We're all barren here you know!'

'Hello. Is there anyone at home?' called a disembodied male voice from the passage at the side of the house.

Rachel sat up with a start, sloshing coffee into her lap. Who the hell was it? Had *Betterware Linda* sent the boys round? Had she been late returning the catalogue once too often? Biting anxiously on her cigarette she decided to sit it out, in the hope that whoever had come to bug her would soon give up and go away.

'Hello … Rachel. Are you there?'

Damn; it was Andrew. She'd have to let him in as he'd only agreed to come over as a favour. Reluctantly, she stubbed out her cigarette and reached for her sunglasses, grateful she'd chosen an Aviator style that masked half her face. She opened the gate and remembering her spilt coffee, offered him a drink.

'That would be great, thanks. It's going to be a hot one I reckon,' he said, following her through the French doors into the kitchen.

Rachel pulled two beers from the fridge and handed him one. She watched his Adam's apple slide gratefully up and down, as he downed its contents in one. Blonde, muscle-bound and with mud-streaked tanned legs emerging from dusty work boots, he reminded her of an Australian lager advert.

'What plans have you got for the garden?' he asked, waving the empty bottle towards the pool of sunshine beyond the French doors. 'Shall we?'

'I'm not sure really. Somewhere private to sunbathe and …' she said, stepping onto the patio she remembered the butterfly and quickly added, 'lots of flowers…you know for the wildlife. I hope that doesn't sound too Miss World. I'm not really a save the planet, help old people type of girl, but a bit of colour wouldn't go amiss.'

'Well, that's a very good place to start.' He laughed and bent down to right a pot of geraniums that was lying on its side, its petals scattered and torn. Rachel blushed remembering the furious kick she'd given it on her way out to drip dry her uniform.

'It's very dry,' he said, straightening up and showing her a handful of dusty soil. 'Most of your pots could do with a good soaking. Why don't I get the hose on them now, while you talk me through your ideas?'

'I … um, OK,' she stuttered, realising that until recently, the only thing she'd considered cultivating was an all over tan and her mind was a horticultural desert. She watched as he gave her dehydrated plants a desperately needed drink and doubted that even his green fingers could coax life into the crispy brown husks.

'They're in a bit of a state aren't they?' he said.

Rachel shrugged and bent to stroke the cat who had come to investigate. 'I'm away so much. I fly long-haul you see … everything dies on me, perils of the job I guess. Biggles would be six feet under if it wasn't for Sarah.'

At the mention of his sister Andrew frowned and began to coil the hose onto its wall mounted bracket. Funny, she thought, Sarah's always raving about how close they are and she hadn't mentioned any argument between them, but not wishing to pry, she switched the subject back to the matter in hand.

'The thing is Andrew I'll come clean with you, I know absolutely nothing about plants or gardening. If Charlie Dimmock is here on the scale of gardening knowledge,' she said, waving one hand above her head and pointing the other at the floor, 'then I'm about here! And whatever plants we choose, they're going to end up 'latch key' kids I'm afraid.'

'As in, they need to be able to look after themselves,' Andrew laughed, taking a dog-eared notebook and a pencil stub from his back pocket. 'That's fine Rachel. I've never had such a succinct spec but I can work with it, don't worry.'

'Great, I wasn't very hopeful that you'd want to work in such a small garden. Sarah told me how busy you are.'

'She's right. I've got a list as long as your arm of old biddies wanting an hour's weeding or a shrub moved to a sunnier spot. Sarah's always telling me to charge more or drop them from my list but they get so depressed when they can't manage their gardens,' he said, shrugging apologetically. 'I'm just an old softie I guess.'

'Or a gentle giant?' Rachel suggested, sipping her beer.

'I don't know about that but I'd certainly like to move into horticulture on a much bigger scale. Organic farming, that's my dream.'

'But wouldn't that mean moving away? Surely there's not much agricultural land in the Thames Valley.'

Andrew shook his head. 'There are pockets if you know where to look. In fact there's a small holding on the edge of town that I've had my eye on for years. You might know it; 'Water Meadows', they run the farm shop on the main road. Rumour has it they're planning to sell.'

Rachel nodded. 'I know the place. I imagine it's a bit of a struggle for them with the hypermarket just around the corner.'

Andrew nodded. 'It is but even farm shops have to move with the times and I've got so many ideas. All wishful thinking unfortunately, unless I can come up with some serious cash,' he said, and smiling at the memory of his naked boss, he added, 'although I may have stumbled on a potential goldmine.'

'Oh yes, tell me more,' Rachel asked, intrigued.

'No, I was sworn to secrecy.' He shook his head and a look of concern clouded his face. 'But if I can pull it off at least I'll be able to help Sarah out of that damn hole, her idiot of a husband has got them into!'

'What hole? What do you mean?' she asked, insulted that her best friend should be in trouble and she didn't know.

'She must have told you Rachel, their crippling mortgage and the threatening letters from the building society. They're up to their necks in it!'

Rachel shook her head and without thinking, took off her glasses to rub her eyes. Andrew frowned, noticing how her eyes were red and swollen. 'Here I am going on about my sister's problems, when I shouldn't even be talking about it,' he said, gently touching her arm, 'and you've had a problem of your own today haven't you?'

Rachel looked into his concerned face that was so much like Sarah's and fought back a fresh round of tears. 'I'm fine,' she sniffed, determined not to break her golden rule of never crying in public. 'It's hay fever, lots of people get it at this time of year.'

Andrew nodded sympathetically. 'Poor you,' he said. 'I've never suffered myself, good thing too I guess, with my chosen profession. Well, as long as you're OK I'll start taking some measurements.'

He pulled a measure tape out of his pocket and turned his back, allowing her to regain her composure while he began to measure the depth of the patio. Without knowing exactly why, but unable to stop herself Rachel found herself blurting to his back. 'I just found out that Josh doesn't want a baby, at least not with me anyway.'

'Umm, that would definitely make hay fever worse,' he said, turning around to face her. 'Maybe he just got scared, commitment stuff … it frightens us big strong men you know. Give him time.'

Her face flushed. 'That's just it, I can't afford to wait … I'm forty next year. My eggs are almost OAPs!'

'If that's the case maybe you shouldn't wait. If having a baby is that important perhaps it's time to think about going it alone,' he said quietly. 'We have to be true to ourselves Rachel. We can't go around living other people's dreams, pretending to be what others want us to be. Remember that.'

Rachel stared at him open mouthed, they were

supposed to be discussing her herbaceous borders not the virtues of single motherhood, but he made it sound so simple. Maybe wading through a dearth of reluctant males was merely muddying the waters. Should she cut out the middleman and go straight to the sperm bank?

Andrew returned her gaze, his face as calm and certain as if he'd suggested a nice little evergreen climber to cover the trellis either side of the French doors. She could tell he meant every word, but something told her that he was trying just as much to convince himself and she couldn't help wonder what he was pretending to be and to whom. Unspoken questions darted between them like the swarms of Mayflies buzzing above their heads.

At last breaking the spell, Andrew tapped his notepad with his pencil. 'Must get cracking. Forget all that stuff I said about Sarah, I'm sure they've got it all in hand. I'll take a few measurements and pop back later in the week with some ideas, OK? Cheers for the beer.'

Rachel nodded and feeling overwhelmed by the turn in their conversation, sought refuge in her kitchen. Taking another beer from the fridge she watched him through the open window, pressing the icy bottle into her burning cheeks, her mind tumbling with images of nameless babies, test tubes and how attractive Andrew looked in his denim cut-offs. Through conversations with Sarah she felt she knew him, but in reality they had met only a handful of times. Maybe he felt the same way she thought; it would certainly explain why they had bared their souls over a tub of withered geraniums!

He signalled to her that he was leaving and she wasted no time locating her mobile phone. Sarah was in trouble. The *Lady Chatterley's Lover* fantasies could wait. Glancing at her watch she realised it was lunchtime and Sarah would be up to her eyes feeding her hungry brood. A text would have to do.

Across town, a chrome fridge hummed smugly in it's mortgaged up to the hilt new home and Sarah cursed as she wiped off yet another greasy finger print. She sighed, remembering her old off-white fridge in her old, shabby kitchen.

'Blasted thing I didn't want you, just like I didn't want this stupid house!' she said, jumping as her mobile phone buzzed from the kitchen table. It was a text from Rachel.

Sarah, drink chez moi. 8pm. Need to talk. Urgent.

Urgent sounded ominous. Had Rachel caught someone else playing with Josh's joy-stick? she wondered.

OK. R U OK? Sounds serious!

Rachel's response was instant.

It is.

Throwing her mobile into her handbag, Sarah checked the shoulder of lamb roasting contentedly in the Aga. She hadn't wanted the cumbersome cooker anymore than she'd wanted the American fridge but Dave had insisted. They were all the trappings of his grand plan. Six months ago, he'd come home from work, declaring that they were upping sticks and moving to the famous Royal Regatta town of Henley-on-Thames. Sarah remembered how determined he had been.

'I just don't know why you can't see it darling. The house prices in Henley are rocketing and if we move now we can make a killing in a few years time. Think of the children,' he'd implored, knowing they were her Achilles heel. 'The schools are great. We'll be able to walk into town for the shops and restaurants. Harry will be able to learn to row, you'll be nearer to your mother and to Rachel, everything will be so much more…'

Sarah jumped in. 'Expensive!'

'No, I was going to say up market. Don't you want that for our children?'

'Well, now that you ask I'm not sure that I do. I like it here and if we move it will mean a huge mortgage and I'll have to go back to work. When will I see the kids?'

'Now you're just being melodramatic,' he bristled. 'Of course you'll see the children and yes, you might need to get a little part-time job but think of the fun we'll have at weekends … walks by the Thames, family games of tennis at the club.' His eyes glazed over with his 'up-market' thoughts.

'I can walk by the river here, you great plank! In case

you've forgotten the Thames flows through Reading on its way to Henley! And you've always enjoyed playing tennis at the leisure centre without all that up itself club nonsense.'

'It's up itself for good reason Sarah. I mean, it is actually up there. Half the celebs on telly live around Henley, swanning about at the Regatta, mixing with all the right people, making connections and if it's good enough for them it's good enough for us!'

He had ground her down eventually and that was how they came to be, mortgaged up to their eyebrows, signed up at 'The Club', and completely and utterly out of their depth. As instructed Sarah had signed up the whole family at The Upper Thames Tennis Club but only Dave actually played any tennis.

Sarah threw the dishcloth onto the draining board and slipping on her oven gloves, lifted the lamb out of the oven. She glanced at the kitchen clock. Dave would be home any minute, staggering in just in time for lunch, puce faced, dripping with sweat and gushing over his latest game with his new best pal Rupert Fotheringham-Allen. On cue, she heard his key in the lock and called the children in from the garden. Minutes later the dining room was filled with grubby knees and the delicious smells of Sarah's cooking.

'You know Sarah, as a Club wife you are expected to show your support,' said Dave, waggling a roast potato on his fork. 'Luckily, when I told Rup that you were still finding your feet in the tennis department he came up with a perfect solution.'

A feeling of dread washed over Sarah as she poured gravy for the children. She knew Rupert Fotheringham-Allen, Rup to his friends, was a well known figure around the town, a bit of a lady's man by all accounts, who had made an obscene amount of money from buying and selling property in the Balkan states. Rup knew everyone who was anyone and worked the social scene with the accuracy of a fighter pilot and he *never* missed his target. Sarah shuddered at the thought of him but she needn't have worried, Rup didn't set his sights on women like her; she had no social connections and she was too loyal to her husband to be charmed into Rup's bed. So what, in heaven's name had the lecherous slime bag suggested to Dave? she wondered.

'Please enlighten me dearest, what does Rup have in mind?' she asked, handing him a bowl of honey glazed carrots.

'Tea.'

'Tea?'

Dave nodded. 'Exactly, next Sunday. Tea for us chaps and the visiting teams from Wallingford and Thame. Rup's better half was down on the roster for next Sunday but she had a last minute invite to her sister's villa in Nice. So it makes perfect sense for you to relieve her on teas.'

'Can't I relieve her at the villa instead?' she asked, tying a pink bib around two year old Harry's neck. 'And since when did you become a chap?'

'More to the point when did my son start wearing pink bibs?'

Sarah arched her eyebrows in warning. 'It's one of Millie's old ones, which I thought, considering the state of our current account, was preferable to buying new blue ones!'

Dave ignored the jibe and helped himself to more potatoes.

'Hey, don't eat all the crispy ones!' yelled Naomi, piling the remaining potatoes onto her plate and prompting an indignant cry from her younger sister Millie.

'That's not fair, I've only got two and Naomi's got five. Mum, tell her!'

Quick as a flash Sarah grabbed two potatoes from her elder daughter's plate and plopped them into Millie's gravy. 'There, everyone happy now? I really think I've got enough to do Dave, without making tea for Rupert Fotheringham-Allen and his cronies.'

'Come on Sarah, it's just a few sandwiches and a slice of cake,' Dave said, slicing into his lamb, releasing the aroma of rosemary and garlic, 'and you are such a good cook. This lamb is fantastic.'

Sarah nodded. 'Yes, you're right,' she said, taking on

a Lancashire accent. 'I've got a few jars of paste and pickled onions in the cupboard and I can pick up a couple of lardy cakes from the bakers. I, I'll do it lad and it'll be just grand.'

Dave put down his fork and sighed. 'Sarah, it has to be done properly. They have high standards at the club you know.'

'Lighten up for goodness sake, I was joking,' she said, fantasizing it was his thigh as she stabbed her fork into a tender piece of lamb. 'Rup shall have a tea to make his Norland nanny proud!'

'What makes you think he had a nanny?'

'He's called Rupert for goodness sake, what other reason do I need?'

'Point taken,' he grinned. 'And you'll do the tea?'

Sarah nodded. 'Yes, I'll do the tea. Now let's eat. The food's getting cold.'

Chapter 4

The door bell rang at precisely eight o'clock and Rachel opened the door to Sarah, a supermarket carrier bag under one arm and a bottle of chilled Sauvignon Blanc under the other. 'Hi Babe, still carrying your belongings in nothing but the best polythene I see,' she said, taking the bottle from Sarah's outstretched hand and ushering her down the hall.

'Some of us have more important things to worry about than matching a bag to every outfit,' Sarah said, giving Rachel a playful shove.

In the kitchen, Sarah went to a cupboard and took out two glasses while Rachel opened a packet of roasted pistachios and found a corkscrew. Filling Sarah's glass almost to the brim, she said, 'I guess you're right, a Tesco bag does go quite well with most things, particularly jeans and your old man's rugby shirt.'

Sarah brushed an imaginary crumb from the front of Dave's shirt and laughed. 'Cow!'

'Guilty as charged,' said Rachel, flashing her French manicure under Sarah's nose. 'Could you do some of these pistachios for me? Splitting the shells ruins my nails. Did I mention that I saw your brother earlier?'

'You didn't but he did,' said Sarah, tipping a handful of green nuts into Rachel's outstretched palm. 'You should have rung me as soon as Josh left.' She gave Rachel a knowing look, as if she had been preparing for this very moment.

Rachel pretended not to notice. She knew Sarah had had her doubts about Josh and had tried many times to convince her that the failure of Jet Junior to make an appearance, was due to the sperm strangling designer briefs preferred by her pilot boyfriend. She sniffed and tipped the nuts into her mouth. She'd invited Sarah over to help with her problems, not to be quizzed about her own and she certainly wasn't about to put up with a round of 'I told you so's'. Handing Sarah another handful of pistachios to split, she asked 'How are the kids?'

'Don't change the subject Rachel Ryder. You must be devastated about Josh. What are you going to do?' asked Sarah, wincing as a piece of shell pierced the vulnerable pad of skin at the top of her finger, where a nail should have been.

Rachel shrugged. 'Get on with it, what else can I do? I tried so hard this time, healthy eating, taking my temperature and testing my mucus every day like some nerdy lab technician.' She stroked a pistachio crumb from her wash board stomach, wishing it had a gentle post-pregnancy curve like Sarah's. 'Actually, he's done me a favour; apart from the bedroom department he was really quite boring and immature.'

'Umm, he was several years younger than you … not that you're old or anything. Look at Madonna, she had beautiful babies late in life and you can too.' Sarah hesitated. 'Just not with Josh that's all …'

'Exactly, I can't stay with a man who doesn't want children but how am I going to find another one? I don't polish up as well as I used to,' she said, her fingers stroking her unusually smooth forehead. 'It's a good job I had a dose of Botox and my teeth whitened whilst I was in Jo'burg.'

Sarah shuddered. 'Ughh, isn't Botox a type of poison?'

Rachel shook her head. 'No, everyone's doing it. It's very professional. The clinic sends a car to the crew hotel *and* they drop you back afterwards. What do you think; did they do a good job?' she asked, baring her gums and pulling back her fringe.

Sarah grimaced. 'Nice, you look like Millie's Barbie!' She took a gulp of her wine and leant forward conspiratorially. 'I had cosmetic surgery myself last week.'

Rachel looked at her amazed. 'I don't believe it. You don't even have your legs waxed!'

'I know,' Sarah confessed, 'but I found these funny little bumps on my bra line, senile warts apparently. I'm only thirty-seven for goodness sake!'

Rachel smiled for the first time that day. There was nothing like a good 'warts and all conversation' to make you feel better, especially when the warts belonged to someone else. She raised her wine glass. 'To senile warts, Botox and peri-menopausal babies!'

'Hear, hear!' Sarah clinked their glasses and took a slurp.

'I've been thinking maybe I should cut men out of the picture altogether. After all I only need one happy, little sperm and Bob's your uncle!'

Sarah wrinkled her nose. 'Like a donor you mean?'

Rachel bristled, she had known Sarah wouldn't approve or understand for that matter. Why should she? With a loyal husband and three adoring children hanging off her *Cath Kidston* apron strings.

'You needn't look so shocked; it was your brother that got me thinking that way. We had this really deep conversation about following your dreams and being who you want to be. Come to think of it he's not on anything is he, weed I mean?'

Sarah shook her head. 'God no, Andrew's straight … well, not straight exactly. I can't believe you'd consider a donor when you could have a living, breathing father for your kids.'

Rachel topped up their wine glasses. 'Of course I'd rather have that, wouldn't anyone? But you didn't have to beat your way through a queue of kind, intelligent, good-looking blokes begging to become fathers, to reach my door this evening did you?'

'No, but …'

'Exactly, I've got to be ruthless,' interrupted Rachel. 'I need a plan, work through my options.'

Outside the light was beginning to fade and Rachel got up to turn on the kitchen spotlights. As she sat down again, Sarah was covering the kitchen table with what looked like the contents of a craft store and whilst she concentrated on searching for some lost item at the bottom of her carrier bag, Rachel noticed how the harsh artificial light accentuated the dark hollows under Sarah's pale blue eyes and her thinness, almost a frail look. Even her usually glossy blonde hair, looked dull and unwashed and when she suddenly looked up and smiled, Rachel felt a lump form in her throat.

'What's all this for?' she asked, rifling her hand through piles of card and sticky tape.

'It's a Medusa costume for Naomi, or at least it will be when I've finished it. You don't mind do you, if I carry on with it, only she needs it for school tomorrow?' said Sarah, cutting out a snake from a computer print out.

'Pass some here and I'll help you,' Rachel said, fetching scissors from a kitchen drawer. 'Sarah, I'm worried about you. Andrew told me about the debt.'

Sarah flushed darkly. 'He shouldn't go around blabbing it to all and sundry!'

'I'm hardly all and sundry am I? And it must be worrying him or he wouldn't have mentioned it. You know that's part of the reason he wants to buy the farm business don't you? So, he can help you out.'

'No, I didn't know that,' said Sarah quietly, screwing up her eyes in concentration as she cut around a particularly tricky Puff Adder. 'We've always thought we'd like to work together. Andrew would grow the fruit and veg and I would cook it. He has this idea that I'll run the café. And he's livid with Dave, who he holds responsible for the whole stupid mess. He could barely look at him the last time he came over.'

Rachel, cutting out her fifth grass snake lost concentration and accidentally stabbed herself with her scissors. 'Damn, this snake just bit me,' she said, sucking a pin prick of blood from her finger. 'Can't we just cut out approximate snake shapes? I'm having trouble with the forked tongues.'

Sarah shook her head, so Rachel continued with her cutting. 'So, how bad is the debt?' she asked.

Sarah sighed. 'Leave the tricky ones for me. Have these Florida Water snakes they're nice and smooth, no tongues,' she said, pushing a pile of paper across the table. 'The debt's about as bad as it gets. We haven't paid the mortgage for the last three months and the credit card bills are stacked to the rafters. It doesn't matter how many letters they send us, we simply don't have the money. We've been relying on Dave's bonuses but the company's been going through a rough patch. We'd probably have been alright if we hadn't bought all the new stuff for the house but Dave insisted. He thought our old furniture was too shabby. And I can't work any more hours, it's barely worth it as it is by the time I've paid Harry's child minder.'

'There must be something you can do,' said Rachel exasperated, accidentally decapitating a handful of amphibians. Quickly, she rounded off the blunt ends hoping nobody would notice; who knew what a Florida Water snake was supposed to look like outside of Florida, for goodness sake? She wondered for a moment if there were snakes in the Thames and then it hit her, the solution to Sarah's problem. 'Got it!' she yelled, banging her scissors on the table. 'The Regatta! You could be a Regatta Landlady and host a crew. Most of my neighbours do it and they make stacks!'

Sarah had picked up a handful of snakes and was beginning to staple them to a black baseball cap. Sounding unconvinced, she said, 'How on earth am I supposed to fit all the extra bodies into my semi-detached?'

'I'm not suggesting you put up an eight man crew but a coxless four plus a coach would be no problem. Come to think of it, you probably could fit in a coxswain. They're only tiny aren't they? Seriously Sarah, it would be a piece of cake, the kids bunk up on the floor in your room and the crew sleep in theirs. Throw in a few boxes of cereal and before you can say 'mind where you're putting your oar young man', you've paid off a bill or three!'

Sarah stapled the last of the cut out snakes onto the baseball cap and began sweeping scrap paper into her carrier bag. 'I'm not sure Dave would approve of strange men in the house.'

'What's he got to be afraid off? That you'll run off with one of them, it's hardly likely is it?'

Rachel saw Sarah bite her bottom lip; what she'd meant as an expression of Sarah's loyalty to her husband, Sarah had interpreted as no one would want to run off with her. How had Sarah's self esteem sunk to such an all time low? Rachel asked herself, and back tracking wildly she said. 'You might be tempted though Sarah, they're built like brick houses with muscles from here to eternity! And if they're staying in your house whose job do you think it is to replace the shower gel?' Rachel licked her lips salaciously. 'And it's up to you when you replace it, if you get my drift?'

Sarah smiled, warming to the idea. 'It's sounding more tempting by the minute. Imagine my own daily Chippendale show for free. It sounds too good to be true!'

Relieved, Rachel nodded enthusiastically. 'Believe me babe it's all there for the taking and Auntie Rachel will personally come round and de-scale your shower screen for you! It's the very least I can do.'

Sarah laughed and gave Rachel a high five, and gathering up what was left of the snakes, she prepared to leave. 'Consider yourself the official Crouch family Royal Regatta shower screen de-scaler!'

Rachel got up and hugged her, and pointing to a *FW Schwartz - New York* carrier bag propped against the French doors door, she said, 'Millie's Barbie. I got it on my last stateside. I warn you it is very pink and I raided the hotel freebies; there's a bunch of magazines for you, *Condé Nasts* mostly.' Rachel pushed open the French doors. 'You may as well go through this way, the side gate's still open from earlier.'

Sarah kissed Rachel's cheek and stepping outside, she said, 'Will do and promise me you'll take your turkey baster to the charity shop!'

Rachel waved her off and closing the patio doors, settled down on the sofa with Biggles. 'Honestly cat, do I look like someone who owns a turkey baster?' she asked and reaching for her mobile phone clicked onto the messaging option.

Josh. Baby. Have a nice life. Rachel.

Chapter 5

The next morning Rachel opened her front door and stepped out into what promised to be another warm day. The sun had already baked the dew from the front steps and Biggles was sprawled, legs akimbo like an Amsterdam hooker, along the low white washed wall separating the small front garden from the street.

'Morning Biggles you dirty stop out,' she said, stopping to tickle him under the chin. 'I'm not joining you for breakfast today. I'm off to the French market to consume my body weight in unpasteurised cheese.'

She walked the short distance to her car and then, changing her mind dropped the keys into her rip-off *Radley* shopper, deciding to walk into town instead. After a pleasant ten minute stroll she arrived at the town square, where the French market was in full flow and to her delight the first stall she came to was a Crêperie.

Savouring bites of a creamy pancake dripping with caramel sauce, she meandered contentedly through the market. Canopies, striped white and yellow and strung with artificial flowers; wisteria, rose and gypsophila, covered stalls laden with stout wooden barrels brimming with fecund bellied olives, and spicy dry cured meats arranged in bell shaped baskets, lined in red and white gingham. As Rachel moved on, the exotic aroma of the charcuterie changed to something else, something musty and over ripe.

'Madam?' The cheesemonger gestured at the refrigerated cabinets in front of him, indicating that she should make a selection.

Rachel hesitated. 'Sorry, I'm a bit out of practice …'

'Perhaps I can make a suggestion?' he asked, his eyes twinkling with mischief.

Rachel laughed enjoying the flirtation. 'As long as it involves cheese, that's fine by me.'

'Tomme Grise de Seyssel?' he said, lifting out an ugly looking cheese covered in a dusty, grey fur. 'Please, try.' He sliced a small piece onto a plate and placed it on top of the cabinet. Rachel picked it up and gagged. Its smell reminded her of an economy toilet at the end of a non-stop flight to Hong Kong! 'No, thank you …,' she said, wrinkling her nose and passing back the plate.

The cheesemonger laughed, winking conspiratorially over her shoulder and Rachel turned round to discover who was sharing the joke.

'He is making a joke with you,' said the man at her shoulder in a broad Parisian accent. 'The grey fur on the cheese, we call poils de chat. Cat's fur in English, I believe. It's an acquired taste.'

'The cat must be in pretty bad shape is all I can say,' Rachel said, noticing the way his long brown hair curled over the collar of his loose white shirt and his eyes, that were liquid Bourneville. She could hardly believe her luck. Standing close enough to breathe in a heady whiff of *Acqua di Parma*, was *Heathcliff, Mr. Darcy* and *Cyrano de Bergerac*, all rolled into one.

His face creased into a smile, accentuating his sensuous mouth and the laughter lines around his eyes. 'I've bought cheese from Jean Luc before; perhaps I can make a more palatable recommendation?'

'Please,' she gushed. *My recommendation is that we forget the cheese and we go somewhere I can play with your hair….*

'Coulommiers, a type of brie,' he said, pointing to a pale yellow cheese, 'it has a sweet, melting texture, perfect with a glass of Bordeaux. And perhaps a goat's cheese?'

Rachel nodded enthusiastically.

'Parfait. Jean Luc has an unusual goat's cheese; it is rubbed with a cloth soaked in Muscadet. It has the most unusual flavour. And finally Bleu des Causses'. He nodded his thanks to Jean Luc who passed him a plate with samples for her to taste. 'It is like Roquefort, an excellent moist summer cheese to have at the end of your meal with a glass of Barsac Moelleux.'

Conscious that he was watching her face for a reaction, Rachel tried each cheese in turn. Her insides softened as the intensity of flavours grew and an involuntary groan of pleasure escaped from her lips. As a satisfied smile spread across her mentor's face, she could feel herself blushing hotly and was suddenly dying for a cigarette.

'Thank you … I'll take a piece of all three,' she croaked, wondering what else this gourmet Sven Gali could teach her. She paid Jean Luc and turned to thank the stranger, at the exact moment his mobile began to buzz.

'Excuse me,' he said, placing the phone to his ear. He shrugged apologetically and pointing to her bag of cheese, mouthed 'Bon Appétit', before disappearing through the crowds. For several minutes she remained rooted to the spot, hopeful for a glimpse of his billowing white shirt amongst the throng. She would happily feign ignorance of all French food, from the pretty pink garlic bulbs to the luminescent glace clementines, if he would only reappear and talk to her again; in his sexy I want to lick honey from your navel voice.

Reluctantly, she moved on to the neighbouring stall and pretended to admire the crude oil paintings of Mont. St. Micheal and a smiling apple cheeked mademoiselle dressed in traditional Normandy lace. Then, spotting a flash of white cotton, her heart skipped a beat and turning to dazzle him with her best smile, she found herself beaming at a heavily pregnant woman in a voluminous white kaftan. Replete with happy hormones, the woman beamed back and offered her an outsize green olive from a polystyrene cup.

'Err, no thanks, it's very kind of you but I'm saving myself for this,' said Rachel, waggling her cheese and backing into the crowd. Everywhere she looked there were pregnant women, tall good looking men with cupid style toddlers giggling from their shoulders and couples meandering arm in arm choosing French delicacies for their Sunday lunch à deux. Feeling like the token Billy No Mates and Billy No Partner / No Kids / No Sexy French Stranger, she made her escape.

On the way home she considered her options. Drop dead gorgeous strangers were all well and good but if they didn't hang around long enough to be separated from their telephone number, they were no use at all. No, what she needed was someone much more reliable and down to earth. While she didn't know Andrew all that well, she liked what she knew, and as she and Sarah were so close they could almost be regarded sisters, why not go the whole hog and become sisters-in-law?

Chapter 6

A row of spindly legged trestle tables groaned under the weight of the Tennis Club tea; sandwiches cut into delicate triangles, a generous cheese board and cake stands layered with squares of rich organic chocolate brownies, feather light sponge with a sharp, crunchy iced lemon topping and generous slices of heavily fruited, moist Dundee.

As she surveyed the feast, Sarah gave herself a small congratulatory hug. Preparing the tea had been an enormous amount of work, not to mention expense, but single handed she'd pulled it off. Suddenly the doors of the pavilion swung open and the ladies doubles champions strolled in, immaculate in tennis whites and not a stray hair or a smudged lip line between them. Self conscious of her 'World's Best Mum' apron, Sarah felt her cheeks instantly flame. 'Please help yourself, everything is ready,' she said, before darting back through the galley doors that led to the kitchen.

No sooner had the doors swung closed behind her, did they swing open again. Sarah braced herself for a criticism of her sandwich fillings, but to her relief she saw that it was Rachel, come to lend a hand.

'I don't report for work until seven, so thought I'd come by and help with the washing up!' she said, picking up a pair of yellow washing up gloves from the draining board and holding them against the vivid reds and oranges of her 'God Save the Queen' top, hastily dropping them again in disgust.

Sarah smiled. 'Am I pleased to see you? When I agreed to do this I hadn't thought about all the clearing up. I was up until three this morning baking.'

'You poor baby, you must be knackered!' Rachel said, peering over the galley doors. 'Where are the kids, I didn't see them as I came in?'

'They're with Andrew. They wanted to come but Dave wouldn't have it, he thought they'd spill juice and run amok.'

'Shame, I bet the girls would have liked to play waitress,' said Rachel, taking a compact mirror out of her handbag and checking herself. 'Andrew could bring them up to the club house if you rang him on your mobile.'

Sarah shook her head. 'Dave would kill me, that's if Andrew didn't clock him one first. I told you, they're not getting on at the moment. Why are you so keen to see him anyway?' asked Sarah, nudging Rachel out of the way so she that she could rinse a colander of strawberries under the tap.

Rachel spotted a pretty glass bowl on the table and held it up ready. 'I keep missing Andrew at home. It seems every time I go out, he comes in to do the garden and he always manages to be gone before I get back. Just thought we could catch up about plants and…stuff.'

As she tipped the fruit into the bowl Sarah caught Rachel's eye and slowly the penny dropped - Rachel's flushed cheeks were a dead give-away. Rachel was on a man hunt - and the man was Andrew. Sarah frowned, Rachel couldn't be more wrong for Andrew. Trouble was how to tell her. Letting Rachel carry on with her fantasy was bad enough but explaining to her, why Andrew, in spite of his good looks and charm, would not be a good catch was unthinkable. No, she decided, taking the bowl from Rachel and sprinkling the top with castor sugar, Rachel would have to work that one out for herself.

'Are you alright? You've gone all quiet on me,' Rachel asked.

Sarah nodded. 'I'm fine. I'd better check how it's going,' she said, cocking her head towards the club room.

'Stay where you are and put your feet up for a moment. If I can clear an economy cabin with 10 minutes to landing, I sure as hell can clear a few tea plates!'

The club room was filled to bursting with tennis players, tucking into tea with gusto. Sarah had done a great job thought Rachel, as she tided the buffet area, she'd make someone a perfect sister-in-law someday and the more she thought about Andrew, the more she convinced herself that he was the perfect match. They wouldn't be rich but if she continued to fly part-time, after the children had inevitably arrived, they might just scrape a fortnight in Martinique once a year using her travel concessions, especially once she'd put a stop to Andrew working for old ladies, for nothing more than a cup of weak tea.

Suddenly, despite a generous lunch from the spoils of her market trip, her stomach grumbled and now, having re-established a taste for it , she scooped up a piece of brie from the cheeseboard and popped it into her mouth. Its creamy texture coated her tongue and in an instant, she was reminded of the mysterious stranger from the market. He was gorgeous, sexy and if his knowledge of cheese and wine had been anything to go by, intelligent too; but also, she reminded herself, firmly out of reach. Refusing to allow the memory of him to distract her, she decided that from now on she would declare herself lactose intolerant and avoid cheese like the plague.

Outside, behind the high laurel hedge that separated the car park from the tennis courts, Rupert Fotheringham-Allen was parking his Mercedes convertible. As he climbed out of the car and picked up his tennis racket from the back seat, he could hear that a match was already in progress. Smiling to himself, he decided to play his usual game of 'Guess the Filly'; to his delight, he had noticed that the noises his bedfellows made reaching orgasmic bliss between his thighs, were almost identical to the noise they made on the tennis court, hitting a strong service or returning a lethal backhand. And now, as he stood behind the hedge out of sight of the players, he prepared to guess the identity of the female players by sound alone. Soon, he was rewarded when a deep groan penetrated the foliage. Rup sighed, 'Gillian. Lovely Gillian.' He waited until the point had been played and then called out, 'Good afternoon Gillian.'

A high pitched disembodied voice called through the hedge. 'Afternoon Rup, how are you darling?'

He rounded the hedge just in time to hear the 'lovely Gillian' turn to her partner and ask 'How on earth does he do that? He must have sixth sense or something.'

Rup saluted and bounded up the stairs to the club room, two at a time.

Rachel had her back to the pavilion door and was busy

filling a cake stand when she heard Rup's voice.

'I'll have another slice of cake, Miss, and make it a large piece, one with plenty of icing so I can lick it off ... very, very slowly,' he said, picking up a vol-au-vent and scooping the contents out with his tongue.

Remembering the last time they'd met, Rachel glared. She and Josh had visited the tennis club, thinking they might like to join and when Josh had nipped to the Gents, the Club Chairman Rupert Fotheringham-Allen had made a clumsy pass. And now the lecherous pillock was showing off to his cronies, who she noticed to her disgust, included Sarah's husband Dave.

'Still servicing passengers are you Miss Ryder?' Rup said, licking coronation chicken from his lower lip.

Being used to the uninvited attentions of male passengers, who mistakenly believed that all stewardesses were gagging to join the mile high club, Rachel knew exactly how to put him back in his box. 'Oh, yes', she smiled sweetly. 'And we're always looking for Bob of course.'

Rup leered. 'Who's Bob when he's at home, the pilot with the biggest joystick?'

'B.O.B. the initials stand for Best on Board. You can do it with your own initials. Now let's see ... Rupert Fotheringham-Allen, R.F.A., that's easy.'

Rup looked smug.

Rachel continued. 'I looked at you Rupert and it came to me in a flash - Right Fucking Arsehole!' And swinging on her heels she marched towards the kitchen, turning briefly to smile at Rup's astonished face and discreetly give him the bird.

Furious at being upstaged in front of his friends Rup leapt up from the table, knocking over a cup of tea and sending a plate of sandwiches crashing to the floor.

'Steady on Rup, you did ask for it,' said Dave, slapping him playfully on the back.

Rup shook him off crossly. 'Right, that's it,' he snapped, pushing back his chair, 'bugger you lot, I'm off to find more accommodating company.'

His friends laughed at his retreating back.

'Silly sod! Always after the next bit of skirt. I don't know why Carolyn puts up with him, such a lovely girl. They've only been married five minutes, couldn't blame her if she left the randy bastard!' remarked Rup's best friend and doubles partner, Nigel.

'Is she here? I haven't seen her all afternoon,' asked Dave, a picture of innocence.

Nigel sighed. 'No, in the South of France apparently. Now, if I'd hooked a beauty like Carolyn I'd never let her out of my sight, let alone chase a silly little tart like Lucy.'

In the kitchen Rachel took over and Sarah, carrying two steaming pots of tea, went into the pavilion. As she refilled tea cups, she received compliments from every quarter.

'Are you the young lady responsible for our tea this afternoon?' asked an older gentleman in immaculate whites.

'Yes I am,' Sarah replied nervously, wondering where the conversation was going.

'Well, may I just say that I've been playing at this club for over twenty years and that was the best tea I've tasted!' said the man, looking around his table for confirmation and being rewarded by several tea cups raised in unison.

Sarah blushed with pleasure and as she turned away she caught sight of Dillys Forsyth, the club secretary, working the room with a red clipboard and handing out pens and paper. How cheesy she thought, they're going to have a quiz, but in spite of herself she glanced at one of Dilly's papers to see if she could answer any of the questions. At the top of the page she read, **Tea Appraisal: Visiting Teams**, followed by a set of questions about quality, variety and presentation.

Hells bells! It was worse than appearing on *Strictly Come Dancing*! The Club was actually planning to give her marks out of ten for creative bloody impression! No wonder Rup's wife had cut and run to the South of France, someone must have tipped her off. Grabbing a handful of dirty plates, she escaped to the relative sanctuary of the kitchen and dumping the crockery, opened the fridge to let the cool air fan her burning cheeks.

'What's wrong babe? You look like your head's going to explode!' asked Rachel from the sink, where she was up to her elbows in soap suds.

Sarah knelt on the floor fanning the cool air onto her face. 'They're marking me! Or rather my tea … marks out of ten!'

Rachel patted Sarah's shoulder with a soapy black glove. Sarah raised her eyebrows. 'What happened to my Marigolds?'

'Safe and sound in your bag. I found these under the sink. The black goes much better with my top don't you think? And don't worry about that lot in there. You'll do fine and if you don't, they won't ask you back, which means you won't have to go through this silly palaver ever again!'

'Yes, you're right and who cares anyway?' said Sarah, getting up and busying herself stacking crockery. Trouble was she did care, her score on teas meant as much to the club and therefore to Dave, as his score on the court but she couldn't help wonder, hope even, if a few fancy sandwiches and a slice or two of fruitcake could raise her score with him? She knew it wouldn't feature on *Relate*'s top ten ways to save a marriage but she'd felt invisible to him for so long, she couldn't afford to be choosy.

Later, when Rachel had left for the airport and Sarah was rinsing through the last cups and saucers, she heard the unmistakable voice of Dilly's Forsyth. The kitchen door swung open and Dilly's ample bosom made its entrance, for what seemed like several seconds before the woman herself. Sarah smiled, the last time she'd seen such a stout chest was on the figurehead of the *Cutty Sark*.

'Ah, there you are dear. I've just come to break the news, thought you should be the first to know,' Dillys said.

Oh, no here it comes, thought Sarah, she's going to tell me that someone found a pubic hair in their lemon sponge and Dave's been barred from the club for good and I'll have a divorce on my hands before sundown.

'What news is that Dillys?' she croaked.

'Ten out of ten, dear! A new club record ... your exquisite tea ... ten out of ten! Your husband didn't mention that you were in catering.'

Sarah flushed with relief. 'That's because I'm not.'

'You should be dear, with a talent like yours and all organic too I gather? Perhaps you should consider it dear, run your own little business? A cousin of mine in Dorset went into catering and never looked back.'

'It's certainly food for thought,' joked Sarah, but her pun was lost on Dillys, who made a bee line for a plate of left over cakes.

"I don't suppose you've any use for these have you dear, perhaps I could take them for supper?' she said, balancing the plate on her red clipboard.

Sarah nodded and Dillys swept out of the kitchen in much the same manner as she'd entered it, only this time Sarah's cakes led the way. Still glowing from Dillys's praise Sarah went to find Dave who was practising his serves on an empty court. Spotting her, he came over to help load empty Tupperware boxes and other kitchen paraphernalia into the car.

Flushed with excitement Sarah asked, 'Did you hear the good news?'

Proudly, Dave nodded. 'Yeah, it's great isn't it? We thrashed the pants off the men's doubles from Thame and Wallingford.'

Sarah stopped in her tracks, a Tupperware of lemon sponge hovering in mid-air like a rhetorical question. 'Oh, did you?' she asked, suddenly realising that she hadn't taken notice of the tennis, or his part in it. 'That's great news. I did rather well too....my tea got ten out of ten. Dilly's said it's a club record.'

'That's great Sarah, well done. I knew you could do it,' he smiled, patting her backside.

Grinning, Sarah placed the Tupperware in the boot and slid into the driver's seat. Relieved that all the hard work had been worth it, she said, 'It's just the confidence boost I need. If Andrew finds a way of buying the farm, I'd like to take him up on the offer of running the café for him.'

They drove off and Dave sniffed, pointing out that a tractor had turned onto the road ahead of them. 'You two are as bad as each other, always daydreaming. Andrew will never afford to buy the farm shop and I hardly think serving up a few sarnies qualifies you to run a restaurant.'

His words stung. Concentrating on the road ahead Sarah tried hard not to cry and after several minutes, Dave noticed how quiet she was and said, 'All I'm saying is Sarah, don't run away with yourself. Imagine how disappointed you'll be if it doesn't come off.'

Without looking at him she nodded, and they drove the rest of the way in silence. Arriving at Andrew's to collect the children, Dave stayed in the car claiming to want a snooze. As she rang Andrew's bell, Sarah found herself wondering whether she'd left the handbrake on and was about to rush back to the car, when Andrew opened the door and offered to make her a cup of tea. She glanced over her shoulder. The road wasn't on a hill she decided; more what you would call a gentle slope. 'That would be lovely, you can fill me in on your progress with the farm,' she said, closing the front door behind her with a satisfying click.

Chapter 7

The next morning, Sarah prised open her eyes and squinted at the neon display on the bedside clock. It was 7.15. Tentatively, she edged her foot towards the other side of the bed and made brief contact with Dave's shin. Damn! Why was he still in bed? He always left for work by seven and this morning of all mornings she did not want him hanging around. There must be no hint of what she had planned or all hell would let loose. If he found out that she had an appointment with 'Debts 'R' Us', he'd insist that they could sort out their finances themselves and forbid her to go. If the plan had any chance of succeeding his fierce male pride had to remain firmly intact.

Putting off the day for a few moments more, she lay listening to the household noises, telling her who was up and about. Millie was singing and talking to her Barbies and the snuffling chatter coming from the box room meant that Harry was also awake. Only Naomi was still sleeping.

Sarah reached for her dressing gown and padded into the bathroom for a pee. As she sat down, the cold wet feeling on the back of her thighs was instantly recognisable. Millie! The child's toilet habits were bordering on Elizabethan! Standing up, she wiped the back of her legs and sat down again, resigned. The twenty first century luxuries of quilted toilet tissue and full flush cistern held no fascination for her youngest daughter. Sarah consoled herself with the thought that it could be worse, at least urine was supposed to be sterile. She remembered reading somewhere that some weirdos actually drank the stuff, believing it had miraculous health benefits.

Lifting her dressing gown she twisted round to look at the backs of her thighs. There was no way she'd consider drinking pee but maybe the benefits still worked if it was applied topically, perhaps it might even do her cellulite some good! She imagined herself creating the world's first cellulite cream that *actually* worked and being asked how she discovered it. 'Oh, it was so simple,' she imagined herself saying to the intrigued beauty editor of Vogue magazine. 'I sat in my seven year olds pee on a daily basis, not on purpose you understand, and one day I noticed that my cellulite had gone. I put two and two together and hey presto!' After the interview, the beauty editor would be *sooo* grateful she would be introduced to the fashion editor, who in turn would be delighted to advise her which designers she should be spending her new found millions with!

Suddenly the bathroom door swung open, bashing against her knees and Dave looked at her bemused, as she clambered off the loo.

'What an earth were you muttering about? Something about Millie's pee and London Fashion Week?' he asked, yanking her up. 'Daydreaming again I suppose?'

'No I wasn't,' she said. 'I was thinking how lovely it was to be marked ten out of ten for my teas. Did I mention it was a new club record?'

'Yes, several times,' Dave said, reaching for his shaving foam. 'And there's a ten out of ten smell coming from Harry's nappy, so you'd best forget about becoming the next Delia Smith for the time being!'

Sarah stared at his profile as his face became lost in foam, camouflaging his features. What did it matter? He was turning into someone she hardly recognized anyway. Was she really married to a man who couldn't bring himself to say thank you? She was beginning to wish that she'd planted a nice curly black hair in the Dundee, just to spite him. 'Aren't you supposed to have left for work by now?' she asked.

'No, my meeting starts at ten, so I thought I'd treat myself to a more leisurely morning.'

That just about sums things up, thought Sarah, I haven't used the words 'leisurely' and 'morning' in the same sentence for almost a decade! Still fuming she changed Harry's nappy, secured him happily in his highchair, put on a whites wash, unloaded the dishwasher from the night before, showered (and noticed that the cellulite was still very much in residence), filled in a slip giving Naomi permission for swimming lessons, attached a hand written letter giving her permission to use goggles (since when did goggles become scary, dangerous things? Parental permission for flame throwing or juggling machetes she could understand, but wearing goggles to go swimming?), cobbled together two packed lunches, tipped away yesterday's water from two school water bottles, refilled them from the filter jug and in a state of near exhaustion gathered the children for their breakfast.

Naomi and Millie were arguing over who had the right to read the cartoons on the back of the cereal box and Harry was trying to see how many corn pops he could load into his left ear, when Dave appeared at the kitchen door.

'On second thoughts I think I'll just grab some fruit and go. Should be home about seven,' he shouted above the din. 'Could you see if you can track down my passport, I can't find it anywhere? I've got to go the States for a couple of days, sort out a new contract.'

Sarah threw him a banana from the fruit bowl. 'Fine, have a good day.'

'By the way Sarah, Harry has corn pops in his ear.' He winked and swept out of the door.

Sarah glanced at her watch and felt beads of perspiration pop onto her top lip. She had ten minutes to get herself ready.

'Naomi, please could you clear away the breakfast things and get the corn pops out of Harry's ear?'

'Oh Mum, I did it yesterday. Can't Millie do it today?'

'No, she can't she's too little and besides she takes so long to do her teeth, she won't have time.'

Naomi glared and Sarah chucked her under the chin. 'Don't look at me like that. One day when you're an eminent ear, nose and throat surgeon you'll thank me!'

Throwing on jeans and t-shirt from the day before, Sarah grabbed a bundle of letters with angry red font threatening bailiffs, from their hiding place in her knicker drawer and herded the kids into the car. Catching sight of herself in the rear view mirror, she scowled at her reflection. In the rush, she'd forgotten to brush her hair.

'Has either of you got a hair bobble on you?' she asked the girls in desperation.

Millie handed her a grotesque confection of purple froth. 'Here you are Mummy. It's my favourite one with the purple, twirly bits.'

'Oh! It's … lovely darling, thank you,' said Sarah, scraping her hair into a pony tail and making a mental note to buy more tasteful hair accessories for the girls in future. 'Millie, put your seat belt on.'

'I can't.'

'Why?'

'Because there's a five pence in the slot.'

'For goodness sake! How on earth did five pence get in the slot?' Sarah glared at her in the rear view mirror.

'I don't know.' Millie shook her head slowly and shrugged her shoulders, as if in sheer disbelief.

'She put it in there, Mum. I saw her do it.' Naomi nodded pompously, delighted to be her sister's judge, jury and executioner.

Sarah leant her head on the steering wheel and tried to slow down her breathing. Rachel had told her she should imagine walking through a beautiful garden when the kids stressed her out but all she could imagine was being taken away by the men in the white coats, gibbering and snarling, 'eat up your goggles, don't forget to wear your corn pops for swimming, eat up your goggles, don't forget …' She had to get a grip! They all had to get a grip!

'I just don't get it with you kids. It's the same routine every single morning. I have to remind you to do everything. Get up, get dressed, eat breakfast, brush teeth and hair, put shoes on, put your seatbelt on …what happens between midnight and seven o'clock? Does some alien life force erase your memory, so that every morning you have to start over?'

Naomi sighed and stared out of the window and Millie, trying to bend a hair clip into the door lock pretended not to have heard, and Harry, oblivious to the drama, beamed back at her. With the threat of the men in the white coats ever nearer, Sarah extracted the coin from Millie's seat belt with a pair of tweezers.

Ten minutes later, with overwhelming gratitude she waved the girls into the respective care of their teachers and drove to Andrew's.

'Are you sure you don't mind having him this morning? Are you sure he won't get in the way?' she asked as she handed Harry over.

'Of course he won't be in the way. We'll have a great time, won't we my boy?' Andrew threw Harry high into the air, making him squeal with delight. Then, noticing Sarah's look of concern he ended the throwing game and whisked Harry around to sit on his shoulders. Harry beamed at his mother and yanked his uncle's hair.

'Ow! You be careful up there! I'm going thin up top as it is; I certainly don't need any help from you! We're going to the garden centre to pick up some plants and then you're going to help me make some hanging baskets. Which means you're allowed to get all muddy!' he grinned at Sarah, 'that's if it's alright with you of course?'

'Harry loves getting dirty, don't you sweetie?' said Sarah reaching up to tickle his tummy. 'Have you got a kiss for mummy then?'

Andrew bent forward so that Harry could give her one of his special extra slobbery, but exquisitely sweet toddler kisses.

To her surprise, she quickly found a parking space in town and decided to make use of the spare twenty minutes before her appointment, to whiz into the supermarket. On auto-pilot, she pushed her trolley through the fruit and veg section, trying to imagine what the 'debt man' would ask and how she would explain, as mature mother of three she'd allowed her family finances to get into such a mess.

Rounding the corner into the cold meats aisle she was immediately confronted by two oversized trolleys being loaded with groceries for internet shoppers. The supermarket versions of the 4 x 4 were parallel parked, making it difficult for non-virtual shoppers to squeeze through the gap. One of the giant trolleys was stubbornly blocking the cheap ham section; the meat tasted of nothing and was just a layer of pink water, sugar and salt but it was the only filling that Millie and Naomi would eat in their sandwiches. Sarah appealed to the owner of the giant trolley, 'Excuse me. Please could you move your trolley back a little, so that I can reach the ham?'

The woman sniffed and swung the gargantuan trolley into the middle of the aisle, narrowly avoiding a toddler, who ran off screaming for his mother. Still shaken from witnessing the near miss, Sarah stumbled into the wine section and chose a decent looking Chablis to give to Andrew, as a thank you for looking after Harry.

'Excuse me, I think you'll find that's my trolley!' said a large, red faced woman pointing accusingly at the wine Sarah had chosen.

Both women stared at the wine, as if expecting it to stand up and declare its rightful owner.

'And do the tomatoes and ham belong to you?' accused the woman, glancing round, as if keen to conjure up an audience.

Sarah flushed, realising she'd trolley-napped the woman's shopping and hadn't a clue where she'd left her own.

'Sorry … I'm a little distracted you see, I've got a difficult appointment later and the kids were a nightmare this morning, and then this mad woman with one of those giant trolleys nearly killed a toddler …'

'I see,' said the woman, when she clearly didn't.

Emptying Sarah's groceries from her trolley the woman backed away slowly, like a wildlife photographer who'd over stepped the mark with an unpredictable wildebeest and Sarah, rooted to the spot in embarrassment, waited until the woman had disappeared around the next aisle, shoved her groceries next to a row of Kooma Creek Bin 47 and fled the shop empty handed.

In the street, even the Regatta bunting, miniature flags of red, white and blue fluttering prettily in the warm morning sunshine, did little to lighten her mood. In anticipation of the thousands of visitors who would soon be descending on the town, everything had been spruced up, from the polished brass coloured oars on the town sign to the fastidious hanging baskets, without a dead head to be seen. Over-night Regatta frenzy had gripped the town; boutiques advertised 'Regatta Gowns' and cafes offered 'Regatta Specials.' There were even signs attached to lamp-posts promoting 'Regatta Radio.'

As Sarah walked into the reception of 'Debts 'R' Us', she wondered if 'Regatta Landladies' were also obliged to offer 'specials'. The way she was feeling about Dave, she thought she might be tempted.

As she waited in the reception area she caught sight of herself in a mirror and gasped in horror at the scruffy woman staring back. She'd planned to wear a dress, put her hair in a French plait and wear subtle make-up, to give the impression of a woman perfectly in control, who had simply bought one too many exquisite lamps from House of Fraser. Instead she looked like a serial spendthrift who fed her children on wine gums and spent her child tax credits on tasteless hair accessories!

'Mrs. Crouch?'

Instantly she recognised the bossy voice. The debt advisor and the nasty woman from the supermarket were one and the same! Deciding she would rather stick pins in her eyes than share her financial crisis with the woman, Sarah pretended to be engrossed in a dog-eared copy of *National Geographic*.

'I'm sorry dear, I think that's you,' said the elderly receptionist whom she'd booked in with. 'You are Mrs. Crouch aren't you dear? That is the name you gave me when you came in, isn't it?'

Blood rushed to Sarah's cheeks and to her horror, she knew she was blushing. That just takes the bloody biscuit she thought, 'Mrs. You Can't Even Manage a Current Account - Duh!' has already got me down as some half-brained crazy trolley snatcher but now the old cow- bag will think I'm working under a fraudulent alias to boot!

'Mrs. Crouch'.

It was cow-bag again.

'Pleased to meet you ... again. I'm Margery Willis; would you like to come through?'

Sarah saw her tap her watch discreetly at the receptionist. Probably a coded signal, thought Sarah, for I've got a right nutter here and if I'm not out in twenty minutes send for the constabulary!

Forty-five minutes later, Sarah emerged onto the street in a trance. While cow-bag Margery had explained how she could free herself from debt, Sarah had conjured an out of body experience, one she normally reserved for visits to the dentists, baby inoculations and smear tests. While half of her brain had listened to how she must draw up a two- part plan - part one required getting up close and personal with the creditors and made the assumption that credit card companies and building societies appreciated almost any offer, of any sum of money as long it was going in the right direction, and part two meant 'exploring' ways of adding to the family income, such as taking in lodgers - the other half of her brain had been working through a recipe for Boeuf Bourguignon.

Relieved to make her escape, Sarah crossed the bridge leading to the Henley Royal Regatta headquarters. As she pushed open the door, the receptionist looked up and smiled. Sarah explained how she wanted to become a Regatta Landlady and launched into a well practised spiel of how she would arrange the bedrooms and what a varied and healthy breakfast she would provide the young athletes. The receptionist shook his head, and for a moment, Sarah thought he was going to tell her that her domestic possibilities were not up to scratch. After all, she knew that many homes in and around Henley had tennis courts and swimming pools and some even had direct access to the Thames itself, meaning those very same athletes could simply row to the Regatta, using it as a convenient warm up.

Instead, he explained that she was too late; all the visiting crews and families had already been allocated somewhere to stay. Feeling a fool for the second time that morning she turned to leave, but at the last moment, the receptionist pushed a piece of paper across the desk, saying,

'Leave your details. If we get a call from any last minute visitors, we'll be in touch. But I must emphasise it is extremely unlikely'.

Sarah nodded her thanks, understanding that he must have registered the desperation in her face. Walking back across the bridge she stopped to help a woman, who'd upended a box of art materials over the pavement.

'Thanks,' smiled the woman, picking up tubes of oil paint from the gutter. 'I'm painting the bridge today. I was just looking over the edge, for a good spot to perch myself and my box fell open, I can't have fixed the catch properly.'

Sarah grinned; at least she wasn't the only ditzy woman in town. 'No problem, you've got a great day for it.'

'I have indeed and I'm hoping to capture Isis today.'

'Isis?' asked Sarah.

'Down there.' The woman pointed to female face sculpted into the side of the bridge. 'Tamesis, the man is on the other side. Did you know they were sculpted by a woman?'

Sarah shook her head. She wasn't one for local history. 'No, I always assumed that the whole bridge was built by men, considering its age.'

The woman nodded and clipped her paint box shut. 'A common assumption, but in fact they were sculpted by a woman. She turned her hand to sculpture after her husband lost all their money gambling and then shot himself in the head. Just goes to show what a woman can do if she puts her mind to it. Anyway nice talking to you and thanks again for your help.'

Sarah walked up the High street, mulling over the woman's story and passing 'Debts 'R' Us', she considered popping in to tell Margery that part two of the plan; adding to the family income by becoming a Regatta Landlady was a non-starter, and to ask whether a husband blowing his brains out and leaving his wife the life assurance, could be considered instead.

Finally, thinking better of it, she decided to collect Harry and head home to write to her creditors, who, as

Margery had reminded her, were not going to give up and go away.

Chapter 8

Resisting the temptation to add one for herself, Rachel poured champagne into half a dozen fluted glasses and added them to a tray of mineral water and fresh orange juice.

'Just pop these through would you, Sally,' she said, handing the tray to the junior crew member who was still bright eyed and bushy tailed at landing herself her dream job.

Rachel watched Sally's willowy figure sashay down the aisle and a male crew member bustle past her with an armful of passenger's jackets, winking as he did so. He's already singled her out for a down route bunk up, thought Rachel suddenly feeling old. As a rookie Sally was easy pickings; a naïve girl plucked from the Home Counties, about to be wined, dined and wooed on airline expenses in glamorous downtown Manhattan. Rachel knew, Sally's virtue, if she had any, didn't stand a chance.

All the passengers were now on board and the doors were closed. Economy travellers were eyeing up empty seats like vultures over carrion, judging when to make the dash to claim the extra space that would make their flight more bearable and mothers with flushed cheeks and tired eyes were pleading with over-excited youngsters not to upend their cabin bags and eat *all* the sweets and fill in *all* the activity books before the plane had taxied onto the runway. Meanwhile, passengers who'd had the privilege of turning left, sipped from glasses of something chilled and disregarded the glossy in-flight magazine, most having read this month's copy several times already.

As Rachel wiped up a drop of split orange juice from the galley work counter, a familiar face appeared at her shoulder.

'Everything alright, Rachel? Here's your passenger list, it's a light load in Business today.'

Mike Mathews, the silver haired, perma-tanned Cabin Service Director had been airborne since the days of the Wright brothers, or at least it appeared that way to Rachel. Over the years they had crewed many flights together and had become friends.

Rachel laughed. 'I'm fine Mike, thanks. I've got a good team today, although some of the crew are sniffing round Sally like dogs on heat.'

'I'm sure you can give her a few tips on how to handle that,' he said, giving her arm a friendly squeeze before leaving the galley.

Rachel ran her finger down the list of passengers, checking for special meals; Kosher, Gluten Free, Lactose Intolerant; the list of 'specials' grew all the time. The passenger names, like a United Nations roll call fascinated her and she enjoyed trying to second guess the nationalities - Brad Hunter seat 12A - American or Australian, Hans Kohl seat 13J - German, David Crouch seat 17A – British ... DAVID CROUCH! Was that David Crouch, as in married to Sarah Crouch, best friend and confidante to Rachel Ryder and father to three beautiful children? And sitting in seat 17B was a Gemma Jacobs. Why would check-in have sat two strangers next to each other on such an empty flight? ... unless ... a knot of anxiety twisted in her stomach ... surely Dave wasn't playing away?

'Are you OK Rachel? You look like you've seen a ghost,' asked Sally, strapping herself in for take-off.

Rachel nodded and stared out of the small lozenge shaped window as the plane roared down the runway. As soon as the plane had cleared the first cotton puffs of cloud, the captain signalled that the crew could leave their seats. Rachel ensured that hot towels were handed out and that the bar round was under way, and as she prepared for the meal service she racked her brains for a plan. To discover whether Gemma was merely an innocent fellow traveller or planning to take Dave to the Mile High Club, she needed to observe them without Dave spotting her. Fortunately, Dave was sitting in a rear facing window seat and would have his back to her, as she pushed the trolley along the aisle to serve Brunch. 'Innocent Fellow Traveller Gemma' or 'Scheming, Husband and Father Snatching Bitch' on the other hand would be facing her, but would have no idea that she was being observed or by whom.

Performing their own airborne double act, Rachel spread crisp white cloths on passenger's food trays before Sally added plates of steaming breakfast. Looking over Sally's shoulder Rachel had a covert view of row 17. Between highly glossed lips, Gemma Jacobs was sipping a glass of bubbly and playing coquettishly with a strand of her long strawberry blond hair. Suddenly she laughed at something said by her companion and leant forward in her seat. Frantically Rachel signalled to Sally to pull the trolley forward and to her horror, saw that the lips reaching forward from seat 17A to join with the lips in seat 17B, belonged to none less than her best friend's husband.

Instinctively Rachel tugged the trolley backwards, not wishing to watch anymore of the Dave and Gemma floor show. Sally looked up, alarmed at the change in routine but the look on Rachel's face told her not to comment.

Reversing up the aisle towards the galley, Rachel said, 'I'm sorry Sally … I don't feel well. I've come over all faint. Can you get one of the boys to help you finish the meal round? I need to sit down.'

Pouring herself a glass of water, Rachel sat on a crew rest seat until her heartbeat returned to normal. If Dave thinks he's going to get that little bitch to tuck her legs behind her ears in New York, while Sarah's battling to keep a roof over their heads he's got another thing coming, she thought bitterly.

By the time the crew returned with the empty trolley she had applied a new layer of lippy and composed herself. All in good time, she told herself, you're on my turf now sunshine! Reassuring Sally that she was now feeling much better she helped with the rest of the service, clearing dishes and topping up drinks while keeping out of Dave's range of vision. After sending one of the crew for their rest she made Sally a much needed cup of tea and decided to take her into her confidence.

'I need to ask you a favour,' she said, handing Sally a steaming mug. 'A friend of mine is on board and I want to surprise him. I'm going to wait for him in Mike's office and I want you to bring him to me, on the pretence that he's being offered a visit to the Shite Deck.' Seeing Sally's look of confusion Rachel explained. 'Shite Deck - Flight Deck, you'll get used to the jargon after a few trips. Anyway, my friend is travelling with someone, a woman; I don't want her tagging along. You can make something up about rules of one person at a time or something, OK?'

Under the stairs to the 747's upper deck, hidden by a curtain Rachel slipped unseen into the miniscule office. Mike's paperwork was piled neatly on the desk and there was hardly enough room for her, let alone company. It would be up close and personal she thought, anticipating the whites of Dave's terrified eyes when he saw her.

Moments later she heard Sally's gentle chatter. 'No, not up there sir, through here please.'

Dave had obviously started to mount the stairs to the upper deck, knowing that it led to the cockpit.

'Ha, they've fitted a lift now have they? How civilized,' he said.

Dickhead, thought Rachel and braced herself as the curtain swung open.

'Dun-naaaaaaah!' squealed Sally, giving Dave a gentle push and closing the curtain behind him.

Dave gasped, the colour draining from his face. 'Holy shit! Rachel! What are you doing here?'

Rachel raised her eyebrows in mock disbelief. 'Do you want to work that one out for yourself, pea brain?' she hissed, pushing him onto Mike's chair. 'And while you've got your thinking cap on, which in your case must be the size of a thimble; do you want to tell me what the hell's going on with you and Gemma bloody Jacobs?'

'How do you know her name?' he asked, beads of perspiration popping out on his forehead like sherbet pips.

Rachel shook her head. Could he really be that stupid? 'You really are going to have to start taking your fish oil capsules, aren't you? Shouldn't be too difficult, I believe Sarah gives them to *your* children every day at breakfast! As one of the Pursers on board this magnificent flying machine I get something called a passenger list. And in case you're struggling with the concept, it's a list of passengers!'

Trying to regain his composure, Dave mopped his forehead with his sleeve. 'You're jumping to conclusions. Ms. Jacobs is a business colleague, there's nothing going on between us.'

'So you make a habit of playing tonsil hockey with your business colleagues do you?' said Rachel, hearing Dave's sharp intake of breath.

'No, I...'

'I didn't think so, just Ms. Jacobs!'

Dave stared at his feet like a little boy caught nicking sweets from the post office and Rachel continued, blood rushing to her cheeks. 'I'll tell you what you're going to do with Ms. Jacobs and it won't involve your dick at any point I can assure you! You're going to send that adulterous little cow back to London on the next flight. I don't care what excuse you have to make, quite frankly that's your problem. And don't think for one moment that you can sneak her into New York behind my back because one word to tonight's crew and I'll know whether you've done the decent thing or not!'

When he looked up Rachel saw panic in his eyes.

'OK, whatever you say I'll do it … what about Sarah?' he asked sheepishly.

Rachel felt a jolt at the mention of Sarah's name, the innocent in all of this. 'Good question. While you were planning to have your end away, your wife has been trying to bail you out of the financial shit you've put your family in! I suppose it's escaped your notice that she's planning to take in rowers over Regatta to help make ends meet.'

At least, Rachel noticed, he had the decency to blush. 'No, I didn't know,' he said quietly. 'I've been an idiot, I know that. Business trips to the States, Gemma … it's all been an easy way to block out the trouble at home. I swear to you Rachel, nothing has happened between me and Gemma, this trip was kind of …'

Rachel snapped the words from his mouth. 'When it was going to happen?'

'I guess so. She was just a diversion, nothing more.'

Rachel shook her head, unimpressed. 'Don't think that puts you in a better light because it doesn't. Diversion or not, do you honestly think that the building society and the credit card companies are going to just give up and go away? And how long was Sarah supposed to keep going, shouldering all the pressure on her own?'

Crestfallen, Dave seemed to shrink inside his business suit. 'I know, I know. I just don't know what to do, I'm supposed to be the man of the house and I'm steadily bringing it down around our ears.'

He looked on the verge of tears and knowing that making a business class passenger cry would not go down well, Rachel decided to cut him some slack.

'Look, it's not insurmountable. If you get some good advice and if you support Sarah instead of running away, you two can get this thing licked.'

Dave looked up, mollified. 'Thanks Rachel, you are a good friend. Sarah's lucky to have you around … we both are. Can I go now?' he asked, pushing the curtain aside.

'Dave,' she said as he stood up to go, 'Sarah is your wife and the mother of your children but she's a woman too, don't forget that will you? She's worth a thousand Gemmas.'

Dave nodded and made his escape. Rachel waited a few moments before returning to the galley and sending Sally for her break, but seconds later Sally dashed back into the galley and grabbing handfuls of paper towels.

'The blond in seat 17B has chucked up. Can't say I'm surprised, your friend's been plying her with champagne and chocolates since take-off. It looks like a scene from 'The Exorcist' out there,' she grimaced, searching for a disinfectant spray. 'Mind you, he copped a lapful too!'

Rachel laughed. 'Serves him right,' she said, imagining Dave with a crotch covered in vomit. 'He's married to my best friend and the bimbo in 17B is his bit on the side. He was planning all along to get her face in his lap but I don't think that's quite what he had in mind! Poetic justice don't you think?'

Sally grinned and put the disinfectant spray back in the cupboard. 'Shall we forget the nice smelling spray then? The smell of her vomit on his cock should put him off adultery by the time we get to JFK.'

Rachel smiled to herself. Perhaps Sally wasn't as green as she'd thought. Maybe she'd give the male stewards a run for their money after all. Pity thought Rachel, that the same couldn't be said for Sarah, who seemed to hold Dave on a pedestal and would do anything to please, even if it meant staying up all night to make cakes for players like Rupert Fotheringham-Allen!

A short while later, Rachel took her meal break and still reeling from her discovery, forgot her new diet rule and plumbed for a plate of cheese and biscuits. Having the galley to herself, she settled down for a daydream in which she would return from a trip, Rio de Janeiro or maybe Los Angeles, tanned and gorgeous; Andrew would be waiting for her wearing only his denim cut offs, his muscles still hot and mud streaked from the garden…a veggie casserole already prepared for their supper.

Slicing into the camembert on her plate she spread it lovingly onto a multi-grain cracker and instantly the image of Andrew vanished from her mind, to be replaced by the French stranger, standing in her kitchen as though he owned it and pouring two glasses of Burgundy. Bugger! If only I'd gone to Waitrose and been satisfied with a pound of mature cheddar she thought crossly, tipping her meal into the waste disposal. She settled instead for an organic vegetable hot-pot, in the hope that it would help focus her mind. Unfortunately, it didn't and as thinking about the right man seemed fraught with difficulties, she decided to worry about Sarah instead. Should she tell her about Dave? If he kept his word then there was little harm done, hardly worse than a drunken kiss at the office Christmas party but if he didn't send the little tart back to London, she would have no choice but to tell.

After leaving notes for the London bound crews,

asking them to call her mobile if a Gemma Jacobs showed up on their passenger lists, Rachel took Sally on a heads up tour of her favourite shops in Manhattan; *Gap* for basics, *Duane Reade* for 'useful stuff' only available on prescription in the UK, *Target* - the US name for Woolworths, but as Rachel was quick to point out, pronounced 'Tar-jaay' by crew to make it sound more up-market- for just about *anything* and *Ross Dress for Less*, where an eagle eye and a sharp elbow might nab a bargain, and while Sally blew her expenses on her first East Coast shopping trip, Rachel's mobile remained worryingly silent.

Then, just as she and Sally were finishing their Bellini nightcaps in *Fitzpatrick's* bar (native new Yorkers were still at work but the sun was well over the yard arm in London) the call came through - Miss Gemma Jacobs was on board the six o'clock flight to Heathrow.

'I'd like to make a toast,' said Rachel. 'To Gemma bloody Jacobs, who will be so jet-lagged by tomorrow morning, she won't know her arse from her elbow.'

'Cheers,' said Sally, raising her half finished cocktail. 'I think this calls for another one of these, don't you.'

Rachel laughed and clinking her glass against Sally's, she said, 'I couldn't agree more. I'll dedicate my next one to Dave. Make mine 'A Slow Comfortable Screw'. A rude cocktail's the closest thing to a shag he'll be getting tonight.'

Chapter 9

'Hello.'

'Hi Mum. It's Sarah.'

'Hello darling! How is my gorgeous daughter today and what are the little poppets up to?'

She would know how I am and what the 'poppets' were doing if she ever bothered to visit us, thought Sarah crossly. The trouble with Sarah's mother was that she was a 'New-Granny'. She had shunned the traditional title, in favour of 'Glo', deciding on the name after hearing an interview with Gloria Hunniford on *Women's Hour* and although her own name was Jean, she thought Ms. Hunniford's alternative conjured up just the right image. After all, she didn't feel remotely like a granny. She still cut a trim figure in her golfing trousers and in spite of regular tutting and sighing from Sarah, whom she knew was desperate to turn her into a bootee knitting (she sent all her little sewing jobs to *Sketchleys* for pity's sake), jam making, 24/7 babysitting service, she felt far too young to fully embrace the traditional role and was more inclined to spend her time trying to catch the eye of George Fairweather, the dashing silver haired captain at her golf club.

Sarah heard her mother sigh and shook the idea of 'Ban HRT, Bring Back Granny' campaign t-shirts from her head. 'I'm fine Mum and the kids are great. How was your match on Saturday?'

'Fabulous darling! And the lovely George has invited me to partner him in next weekend's charity tournament!'

'Oh Mum, well done! You've had your eye on him for ages!' She heard her mother's throaty chuckle. 'I hate to ask but I need a favour. I don't suppose you could tear yourself away from the lovely George for a spot of babysitting next week could you? Only Dave's off to Paris and he's suggested I go too, for a bit of quality time without the kids.'

'Umm, what a lovely idea darling, let me just check the diary.'

Sarah could hear Jean tapping a pen against her teeth.

'Well, I have Tai Chi on Monday, Bridge on Tuesday, U3A on a Wednesday, lunch with the girls on Friday … and of course there's all the practice matches with George to be squeezed in … sorry darling it's not going to fit. Next time, I promise.'

Sarah held her disappointment in check. 'OK, it was short notice I know. Thanks anyway Mum … jeepers, have to go Harry's in the cat's bowl!'

'You'd better rescue him. Bye darling, have fun!'

Click.

'Have fun! Some chance eh Harry?' Sarah muttered, expertly scooping him up with one hand and rescuing a boiling soup pan with the other. 'I've almost forgotten what your daddy looks like, let alone feels like.'

As she put Harry down for his post lunch nap, she wracked her brains as to who she could ask to look after the kids. Dave's parents lived too far away and in any case, they were too elderly to cope with three energetic young children. She could ask Andrew, he was always pleased to help out if he could but the last time he babysat she'd arrived home just after midnight, to find the house trashed, Harry and his cot covered in lipstick, where Naomi had given him a makeover and Millie playing Barbie at the beach in the bidet! Girlfriends from the school playground were great for the odd hour after school but an overnighter was in a different league altogether. Overnighters were the preserve of grandmothers ('Glos') or friends who have stood the test of time and will forgive two days of snotty noses, *Marmite* smeared curtains and five a.m. alarm calls. So that just left ... Rachel.

Could she ask her, considering the current circumstances? Having three kids to stay and trying to get over the end of a relationship wasn't a great combo. Perhaps Rachel would view it as practice for when babies did eventually come along. As she dialled Rachel's number, Sarah considered that she may in fact be doing her a favour. Maybe, looking after three kids would put Rachel off motherhood completely and she'd be able to ditch the ovulation predictor kits and jet off into a never ending sunset of room service and fake Prada! She heard the phone click at Rachel's end and then a sound like the phone being dropped on something hard, followed by a muffled groan.

'Um, er what? Shit! Have I missed the briefing? I'll be in the lobby in thirty seconds!'

'Rachel, it's me! You haven't missed any briefing, you're at home you batty old bird!'

'Oh, thank God! I was asleep, just done a back to back JFK ... absolutely cream bloody crackered ... sorry Sarah...totally convinced I was still Stateside ...' yawned Rachel, sounding drunk through lack of sleep.

Sarah pondered the wisdom of pursuing with the call. Surely there was a law somewhere about asking for favours when a friend is drugged, drunk or unconscious and Rachel sounded as though she could be a bit of all three. 'It doesn't matter. Shall I call back later when you've had some rest?'

'No!' Rachel screamed down the phone making Sarah jump. 'No please talk to me. I can't afford to sleep any longer ... got stacks to fit in today ... worming the cat ... finding a soul mate and a daddy for my babies ... you know, before I'm off again ... I'm rambling, sorry. How can I help?'

Sarah hesitated. 'It's a big ask, only I was wondering if you'd be able to have the kids for me for a couple of days next week? Ever since Dave got back from New York he hasn't stopped telling me how we need to spend more time together, I don't know what's come over him. Anyway the long shot is he's asked me to go to Paris with him on business. I've tried Mum and she was a no-go as usual and I can't face the havoc that Andrew causes ...'

'Umm, see your point. Let me just look at my roster. I'm supposed to be in Tokyo ... it's a great earner on expenses. It's going to pay for a new cappuccino machine ...' Rachel's voice trailed off sleepily.

'Oh I see, OK. Look it really doesn't matter. Thanks anyway.' Sarah tried to swallow the ball of disappointment that had suddenly stuck fast in her throat.

'No Sarah, it does matter. Listen, it's a long shot but I'll try and get annual leave. Keep everything crossed though won't you? The schedulers are complete bastards and love to say no, especially to us trolley dollies! Leave it with me and I'll call you as soon as I know.'

'Thank you Rachel, so much. I owe you one, a big one!' said Sarah, a grin slowly spreading across her face.

'Don't mention it, now I really must get up and worm Biggles! Ciao Baby, speak to you later.'

Chapter 10

'Harry's due his nap so I'll settle him in his travel cot and then I'll bring the rest of the stuff in from the car, OK?' said Sarah, flushed with a heady mixture of excitement and anxiety.

Rachel took a couple of bags from Sarah's outstretched hands and ushered her inside. 'Fine, just do what you have to do.'

Soon it became clear that what Sarah had to do was prepare Rachel's house for every known disaster known to man/child kind, as bag after bag filled the hallway.

'Sarah what is all this stuff? It looks like we're preparing for nuclear meltdown!' cried Rachel, peering into one of the hold-alls. 'There's enough paediatric medicine in here to start my own branch of UNICEF!'

'Better to be safe than sorry. I wanted to have everything covered. It's not as if you have any experience.'

Instantly, Sarah reddened as she realised the insensitivity of her remark. 'Shit, I'm sorry. What a stupid thing to say. I didn't mean it, you know that. It's just me being a paranoid, neurotic idiot. I'm so sorry.'

'You're right I wouldn't have a clue, not having had kids,' Rachel said, two red spots appearing on her cheeks.

'Oh Rachel, please don't be cross with me. You'll have kids soon, I just know it and in the meantime I'll keep my big, clumsy, mouth shut.'

Rachel looked at Sarah's pleading face and felt ashamed at having snapped.

'I'm sorry too, Sarah. Let's just forget it. We're just two hormonal old bags who need a damn good seeing to. You need recreation and I need procreation. And if I don't do something about it soon I'll end up as one of those sad old bags who hang round maternity units,' said Rachel, her voice catching.

'It's getting worse isn't it?' asked Sarah quietly.

Rachel nodded her eyes filling up. 'It's becoming physical, like a dull ache I carry around all the time. I need a good, kind down to earth guy like … well, like Andrew.'

Sarah was torn. How could she break Andrew's confidence? He had barely come to terms with it himself, but didn't Rachel have the right to know she'd set her cap at a man whose head she had no hope of turning?

'It's never going to happen, Rachel. You're not right for each other, not in a million years. You've got to put Andrew out of the equation,' she said.

Turning on her, Rachel said, 'And I suppose being his big sister qualifies you to make that decision for him does it? Personally, I think he's old enough to make up his own mind about the women he dates.'

Sarah glanced anxiously at her watch, she was supposed to be at Heathrow by now and the last thing she wanted was a row. 'That's just it. He doesn't. He doesn't date *women.*' There, she'd said it, well not quite *it* exactly, but hopefully close enough for Rachel to understand why she wouldn't be Andrew's first choice.

Rachel stared at her, wide eyed and shaking her head in amazement. 'Sarah, are you trying to tell me that your brother's gay? No wonder he didn't bat an eyelid when I offered to help him dead end the geraniums, dressed in my bikini.'

Sarah couldn't help smile at the thought. 'I'm sorry I couldn't say anything before. He's only just getting his act together.'

Rachel shrugged, relieved that it wasn't her powers of attraction in question. 'It's OK. I should have seen the signs. Most of the men I work with are gay and I know so much about their lives I'm almost an honorary gay myself.'

Sarah laughed and looked at her watch again. 'I've got to go or I'll miss my flight. Please don't let on that you know. Maybe you can fool around in your bikini a bit longer so that he doesn't get suspicious,' she said, grabbing Rachel and squeezing the breath out of her. 'And thank you for taking care of my kids, you're a star!'

'Go!' said Rachel, giving her a playful push. 'And remember to have FUN!'

Later that afternoon, Rachel strapped Harry into his car seat and went to collect the girls from school. Forced to park two streets away, she decided to put Harry in his pushchair. She enjoyed pretending that he was her baby, stopping every so often to pick up the toys he'd flung out or to readjust his floppy orange sunhat. Millie was out of school first, swiftly followed by Naomi. Rachel handed them both an apple and bundled their school things into the basket under the pushchair.

'Apples?' asked Naomi, raising her eyebrows at Millie.

'Yeah, Auntie Rachel, haven't you got any sweets instead?' Millie asked, just as Naomi knew she would.

'Yes Millie darling, I've got lots of sweets but they're at home and you can have them after your tea.'

Millie nodded and spotting a school friend, trotted up the path ahead of the pushchair.

'How are you getting on with Harry, Auntie Rachel?' enquired Naomi as they walked along companionably.

Rachel smiled to herself, understanding that Naomi, as the eldest, wanted to be treated as a grownup confidant.

'Fine thanks Naomi, but I'll need your help at tea time. Your mum said that you're brilliant at getting Harry to eat lumps and I've made shepherd's pie, so I'll need all the help I can get.'

'No problem,' Naomi grinned. 'Auntie Rachel, mind if I ask you something?'

'Fire away.'

'What's pole dancing?'

Rachel stopped pushing Harry and turned to stare at Naomi in amazement. 'Sorry darling, did you say pole dancing?'

'Yes, some girls from year six were talking about it in the playground and they all seemed to know what it was and how to do it, but I was too embarrassed to say I didn't know what it was.'

Shit, thought Rachel, how in a lap dancer's name do I answer this one? Sarah had told her that Naomi and Millie always asked the most awkward of questions when she least expected it and how she always tried to answer their questions honestly. It was a hard act to follow but as she'd agreed to play mum for the next twenty four hours she had no choice but to follow Sarah's example.

'Umm, let's see, pole dancing you say,' she said, walking slowly, playing for time. 'Well, it's a dance that ladies do … normally in bikinis … around a pole … that's how it gets the name and people pay to watch and … nice girls don't do it.' Rachel looked at Naomi to gauge her reaction, to find her intently shredding a leaf she'd ripped off a nearby bush. Good, perhaps she wasn't even listening.

By the time Rachel had unloaded all three children and their various paraphernalia from her car and into the house, she felt quite exhausted. Naomi raced into the lounge and switched on the television. She and Millie had a minor scuffle about who was going to sit on the outsize leather beanbag and after a few seconds negotiation, regarding what programmes they were going to watch, both girls settled on the sofa, using the beanbag as a giant footstool.

'Shall we look after Harry for you Auntie Rachel?' called Naomi without taking her eyes from the screen

'Do you mean play with him?' Rachel asked hopefully, balancing Harry on her hip.

'Nah, he just likes sitting between Millie and me and he loves *Bob the Builder*, it's on next. Mum says it helps distract him whilst she makes our tea.' Naomi winked and cocked her head towards the kitchen. 'You know, give you a bit of peace and quiet for five minutes.'

Rachel stifled a grin and winked back. 'Yes of course. Five minutes peace, that's just what I need.' Reaching over the back of the sofa she placed Harry in the space between his sisters, who instinctively moved inwards, wedging him between them. Harry, obviously used to the routine, promptly stuck his thumb in his mouth, leant his head against Millie's arm and was quickly mesmerized by the flickering screen.

With Naomi and Millie happy to be mother's helps, Harry obliged everyone by eating up his tea with minimal fuss and was soon bathed and put to bed in his travel cot. As a treat, Rachel promised the girls they could watch *Eastenders* in bed if they were tucked up by 7.30. Televisions in bedrooms were off-limits at home and the girls didn't need to be asked twice. Rachel popped her head around the door as the credits were rolling.

'Right girls, it's time for lights out now,' she said.

Naomi flew out of bed and onto her knees. 'But we haven't said our prayers yet Auntie Rachel!'

'OK, I guess you better had then,' said Rachel, struggling to remember whether Sarah had written anything about prayers on her childcare notes.

Naomi placed her hands together piously and took a deep breath. 'Our mother who art in supermarket, Tesco be thy name, Thy shopping come, Thy dinner will be done ...'

'Hey, that's not a proper prayer. You're trying to have one over on me. Now get into bed before we're all struck down by a thunder bolt!'

Naomi protested and began again. 'But I haven't got to the best bit - give us this day our daily burger!'

'That's enough,' said Rachel, stifling a giggle.

'Can we have a lullaby? Mummy always sings to us to get us to sleep,' asked Millie.

With her golden hair spread like a halo across her pillow, she looked too angelic to pull a stunt like her sister's.

'Umm, I'm not sure I can remember any,' said Rachel warily.

'That's ok,' smiled Millie sweetly. 'I know one. Shall I start you off?'

Relieved, Rachel nodded and Millie began to sing a familiar tune.

'Hush little baby don't say a word, mummy's going to buy you a mocking bird and if that mocking bird don't sing, mummy's going to buy you some BLING, BLING, BLING!!'

Both girls convulsed with giggles and Rachel turned her face so they wouldn't see her grin. 'Night, night you two. See you in the morning.'

Calculating just how many babies she could pop

before her ovaries really did pack their bags and head for a nice little bungalow in Bognor, she switched off the light.

Chapter 11

Sarah was ravenously hungry. By the time she'd written a tome of childcare notes for Rachel, said her goodbyes, gone back twice to deliver a forgotten bear and a bottle of *Calpol*, she'd somehow forgotten to feed herself. Like a woman possessed she jabbed at the buttons on the hotel phone.

'Room service? Parlez vous Anglais?...Great, can I order steak well done, pommes frites, profiteroles and 2 bottles of Stella Artois to Room 314. Merci.'

Sarah glanced at her watch, her feast would arrive in forty minutes, giving her time to shower and de-fuzz. In the marble clad bathroom, she peeled off her clothes and sucking in her stomach, scrutinised her reflection in the floor to ceiling mirror. Not bad, she thought, for a woman who'd delivered three kids and averaged twenty-three and a half minutes a week on personal grooming, including showers! Although looking down she realised her bikini line was in serious need of a trim and as Rachel often reminded her, when they discussed the pros and cons of intimate waxing, a knicker beard is never attractive. Secretly though, Sarah believed that bikini waxes were in the same league as the cyanide capsules carried by Resistance Fighters in World War Two, something to be kept in reserve for dire emergencies only.

She wondered, did your husband turning his back to you in bed for the third month in a row, count as such an emergency? And sighing she thought of the tiny lace thong she planned to wear later and all the hopes she'd pinned upon it. Wasting no more time and with the poise of a Sumo wrestler, she squatted over the toilet, and imagined what it would be like, if finding the necessary courage she could leave it, like Rachel, up to the professionals. Would the 'bushdresser' ask about cut, commenting that she'd gone short last time and suggest that she try layers? Would she (or God forbid, he) tweak her pubes looking for her natural parting!

Sarah shuddered and taking her nail scissors from her wash bag, trimmed her bikini line into a neat triangle. If the 'bushdresser' did the same she wondered, would she suggest different ways Sarah could style it, flicking it out or curling it under, depending on mood and occasion. And just when the indignity was it seemed, at last over, would the 'bushdresser' do the hard sell on products, promising a conditioner to loosen out tight curls. It didn't bear thinking about and resolving to stick to D.I.Y. Sarah flushed the toilet, watching in horror as her efforts at depilation formed a defiant hairy lilo on the surface of the water.

Leaving it to settle, she stepped under the shower and considered whether she should make *Greenpeace* aware of her discovery, imagining the headline - 'Pubes Mop Up Oil Slick' - until a knock at the door announced that room service had arrived.

Half an hour later, she popped the last exquisite profiterole in her mouth and sighing with pleasure, sank into the mountain of pillows piled up on the bed behind her.

'This is so what the doctor ordered,' she said to herself, switching on the television with the remote control, but the warmth of the room, the comfort of her full stomach and the heavy duty French evening news proved too great a challenge for her tired eyes and within moments she fell into a deep, contented sleep. Soon, regular snores rose up from under the silky eiderdown.

BEEEP,BEEEP, BEEEEP

Sarah sat bolt upright in bed, head spinning. 'What the! Where am I?' she asked the unfamiliar room. Apart from the flickering grey light from the television the room was in darkness. She fumbled her hand over the bedside table … where was the mouldy *Play-Doh* heart Millie had made her for Mother's Day? HARRY! Oh my God where was Harry?

BEEEP, BEEEEP, BEEEP.

The phone on the bedside table began flashing and beeping in unison, demanding her full attention. Lunging at it she yelled, 'Yes, what? Where are my children? Where's Harry?'

A bored French voice replied, 'I am sorry madam. I do not know where the children are or 'Arry, but Monsieur Crouch is in reception and he asks me to inform you that he has a taxi waiting to take you both to dinner.'

'Shit! Sorry, pardon I mean. Please tell Monsieur. Crouch I'll be down in two ticks.'

'Madam?'

'Sorry, pardon, five minutes. I'll be down in five minutes.'

Scrambling from the bed she pulled her evening dress from her overnight bag. Damn! She'd meant to decrease it in the steam from her shower but had been so wrapped up in the thought of steak and chips that the dress had remained in a crumbled heap. Next, she eased on her seven denier stockings, bought solely to stoke the embers of her lumpish love life and snagged them on a toenail. Damn again! Why hadn't she booked the pedicure as Rachel had suggested? Ah yes, she reminded herself because of three kids, a job, a house … she ditched her frustration along with the ruined stockings into the waste basket. Then, wriggling nude toes into strappy heels she straightened up, and catching sight of herself in the mirror, she gasped.

Having fallen asleep with damp hair, half of it was plastered against her skull while the other half stuck out at absurd angles. Desperate times called for desperate measures, grabbing the hotel hair dryer and a can of firm hold hairspray, she set to work. She finished several minutes later and red faced and breathless, reached into her bag for her jacket, a hand-me-down from Rachel - all zips and Velcro - and headed for the lifts. Two minutes later she emerged into the brightly lit lobby.

'Pants!' hissed Dave, as she approached.

'Thanks a million, I did my best you know!'

'No. Pants! There, hanging on your jacket!' Dave said, reaching over to the Velcro edged fastening of her jacket and peeling off a pair of voluminous white knickers.

Sarah blushed crimson as he stuffed them in his pocket.

'Christ Sarah, what happened to you? You look like Tina Turner in *Beyond the Thunderdome*.'

Sarah shrugged and looking over his shoulder saw that

the lobby was buzzing with chic women, and instantly she was Quasimodo in a sea of Esmeraldas. She sniffed and tried not to cry. 'Damp hair, two beers, comfy pillows … look it's a long story. Can we go before I grow a hump and start slurring my speech?'

'What?' Dave said, pulling his 'I'll never understand you as long as I live' face.

Grabbing his arm Sarah propelled him towards the exit. 'Doesn't matter let's just get out of here!'

Later in the taxi back to the hotel, edges softened by several glasses of wine, they giggled like teenagers on a first date.

'Can you remember the expression on the maître d's face when we walked in? He looked like he'd been told it was Anglo culture week at the Louvre!' laughed Dave, draping his arm around Sarah's shoulders.

Sarah's 80's rock chick appearance had raised a number of perfectly plucked eyebrows but the maître d', wanting to avoid a scene, had shown them to a discreet table and ensured that they were fed and watered quickly. She smiled at the memory and mentally glossed over the fact that, whenever she'd bought up the subject of the Café or their money problems he had changed the subject, steering the conversation around to how great the food was or whether they should order another bottle of champagne. Snuggling into his chest, she wondered briefly where this new romantic Dave had come from and when wondering began to feel ungrateful, she gave it up and let the journey to the hotel pass in a warm, alcoholic haze.

'Great, now for dessert!' Dave said, pulling her into their hotel room.

Sarah giggled as they fell onto the bed. 'Oh la, la Monsieur Crouch, are you planning to have your wicked way with me?'

'Too damn right Madam Crouch. Now, where can I find my little French letters?'

Sarah yanked away from him. 'What? Why are you asking me? Surely that's your department?'

'Packing has always been your thing. I thought you'd take care of it,' Dave said, staring at his hands as if he could summon a condom into them by will power alone. 'I'm sorry Sarah.'

'Rachel had to give up a Tokyo trip to look after the kids,' Sarah said crossly. 'She was going to treat herself to a cappuccino maker from her expenses and for what? So we can have a romantic trip without the romance.'

Dave grinned at her sheepishly. 'A cappuccino maker, really? I'm so sorry Sarah, if only I had known what sacrifices were being made on our behalf.'

In spite of herself Sarah grinned. 'I'm sorry I snapped, I so wanted this to be a special time for us,' she said, reaching out to stroke his cheek and enjoying the sensation of his stubble under her fingers. 'It's been such a long time, no wonder we forgot the condoms.'

She saw him wince and tried to make light of it. 'Don't worry about Rachel. She's on first name terms with the guys in Starbucks so she won't go cold turkey! Pity the same can't be said for making love with my husband, I can't get that in a disposable cup with chocolate sprinkles! Still, when I'm running the café we'll have cappuccino on tap.'

It was the wrong thing to say she realised, as a cloud past across his face, and then she saw something else, something new. He wouldn't look at her. Instead he was staring at the carpet between his feet, as if the swirls of brown and red fleck were suddenly the most interesting things in the world.

She recalled a moment recently - the way Millie wouldn't look her in the eye when she had been caught giving her Barbie a make-over with Sarah's best lipstick - guilt didn't make for eye contact. Sarah wondered why she hadn't thought of it before. It hadn't occurred to her that Dave might be ashamed of their financial crisis or the fact that it was Andrew and not him, who had the potential to get them out of it and to make her dream of running her own business a reality. And if Dave no longer felt like the provider for his wife and family, then surely it followed that he no longer felt like 'the man' of the house. Did it explain why he shunned her in bed? They had to talk about it, get it out in the open before anymore damage was done.

She laid her hand on his knee and was about to speak when Dave's mobile sprang into life, precariously vibrating itself towards the edge of the bedside cabinet.

A look of relief swept over his face. 'I'd better take it. Can't avoid the boss, even at this time of night,' he said, scooping the phone into his hand and pressing it to his ear. 'Phil. Good to hear from you.' He shrugged at Sarah apologetically and dived into his briefcase for his laptop.

Reluctantly, Sarah got up and went to the bathroom, closing the door on his conversation she began to undress. Standing in her bra and pants she ran her fingers over her newly trimmed bikini line – it wouldn't be the first time a new haircut went unnoticed. Taking her time, she removed her make-up, re-applied mascara and sprayed perfume on her pulse points, mustering up the courage to try again. Dave couldn't talk to his boss all night, and so what they didn't have condoms, maybe what they really needed was to talk things through, rather than a night of unbridled passion. She unhooked a hotel bathrobe from the back of the door and wrapped it around her - it was man-size and could have gone round twice - it was comforting but hardly alluring so she took it off again and flung it on the edge of the bath.

When she opened the bathroom door, she could no longer hear Dave's voice and the lights were off. Hoping that he had popped out to find a late night chemist, she slipped into the bed and nudged against something hard and bony - an arm. Tentatively, she stretched out her foot and found a leg.

Instead of making a late night dash for a condom, Dave was slumped diagonally across the bed like a bloated starfish, still dressed in his pants and socks. His regular breathing, broken with the occasional rattle of spittle meant only one thing, he was out for the count. Motionless, Sarah lay in the awkward triangle between his outstretched limbs, and tears trickled through her stiff hair-sprayed hair to lap in cold puddles in her ears. She wanted to scream and shake him awake. How could he sleep when she was wracked with loneliness and disappointment? Didn't he want to make love to her? Who was she kidding? They didn't have proper conversations anymore, what chance did they have of making love? But couldn't he see where this was heading? Didn't he want to try and fix it? Unless…her stomach bunched into a hard fist ... he was making love to someone else?

She awoke a little after dawn, raw eyed and exhausted, to find that Dave had already left. The only indication that he had shared the room was his dirty washing, bundled considerately into a neat pile next to her overnight bag.

Chapter 12

Rachel closed the front door on Sarah and her brood and pressed her forehead on the smooth wood, enjoying the peace. Motherhood, she decided was a schizophrenic mix of fun and mind numbing exhaustion.

As soon as Sarah arrived the kids had swamped her with kisses and demands for souvenirs and she'd seemed keen to get them home. Rachel had put her lack of conversation down to missed sleep, the dark shadows under Sarah's eyes certainly indicated as much. Delighted that Dave had used the trip to Paris to put the romance back into his marriage, Rachel congratulated herself in her part of the plan, so obviously well delivered and poured herself a large glass of Merlot. With her faith restored in long-term relationships and Andrew being 'out' in more ways than one, she decided it was time to put her own house in order and sweeping thoughts of the elusive Frenchman aside, she typed the words 'Dating Agencies' into the search engine on her computer. Within seconds the internet responded with 356,000 potential sites.

'Gordon Bennet!' she said, shaking her head at the monitor as if it was a naughty child. 'By the time I've shifted through that lot you silly arse of a PC, the only things I'll be getting up close and personal with will be earth worms!'

Wracking her brains she tried to remember the conversations she'd had with Naomi, who had, on several occasions, attempted to teach her how to surf the web. What had she said? Something about refining your search? Rachel sighed. Rich, kind, sexy, intelligent, available man with no baggage, expensive ex-wives or neurotic kids living within a ten mile radius of Henley and who doesn't already know Rachel Ryder, probably didn't count as a refinement and wouldn't throw up too many results on Google!

Numerous searches later she stumbled across 'Divine Dinner Dates.co.uk', an agency run by a Ms. Sophia Sanderson. She read the blurb and was impressed by Sophia's hands on approach; 'Sophia Sanderson personally interviews each client and with great sensitivity and skill selects a small group who will enjoy a delightful and completely discreet dinner event.'

Rachel lent back in her chair and sipped her wine, imagining herself sitting at an elegant dinner table, making intelligent small talk while a handsome stranger coaxed her into a game of footsie. It was a far more appealing way of rejoining the singles market than terrifying blind dates in the local pub. She shuddered involuntarily at the thought. Sophia Sanderson's joining fee of £500 seemed reasonable in the light of alternative options and besides, Josh would be paying.

She'd tell him the washing machine had packed up. Since declaring he didn't want to play 'mummies and daddies', he'd only called by the house once, and that had been to clear out his belongings, while she was conveniently away on a trip. Though what difference would it make if he did pay a visit? He'd never used the washing machine when he had been at home. Even if by sheer bad luck, he did find his way into the utility room, she knew hell would freeze over before she'd hear him shout 'Rachel, I thought you said the washing machine had packed up, this looks just like our old one.' Besides, she reasoned, if Josh hadn't lied about wanting children she wouldn't be joining Sophia Sanderson for dinner, no matter how divine!

Feeling secure in her plan, she clicked on the send box and launched her application to join 'Divine Dinner Dates' into cyberspace. Sophia's website invited prospective clients to email or call with queries regarding finding love the 'divine' way. Taking a large swig of Merlot for Dutch courage, Rachel dialled Sophia's number and as soon as she answered, launched into her concerns about the suitability of the male guests. Sophia was keen to put her at her ease.

'You'll have the most wonderful time! All my gentlemen are absolute treasures and, how shall I put this delicately? ... very well connected.'

'I'm sure they are Ms.Sanderson but ...'

'Do call me Sophia, please. I don't stand on ceremony you know. If we're too formal we can't expect to break down those barriers can we? And after all, I am in the business of bringing people together.'

'Yes ... Mrs. Sander ... I mean Sophia, I wanted to ask you what checks you do, you know to make sure these men aren't married and just looking for some extra-marital fun.'

Sophia replied in an affronted tone. 'I'm quite shocked that you need to ask. I have interviewed each and every one of them personally and can give you my word that they are all very genuinely single and most importantly, looking for that special lady.'

Rachel grimaced, thankful that Sophia couldn't see her face. Ladies, gentlemen and interviews sounded like she was trying to get into Eton rather than take a shortcut to long-term passion with an alpha male! Never mind, beggars, or in her case women with biological clocks doing the hundred metre dash towards peri-menopause, couldn't afford to be choosers. Resigned, she decided she may as well bite the bullet.

'OK, Sophia, thanks for explaining it to me.' Rachel crossed her fingers. 'How do I get started?'

'I have your application form open on my computer as we speak and I think you'd fit in perfectly with a dinner that I am planning for Friday evening.'

'Friday ... but that's tomorrow!'

'If it's too short notice I do have a lady from Burnham Beeches I could ask instead. In fact she may be better suited. She's a theatrical agent and I have another media person coming along so ...'

Rachel almost shouted down the phone. If she didn't make this dinner date who knows how long it would be before she could make another one. Over the next six weeks, her flying roster was full on; she would be out of the country almost every weekend. 'Please don't invite the lady from Burnham Beeches. I would love to come to dinner tomorrow and I'm sure I will get along with your media client. I once flew Madonna to New York you know,' she said, hoping that Sophia would be suitably impressed.

It wasn't a fib, she told herself, more of a half truth. Several years ago Madonna had been on board one of her flights, travelling First Class and Rachel, working in Business, had brushed past her, on her way to raid the First Class galley for extra salad.

'Oh, how marvellous!' Sophia gushed. 'I hadn't considered all the celebrities you must have met on your travels. You are quite right Rachel. You must come to dinner tomorrow. I'll email you directions. I just know it's going to be absolutely splendid!'

As she replaced the receiver Rachel uncrossed her fingers and hoped that Sophia wasn't doing the same. She jumped suddenly, as warm fur brushed against her shin. 'Christ Biggles, you scared me half to death! You're always creeping up on me. Come here and sit on my lap like a proper cat,' she said, scooping him onto her knees, where he immediately turned three circles and curled up, purring with pleasure. A beep from the computer signalled she had a new email. 'Look Biggles, it's from Sophia. She's prompt with her admin, I'll give her that.'

As promised, Sophia had emailed directions to her Windsor address and a short note asking her to read the attached profile of client 700, who would also be coming to dinner on Friday. Clicking open the attachment, Rachel was disappointed to find that it didn't contain a photograph but as she read through the profile she began to feel excited.

Client 700

Age: 44 – *mmmm mature, sexy, knows who he is and what he wants.*
Build: 5ft 10 medium build – *the Bangkok Jimmy Choo rip-off stilettos would have to go!*
Career: Owner of a private company- *he's his own boss and can take gorgeous new girlfriend on long romantic holidays.*
Address: Oxfordshire - *good, long distance relationships are just extra hassle and this tart with the cart's carbon foot print is already way too big!*
Family: Sadly no, but I would like a houseful of children – *hallelujah!*
Interests: Tennis, Fine Wines, Travel – *tanned legs, firm*

buttocks, serves his Chablis perfectly chilled and knows a perfect, sun kissed atoll where we can frolic in the waves undisturbed.

Favourite Film: 'The English Patient' – *hopeless romantic, likes adventure and steamy sex in exotic places.*

Favourite Book: 'Notes from a Small Island', Bill Bryson – *great sense of humour, say no more.*

Personal Statement: I have everything I want and need in my life except a warm, sexy, confident woman to share it with. If you are that special woman then the best is yet to come - *hang in there baby, mama's coming!*

Chapter 13

The following evening, Rachel poured herself into the made to measure silk shift dress she'd picked up for a song in Mumbai and admitted to herself that had she had longer to prepare for the evening, she would probably have chickened out. In the twenty four hours since her phone call with Sophia, she'd run through hundreds of imaginary 'what if' scenarios. Worst of all ... what if someone recognised her? It was a reasonable probability, considering the Windsor venue's proximity to Heathrow airport. What if all the men had their baby radar on full alert and gave her the cold shoulder? What if she choked on a canapé and had to be given the Heimlich manoeuvre, spraying the contents of her stomach over the only decent looking guy in the room?

With butterflies playing havoc with her stomach she turned on her satellite navigation gadget (last year's practical but crushingly unromantic Christmas gift from Josh) and set the co-ordinates for 112 Castle View, Windsor.

Lying in the shadow of a sprawling 'Shopping Village' on the edge of a toy town estate six miles from Windsor, 112 Castle View was as optimistic about its outlook as it was about the authenticity of its Tudor façade. Rachel pulled onto Sophia's drive and noticed that a graffiti artist had spray-painted 'bouncy' on the road sign.

She was still smiling to herself as she rang Sophia's doorbell. *Greensleeves* tinkled merrily behind the door and was soon accompanied by the clatter of high heels. Eventually the door swung open revealing Sophia, dressed in a purple kaftan, heavily embroidered with silver beads. Smiling broadly she shook Rachel's hand, jangling the dozens of silver bracelets jostling for position on her forearm. In spite of her Botox smooth face and youthfully plump lips, Rachel guessed Sophia to be in her late fifties, the loose skin, hanging in crepe folds on her neck was a dead give-away. Shuddering, Rachel made a mental note to ask for cashmere polo necks and silk scarves for her fiftieth birthday.

Taking Rachel by the elbow Sophia ushered her

towards the living room. 'Do come through. Everyone's here except Nigel.'

'Nigel?'

'Nigel. Client 700. The gentleman I emailed you about.'

Rachel stopped dead in her tracks. The whole point of the evening was to meet client 700, a.k.a. Nigel. If he wasn't going to show his face then she'd really much rather go home, than spend an evening making small talk with a bunch of lonely hearts.

Suddenly doubt began to creep into her mind. Would a successful man of the world really go looking for love in a mock Tudor semi-detached, a stone's throw from *Carpetland* ? How could she have been so stupid? She'd been well and truly had. Nigel had never existed, he was just a marketing ploy used by Sophia to entice desperate women like her to use the agency. She struggled to find some choice words to fling into Sophia's 'botoxed' face but as her own naivety was as much to blame for the situation as Sophia's duplicity, she found she could only glare at her instead. In a flash of anger, directed far more at herself than at Sophia, she yanked her elbow roughly from Sophia's grasp.

'Are you alright Rachel? I'm sorry. I'm a very tactile person. I should remember that some people don't like to be touched, need their personal space, that kind of thing,' Sophia shook her head sympathetically. 'Finding a boyfriend when you have personal intimacy issues can be such a challenge. I run a half day workshop that might help you. Remind me to give you a leaflet before you go.'

Rachel groaned inwardly, now Sophia thought she was frigid! 'No, it's not that, really.' At the open doorway to the sitting room she hesitated, protesting, but Sophia propelled her forward and she found herself announcing to a room full of strangers. 'I've no problem being touched ...'

Four pairs of eyes swivelled round to stare.

'That's my kind of a woman!' announced a short, balding man in his late fifties. 'Come and sit here love,' he said, patting a space on the sofa with one hand, while carefully balancing a gin and tonic on his pot belly with the other.

'Steady on George. I haven't introduced everyone,' said Sophia tapping him on the shoulder. 'Everyone, I'd like to introduce you to Rachel. Rachel, this is George.'

George winked and licked his lower lip, leaving a trail of silvery spit along the edge of his mouth. 'Nice to meet you my love,' he said, rubbing the sofa cushion suggestively. 'When Sophia's finished with her intros, just you come and sit here and I'll keep you company.'

Rachel grimaced, she'd rather clean out a 747 toilet used by 300 passengers with a gippy tummy, than cosy up on the velour with George.

'Wine?' offered Sophia.

Rachel accepted a glass and steeled herself for the rest of the introductions.

'Rachel, this is Edward Rhys Edwards. Edward manages his family estate, just up the road, near Oxford I believe. Have I got that right Edward?'

Rachel caught Sophia giving her a discreet conspiratorial wink, as if to indicate that he was a good catch. Edward, however, was refusing to join the party and clutched the mantle-piece like a security blanket. In response to Sophia's question he nodded, almost imperceptibly. The interaction caused him to blush furiously and he stared into his glass of orange juice, desperately trying to avoid eye contact.

Realising the poor man was crippled with shyness and not wanting to prolong his agony, Rachel steered Sophia in the direction of the remaining guests; two women huddled together, presumably for comfort and safety, on a window seat at the far end of the room. A look of relief swept across both women's faces when they saw that Sophia was only bringing Rachel to join them, and that neither of the men appeared to be moving from their comfort zones.

'Amelia, Jan, let me introduce Rachel,' Sophia said.

Rachel smiled, hopeful that some decent female company would be an antidote to an otherwise crap evening.

'Hi, have a seat.' The woman introduced as Jan gestured towards a large floor cushion nearby. 'Please, sit down,' she insisted more urgently.

'Rachel, I'll leave you with the ladies whilst I fetch the canapés. Is everyone alright for drinkie-poos?' Sophia asked.

All three women nodded furiously, desperate to be rid of her and when she had gone, Jan leant forward and whispered. 'I'm sorry I was so bossy, demanding that you sit down, I was just so desperate that *Wallace and Gromit* didn't join us!'

Amelia giggled nervously and nodded in agreement.

'Is it always this awful?' said Rachel, relieved to have found some kindred spirits.

'I have no idea, this is my first time and it's Amelia's first too,' said Jan.

Again Amelia nodded but remained silent. Perhaps she's pretending to be mute thought Rachel, kicking herself for not thinking of it first. She took a sip of her wine and made a lightening assessment of her maidens in arms. Both women were in their late thirties. Amelia dressed in a pretty floral shift Rachel recognised from the *Per Una* range at *Marks and Spencer*, was guarding a handbag at her feet and dangling from the handle was a handbag charm, containing a photograph of two beaming girls, Amelias in miniature. So, Amelia was doing this second time around thought Rachel, trying to get her life together as a single mum.

Jan on the other hand was much more difficult to place. She wore navy linen trousers, a stretchy white t-shirt and a wide, silver bangle and silver drop earrings.

'So how do you two find yourselves at 'Sophia's Divine Dinner Dates'?' asked Rachel, curiosity getting the better of her.

'I've been asking myself that ever since I got here,' Jan laughed. 'I guess you could say I've been driven here by the dearth of men at my workplace. I work at the BBC,' she said, by way of an explanation.

'I'm not sure I understand. Surely there are plenty of men working at the BBC. There must be hundreds of camera men for a start.'

'Sure there are hundreds of men, gay men!' Jan shook her head sadly. 'They're not all gay, of course, just a high percentage that's all and the rest are either married, either to women or their careers and the ones that are left ...' She looked over in George's direction busy helping himself to Sophia's gin, 'you wouldn't touch them with a barge pole!'

Rachel nodded and sipped her wine. 'I couldn't agree more. I'm Cabin Crew, so I completely understand the gay colleague thing. Most of the pilots are straight but then they're either married or like dogs on heat, shagging a new girl every trip.' Rachel paused. She'd been one of those 'girls' on more than one occasion. 'I went out with a pilot for a while, nice guy but desperate to live the playboy lifestyle. Not into settling down at all ...' she trailed off sadly.

'It's not all it's cracked up to be.'

Rachel looked up with a start. Had the voice come from Amelia? Amelia put down her wine glass, saying, 'I said, it's not all it's cracked up to be.'

'What isn't?' Rachel had been so taken back that Amelia was actually engaging her in conversation she hadn't heard a word.

Amelia snapped. 'Has flying affected your ears? I said, that settling down isn't all it's cracked up to be. My husband, or should I say ex-husband was the settling down type, until it came to the actual settling down and then he did a bunk, leaving me with two children under the age of five.' She shook her head and continued in an acid tone. 'Settling down is a mugs game, have fun with as many pilots as will have you, that's my advice. If you asked me to swop places with you I'd leave skid marks!'

'I ... I don't know what to say. I'm sorry that you've had such a hard time but it's a good sign that you're here, it shows you haven't given up hope,' Rachel said, and keen to steer the conversation away from what was obviously still a very sore subject, she decided to ask Jan about her career.

'So what do you do for the Beeb?'

'I direct the news.'

'Wow, that's a big job!' exclaimed Rachel, impressed.

Jan shrugged. 'It's often boring. The number of times we practised for the Queen Mum's funeral you wouldn't believe. When the old dear finally popped off, I was so relieved I nearly cried. It was such a shame.'

'Yes, she was well liked wasn't she?' agreed Rachel, picturing the ever smiley, wrinkled face of the Queen Mum.

Jan shook her head. 'She'd had a damn good innings. I meant it was a shame for the Beeb.'

'Why? If I remember the whole thing took up weeks of BBC airtime,' said Rachel.

Jan nodded. 'Just as we planned. The shame was for years we'd been leasing an apartment as it had the best view of the funeral route, but because Queen Mum kept going past her sell by date and because of all the pressure that the BBC was under to cut costs, we gave up the lease to save money and guess what? A week later the old girl pops her clogs and Sky grabs the best seat in the house!'

Rachel laughed and even Amelia smiled. Rachel began to cheer up, even without client 700, the evening hadn't been a complete washout. Then Sophia had appeared baring a tray of canapés. 'You three seem to be getting on very well. Help yourselves to a crostini whilst they're hot.'

'We're getting on fine thank you,' said Rachel, popping an olive into her mouth. 'Pity the same can't be said for your other guests.'

All four women turned round to see George fast asleep on the sofa, a dark circle forming on his shirt where his saliva had dribbled from his open mouth. There was no one else in the room. The only indication that Edward had been in the room, was the half empty glass of orange juice on the mantle-piece.

'Oh my goodness!' exclaimed Sophia. 'Where an earth is Edward?'

'I think you'll find that he's legged it,' said Rachel. 'He got a call on his mobile from his mother to say that she'd managed to trace a long lost cousin, who he had to marry straight away or the ancestral family home would be lost to a rich American, without an ounce of common sense or good taste!'

'We may as well sit down to dinner. Although I'm not sure how divine it's going to be,' Sophia said crossly.

At her request they followed her into the dining room, which was situated at the front of the house.

'What about George?' asked Amelia.

'What about him?' snapped Sophia. 'He can jolly well stay there and sleep off the gin. He won't remember whether he's had supper or not by the time he wakes up!'

They took their seats around the table and as Rachel passed round a basket of rolls, beams from a car's headlights criss-crossed the room.

Sophia smiled. 'Good that'll be him. Better late than never.'

'Who?' asked Rachel, Jan and Amelia together.

'My other guest of course.'

'You mean … client 700?' said Rachel, choking on a mouthful of bread. 'I thought you said he wasn't coming.'

'No, I simply said he hadn't arrived. He's a very busy man you know. I imagine he's been working on another of his multi-million pound business deals and couldn't get away sooner.'

She was interrupted by the metallic chimes of *Greensleeves* and tottered out of the door, bumping squarely into George coming the other way.

'What's going on?' he slurred, clutching Sophia's shoulder for support. 'I found young Eddy wandering the corridors.'

Sophia peered around George's ample frame to where Edward stood, lurking in the hallway, doing his utmost to hide behind a leopard print raincoat hanging from a coat stand. 'Edward, where an earth did you get to? I thought you'd gone home.'

In response Edward blushed furiously and stared at his feet.

'He went for a jimmy riddle, love. It's all that bloody orange juice you've been giving him. Goes right through you that stuff. Why didn't you give him a proper drink?' He leant towards Sophia and in a drunkard's misguided attempt at discretion, whispered loudly, 'He's not a poofta is he?'

'Honestly George!' Sophia said, pushing him aside. 'Will you stop this nonsense and sit down with the ladies.'

'Alright, alright there's no need to get your knickers in a twist. Come on Eddy my boy, Miss Bossy Drawers wants us to sit down.'

With a tired sigh he sat his 'man at C&A bottom' down between Rachel and Amelia. Edward hovered nervously at the door then bolted for the nearest chair, as if taking part in a personal game of musical chairs.

'Damn,' said Rachel under her breath. Now the only unoccupied chair was between Jan and Amelia. Amelia was no competition but Jan stood every chance of charming the pants off client 700.

'Alright love?' asked George, placing his sweating palm over Rachel's hand. 'You need anything, anything at all, you just say the word.'

Rachel shuddered, the last thing she needed was this slug of a man pawing her as she tried to make an impression. With her free hand she grabbed her fork, saying, 'I'm perfectly alright thank you and if you touch me again I'll kebab your balls with this, got it?'

Before George could reply, Sophia breezed into the room followed by a distinguished looking man dressed in an expertly tailored grey suit. 'Everyone, may I introduce Nigel,' she said, sweeping the air dramatically with her outstretched hand.

Rachel gasped and dropped the fork onto her side plate with a loud clatter.

Client 700, the man of her dreams, the man destined to rock her world and father her children, was none other, than Rupert Fotheringham-Allen.

Chapter 14

Rupert Fotheringham-Allen, an arsehole, who just happened to be a very much married arsehole, was passing himself off as a lonely heart.

'Like the look of him, do you love?' said George, elbowing Rachel in the ribs suggestively.

Rachel ignored him, watching as Sophia pulled out the vacant chair, gesturing to 'Nigel' to sit down. Taking his jacket, she smoothed it lovingly over her arm and spread a napkin over his lap.

'Thank you Sophia, darling,' he said, dazzling her with his most charming smile before turning to acknowledge his fellow guests. He looked upon them benignly until his gaze fell on Rachel, and for a moment his face became a spasm of horror, before twitching back into a pained impression of a smile. Standing behind her favourite's chair, Sophia was oblivious to his change in demeanour and continued on regardless. 'Nigel, let me introduce everyone. Nigel this is Amelia, George, Rachel, Edward and finally, Jan.'

He acknowledged each of them with a cursory nod, keeping his eyes locked onto Rachel's face, not trusting what would happen next.

'Edward, would you be a sweetheart and top up everyone's wine? And I'll fetch the first course,' trilled Sophia, sweeping out of the room.

Reluctantly Edward stood up and reached for the wine.

'Perhaps you'd better serve Nigel first,' Rachel suggested. 'He looks like he could use a drink.'

Still keeping his eyes locked on her face 'Nigel' held out his glass. Rachel returned his gaze with a dazzling smile. He's like a rabbit caught in the headlights she thought, the devious little prick is wetting himself wondering whether I'm going to let the cat out of the bag - all in good time - there was much more fun to be had in making the bastard squirm. 'So Nigel, what kept you this evening? Sophia has told us what a successful businessman you are, so perhaps it was a little domestic problem?' *Like your wife for instance.*

'It was work related of course. I've been trying to tie up some business in Madrid but you know what these continentals are like.' Rup shrugged and cast his glance at George, seeking a potential ally. 'Can you believe it's the twenty-first century and they still insist on a three hour lunch break?'

'I can,' said Jan. 'I quite admire them for it actually. I think they have a much better work life balance than us Brits.'

'I couldn't agree more,' said Rachel, cracking open a crusty roll with a loud snap. 'Perhaps your colleague was at home having a siesta with his wife.'

Rup glared at her over his wine glass and having dismissed Jan for having an opinion, turned his attention to Amelia. 'May I say how charming you look this evening and your scent?' He closed his eyes as if her perfume was sending him into raptures. 'Is it ...*Chanel*?'

'Oh, my goodness, yes!' exclaimed Amelia. 'How on earth did you guess?'

'A man should notice these things,' he said, raising his glass to her. 'And may I say you wear the scent exquisitely.'

Yuk! thought Rachel, who the hell does he think he is, James bloody Bond? Amelia appeared not to share Rachel's disgust and continued to soak up his sickly sweet compliments like a boudoir biscuit. Minutes later, Sophia reappeared pushing a hostess trolley. 'Sorry for the delay. I hope you enjoy your first course, twice baked goat's cheese soufflés.'

Rup was on the charm offensive again. 'Sophia, they look absolutely delicious!'

'Each to their own, they're a lot of hot air if you ask me,' said Rachel, giving Rup a knowing look.

Picking up on her double entendre he couldn't resist sparring with her. 'They seem to get away with it though don't they? Always very popular with the ladies I find,' he said, winking salaciously.

Rachel twitched with anger, how dare he wink at her! This was all a game to him, an opportunity for an extra bit of totty. She watched as he continued his flirtatious assault on Amelia.

'Looks like you've been beaten to it love,' said George, mistaking her grimace of disgust for one of jealousy.

'The game's not over yet George, not by a long chalk,' she replied, stabbing her fork into her soufflé.

When they had finished, Sophia cleared away their plates and served the main course. Determined to help things along, George offered Amelia a plate of vegetables. 'Want some asparagus love? It's supposed to be an aphrodisiac. Not sure that you need it though,' he said winking conspiratorially at Rup, 'you seem to be getting on fine.'

Rachel looked up in time to see Rup winking back. It was all she could do not to grab the jug of hollandaise sauce and pour it all over his arrogant head. Under the table she felt a foot nudge hers. Surely Rup wasn't playing footsie with her? She glanced up to find that it was Jan trying to attract her attention. She was pointing frantically at her cheeks and mouthing, 'There's something wrong with your face.' Rachel placed a hand on her cheek, it did feel rather warm. She made her excuses.

In Sophia's pot-pourri scented cloakroom, she pulled the light cord and turned to look at herself in the mirror. "Holy fuck!" she said, running her hands over the bumpy red rash that had crept across her face during dinner. The beauty therapist had warned her not to apply makeup within twenty-four hours of the micro-dermabrasion but the idea of meeting client 700 without the benefit of a bucket load of ceramides, light reflecting pigments and half a ton of *YSL Touche Éclat* had been unthinkable.

Other parts of her body were hurting too. Her thong was biting into her freshly waxed bikini line and as she adjusted the ribbon of flimsy fabric the elastic caught on an area of left over wax, making her yelp in pain. She winced, remembering how the wax had been much hotter than she was used to and now every inch of her de-fuzzed skin, from her ankles to her armpits, itched like hell; the pain reminding her of a carpet burn she'd picked up after a marathon of lovemaking with an athletic Captain during a stop-over in Los Angeles. Carpet burn after lovemaking was one thing she thought grimly, but third degree burns on your fanny caused by an overzealous beauty therapist called Kylie, was something else entirely. Particularly when that something else turned out to be Rupert Fotheringham-Allen!

Hoping to find a soothing ointment to dab on her spots, she opened the medicine cabinet but found instead, a peach scented room spray, a dried up mascara brush and a half empty packet of tangerine stained wood shavings masquerading as pot-pourri. Rachel closed the cabinet and searched her handbag, jabbing herself on her car keys she remembered that she'd left her cabin bag in the car, and in it was her emergency medical kit containing a packet of super strength anti-histamines.

Creeping out of the house, she pulled a pot of geraniums against the door frame, so that she could sneak back in again without setting off another rendition of *Greensleeves*. Quickly, she found the pills and downed them with a swig of mineral water she kept in the car for emergencies, before flinging the bottle onto the passenger seat, where it gave up its last drop onto her flying roster.

Desperately she tried to soak up the water with a tissue, before it had chance to make the ink run and underneath another piece of paper caught her eye. Staring back at her was the perfect solution for exposing Fotheringham-Allen. Grabbing the evidence, she returned to the house and closed the front door quietly behind her.

'Are you alright Rachel?'

Rachel turned to see Sophia pushing her hostess trolley towards her, laden with deserts. 'Yes I'm fine. I needed something from the car.'

'Is your face alright, it looks very red?' asked Sophia, peering over a large pavlova laden with tropical fruit.

Rachel nodded. 'Bit of an allergic reaction that's all.'

'Nothing to do with the food I hope.' Sophia frowned and her tone became guarded. 'I don't remember there being any food allergies on your registration form.'

'You're quite right Sophia, I didn't tick any of those boxes,' agreed Rachel, 'but then I didn't tick the box marked 'gullible twat', but that hasn't stopped you treating me like one!'

'I haven't the faintest idea what you are talking about and there's no need for that type of language!'

'No? I think there's every need, considering that there's a married man in your dining room trying to seduce a very vulnerable and very single woman!'

Sophia's face turned puce. 'You've got no proof,' she said, crossing her arms across her purple clad bosom.

'Oh, haven't I?' said Rachel, and brandishing her piece of paper like a cutlass; she made a dash for the dining room.

Realising she was about to be exposed, Sophia gave the hostess trolley an almighty shove, propelling it forward to block Rachel's path.

Catching the end of the trolley, Rachel shoved it back twice as hard, saying, 'You've chosen the wrong weapon lady! You've met the tart with the cart. Meet the dragon with the wagon!'

As the trolley whistled across the hall parquet, the pavlova span off the top, landing with a sticky thud against Sophia's kaftan. For a moment the whipped cream acted like glue, holding the dessert fast and then, slowly it slid down her thighs arriving with a satisfying plop on her delicate silver sandals. Sophia's screams bought the others running from the dining room.

'She shoved the trolley at me. I had no chance,' sniffed Sophia. 'She's mad *and* frigid. Completely mad, I tell you. I knew as soon as she walked in.'

'Right that's it,' interrupted Rachel. 'I wasn't going to bring you into this but as you've been so nasty about me; I see no reason why I should protect you. I am not mad, nor am I frigid but I could be considered incredibly naive for trusting a spiteful, incompetent cow like you! Then again, they all trusted you, didn't they Sophia?' she said, gesturing to the others who were staring at her in stupefied silence.

105

Only Jan appeared able to respond, bravely stepping forward and placing herself between the two sparring females. 'What's going on? What on earth has Sophia done?'

'It's more a case of what she didn't do. I think you'd better have a look at this.' Rachel handed her the paper she'd taken from her car. It was a copy of the Upper Thames Tennis Club Summer Newsletter and covering half the front page was a photograph of the Club Chairman, Rupert Fotheringham-Allen with his arm around the new Club Treasurer, his beaming wife Carolyn. Rachel shook her head in disbelief and passed the paper to George, who tutted before handing it to Amelia. Everyone watched as a look of horror washed over her face.

'You bastard!' she shrieked, grabbing a strawberry mousse from the hostess trolley and taking aim at Rup's head.

Not about to have his designer suit ruined, Rup ducked and Edward could only stare open mouthed, as the pretty pink desert slammed into his face. Bursting into tears Amelia rushed into the cloakroom, locking herself in and Edward, smothered in pudding, carefully removed his glasses, revealing two perfect white circles in a mask of pink fluff.

'Here you are mate,' said George, handing him a spoon, 'you may as well make a start; it's probably the only pud you're going to get tonight!'

Taking advantage of the chaos, Rup made a dash for the door but not before George, sticking out a beefy hand, grabbed him by his shirt collar. 'And where do you think you're sneaking off to, you devious little shit?' he said, swivelling Rup around and slamming him against the wall.

Rup tried to respond but George's grip around his neck made it impossible.

'For such a clever businessman you're really very stupid!' George said. 'By the looks of that photo, your wife's a right cracker. Fuck knows why you're trying to get into other women's knickers but keep this up mate and the only thing you'll be getting into is a divorce!'

Having said his piece George loosened his grip around Rup's neck and Rup, running a finger between his skin and shirt collar, cleared his throat. 'Come on old chap, just because one's married doesn't mean one can't have a little harmless fun does it?' Rup said, determined to justify himself.

George pointed at the cloakroom, from where Amelia's sobs could be heard from behind the door. 'Does that sound like harmless fun to you?'

Rup shrugged. 'An over emotional woman. Getting into her knickers, as you so eloquently put it, would hardly have been worth the bother I'd say.'

'You would, would you? Well, I've had all I can take from you, you arrogant little shit!' George said in disgust and with one swift movement he slammed the front door open, swiping the heads off Sophia's geraniums and threw Rup across the threshold. 'And if I ever see your adulterous face again I'll smash it to smithereens!' he hollered after him.

Closing the door he turned to face the others. 'That's got rid of him,' he said, wiping his hands down the front of his trousers as if he had touched something dirty. 'I think we may as well call it a night don't you?'

'Not quite George,' said Rachel, pointing accusingly at Sophia, who had by now retreated halfway up the stairs and was half-heartedly picking off beads of passion fruit from her kaftan. 'I think we should have our money back.'

'He seemed so charming,' Sophia said, nervously twisting her silver bangles back and forth.

'Charming my arse!' said Rachel. 'He was using your service as a knocking shop and your incompetence meant he got away with it. So, unless you want the truth about Divine Dinner Dates plastered all over the Windsor Gazette, you'll give each and every one of us our money back!'

Nodding meekly Sophia agreed. 'Yes, I see your point ... I'll fetch my cheque book.'

Sometime later, with Rachel's gentle encouragement Amelia emerged from her hideout and was relieved to find that the others had gone and Sophia was nowhere to be seen.

'I think it's time we went home,' said Rachel, handing over Sophia's cheque. 'I'm sorry it didn't work out for you tonight but at least we all got a refund.'

'Thanks,' said Amelia, slipping the cheque into her handbag. 'I can't believe I was sucked in by that slime ball.'

'Don't beat yourself up about it,' Rachel said, opening the front door. 'First impressions can be misleading. I had George down as a dirty old man but he was quite the accidental hero as it turned out.'

As she drove home Rachel recalled the terrified expression on Rup's face as he was flying across Sophia's threshold. It was the second time in a matter of weeks that she'd humiliated him and he wasn't the sort of man to take it lying down. She made a mental note to tell Sarah that if she was planning more teas at the Tennis Club, she'd have to find someone else to do the washing up in future.

Having eaten only a few mouthfuls of dinner, her stomach was grumbling loudly and when she got home, she stuck her head in the fridge for culinary inspiration, Biggles winding himself around her ankles. 'Umm, looks like it's cheese or cheese, Biggles,' she said, dipping her finger into a chunk of goat's cheese and offering the cat a lick.

Unimpressed, he gave her leg a disdainful flick of his tail and disappeared through the cat flap. 'I think for once I agree with you cat,' she said, loading a plate with left over cheese and digestives, 'but I'm starving, so I'll just have to hope that stuff about cheese and nightmares isn't true.'

As she wrapped what was left of the Coulommiers in its greaseproof wrapping, she could hear the voice of the handsome stranger from the market. What had he recommended with the Brie? A glass of Bordeaux? She struggled to recall his words but had no trouble remembering his face. There had to be some way of tracking him down. If only she knew how, she could post herself on *Facebook* and reach millions of people in a matter of minutes but not, necessarily the right *one*. Hopeful that by morning she would have dreamt up plan 'B', she went to bed.

Chapter 15

The next morning Rachel woke in a cold sweat, vowing she would never eat cheese again, so close to bedtime. She hadn't slept well on account of an unsettling dream involving Rupert-Fotheringham Allen raising a mutiny on board a flight to Chicago. It began with a food fight in First Class and ended as the plane made its descent into the windy city, hand luggage blocking the aisles and tray tables down, and Rachel, ensconced in the galley had ignored it all; busy playing *9½ Weeks* with the First Class cheese board…and the handsome French stranger.

Pushing down the damp sheet, she half expected to see Brie oozing from her navel. Ever since their brief encounter at the market, the Frenchman hadn't been far from her thoughts and now he had invaded her dreams. It was a sign she decided. She had to find out who he was, but what did she have to go on? He looked gorgeous in white linen and 'gave good cheese.'

That was it! The answer had been staring her in the face all along. The French market had been back in town since Thursday and she remembered him saying how he'd bought cheese before from…now what was his name? - Jean Luc, that was it. It was a clue - the handsome stranger wasn't a tourist but had some other connection with the town. Maybe Jean Luc, the cheesemonger could help? It made perfect sense - didn't detectives always return to the scene of the crime (the crime she knew, was hers for letting him slip away in the first place) to search for clues?

She showered quickly and drove into town, finding a parking spot in the long term car park. In the rear view mirror, she checked her face for hints of the previous night's rash and was relieved, that thanks to the super strength anti-histamine, her cheeks were back to normal, if perhaps a little flushed. Next, she slicked on *Kiehl's* 'Pink Rider' lip balm, bought not because of the colour but because she thought it sounded like a sex toy and finally, slipped on her sunglasses.

Wandering through the market, she soon came to *their*

stall, recognising Jean Luc who was busy serving a queue of customers. Eventually, he looked in her direction and nodded, which she instantly took to be a good sign.

'Hi,' she said brightly, wondering how to bring the conversation round to a customer that he may, or may not remember. 'I was here the other day and you, er…tried to sell me cheese that smelt of wet cat … Tommes de something, it was grey and furry.'

'Ah oui, Tommes Grise de Seyssel,' he said, grinning he reached inside the cabinet for the ugly grey cheese.

Rachel shook her head. 'Can I take some Coulommier instead? I bought it from you last time; another of your customers helped me make a selection. He was about this tall,' she said, waggling her hand above her head. 'And he was French. You seemed to know each other. Do you remember?'

Jean Luc nodded and positioned his knife above the creamy white cheese for Rachel to indicate how much. 'Oui, he's from Paris. Nice guy; likes my cheese.'

Rachel knew she should be grateful for this nugget of information, but narrowing down the field to the population of Paris, 2.1 million people in old money, could hardly be classed as progress. 'I don't suppose you know his name?' she asked, holding out her hand at a thirty degree angle over the cheese, indicating where he should cut.

Jean Luc shook his head and sliced into the cheese, its silky insides oozing onto the greaseproof paper he held ready.

Great, thought Rachel handing over the right money and slipping the cheese into her handbag, all she had to go on was that the stranger came from Paris and liked cheese. Clues? Yes. Helpful clues? No. Where was *Hercule Poirot* when you needed him? Hastily she scribbled her mobile number on the back of a till receipt. 'If he comes back to buy cheese, will you give him this for me?'

Jean Luc nodded and slipped the scrap of paper into the pocket of his white overall. With the cheesemonger now on the case, Rachel felt optimistic and set up camp on the steps of the town hall; from there she had a perfect view of the stalls and, should he return to restock his cheeseboard, the handsome French stranger. After a couple of hours happily people watching, she felt warm and sleepy and switched on her iPod to help pass the time. It felt like minutes later when she was jolted awake by a foot tapping her leg.

'You won't sell many copies of *The Big Issue* if you fall asleep on the job.'

Shading her eyes from the sun, she looked in the direction of the voice and as they struggled to adjust to the light, her stomach lurched. Blocking out the sun like a storm cloud was Rupert Fotheringham-Allen.

'The only big issue around here is how your wife puts up with you sleeping around and isn't screwing you for the biggest divorce settlement she can get her hands on!' Rachel said, getting to her feet.

Rup opened his mouth to respond but was distracted by his mobile phone buzzing in his trouser pocket. From her elevated vantage point on the steps, Rachel couldn't resist reading Rup's text message over his shoulder.

'07, that's the code for Russia isn't it? Don't tell me you've got some little Babushka knocked up,' she said, noticing how the colour had drained from his face. 'You want to be careful Rup. Look what the Russians did to their Tsar and it hasn't got any better you know, Moscow is one of the most dangerous cities in the world.'

Scowling, he marched off, livid that a two bit trolley dolly who served up mediocre tea and reheated ready meals, had once again humiliated him.

Rachel watched him go and cursed herself for letting him rile her. She knew by the way he spoke to her that he thought spending half her life at 37,000 feet had given her ideas above her station. She saw that he had paused outside the jewellers and wondered who would be the recipient of his purchase, his mistress or his wife. Then, glancing at her watch she gasped. She'd been asleep for two hours! There were only a handful of people milling about; soon the stall holders would begin packing up. Pulling her earphones roughly off her head she shoved her iPod in her bag. Stupid thing! At least her old 'Walkman' would click when it reached the end of a tape, which was guaranteed to wake her up but these iPods went on for hours!

What if the stranger had visited Jean Luc's stall while she'd been asleep? And then she remembered that Jean Luc had her mobile number. Flipping open her phone, she checked for messages and found none. She sat for another hour, watching as numbers in the market dwindled and the stall holders began to pack up their wares. Until at last, on the verge of tears, she stood up stiffly and rubbing her numb backside, decided to call it a day.

A loud rumble in her stomach reminded her that she had no food in her fridge and crossly she trudged off to the Deli on the high street.

'Hey, it's my favourite customer! What can I get for you today my darlin'?' boomed the Italian owner.

'Just the usual thanks, meals for the freezer ... only this time you'd better make it meals for one, please Antonio,' Rachel said quietly.

'Meals for uno? Those men out there must be blind or something! If Antonio was twenty years younger you'd be Mrs. Bertorelli by now!'

Mustering up a smile to make him feel better, she paid the bill and picked up the carrier bag of single sized portions he'd placed on the counter. Walking through the market on her way back to the car, she passed a white van with its rear doors standing open, allowing its owner to load up trays of cheese; in his hurry, he had dropped a large piece of Brie. Rachel bent to pick it up and as she did so, she noticed a pair of black Wellingtons sticking out from beneath the van door and next to them a pair of tan brogues. Both men were speaking French. She paused for a moment to listen, her school girl French enough to understand, that the owner of the brogues was apologizing for getting to the market late and how he had been looking forward to a decent piece of camembert.

Rachel's heart began to hammer. That sensuous voice, it had to be him, didn't it? No, it was just wishful thinking;

hundreds of men had deep voices for goodness sake! She walked around the open door and as she offered the cheese to its owner, promptly dropped it again, as she came face to face with Jean Luc and the stranger. The cheese forgotten she stared open mouthed, rooted to the spot. The stranger paid Jean Luc and looked up in her direction, a smile of recognition spreading across his face.

'Hello, we meet again!' he said, his eyes twinkling, making her stomach flip. 'Pierre Toulon.'

Blushing, she shook his outstretched hand. 'Rachel Ryder.'

Rachel watched him pick up the dropped cheese and hand it to Jean Luc, who winked at her before returning to the task of loading his van. Pierre nodded in the direction of the car park. 'You are on your way home? Please, let me walk you to your car.'

They passed shops and cafes, all familiar to her, but everything else was different, even the pavement, which the soles of her feet could no longer feel. It was as if she were floating, unconnected with her surroundings and it made her dizzy. Taking deep breaths she tried to ground herself, but then Pierre turned to look at her and she felt twice as giddy.

'Are you alright?' he said and concerned he took her bag.

Gratefully she accepted his help, but was terrified that touching him would tip her over the edge and she would collapse in a heap at his feet.

'I think you have had too much sun?' he said, noticing the pink streak across her nose and cheek bones.

Rachel admitted that she had fallen asleep outside, her blush adding to her sunburn.

Pierre grinned. 'Perhaps you are also dehydrated? Would you like a coffee?'

Rachel nodded and let Pierre guide her into one of the pavement cafes. Watching him order their drinks at the counter, she imagined him instead, standing on the terrace of a sun drenched villa dripping in purple bougainvillea. He would wave as he spotted her in her silver Porsche convertible, making her way up the sweeping drive and later after they'd made passionate love in the master bedroom, its balcony doors left open to catch the sea breeze, they'd return to the terrace arm in arm, to sip chilled champagne and admire the sparkling Mediterranean view.

'Sugar?' Suddenly he was back at their table.

Rachel blushed and like the steam from her coffee, her daydream vanished into thin air.

'Sugar?' he repeated.

'Please,' she said, and unsure why, as she hadn't taken sugar in years, she took the sachet from his out stretched hand. His fingers, she noticed, were tanned a golden caramel and stirring her coffee, she fought the impulse to plunge them into the frothy cream and suck each perfect digit clean. Rendered speechless, she was grateful when he spoke, breaking the silence.

'I am glad I caught Jean Luc before he left for the day. His cheese is the best I've tasted outside of Paris. Did you enjoy the selection you bought from him the first time we met?'

Relieved to find her brain and voice box were once again communicating, Rachel said, 'Yes, your suggestions were spot on. Paris, is that where you're from?'

Pierre nodded, pushing back his dark hair as he spoke. 'Yes. My work brings me to the UK at the moment but my permanent base is Paris. I live near La Sacré Coeur, Montmartre, do you know it?'

'Yes, I love the view from up there. I always feel that I could scoop up the whole of the city and take it home in my pocket.'

Pierre smiled and stirred his coffee. 'Please don't, where would I live?'

'I think you'd find my pocket very comfortable actually.'

Pierre paused to drink a mouthful of coffee, not once taking his eyes from her face. 'And if I was to live in your pocket where would we go, what would we experience together?'

Thrilled that he was flirting with her, Rachel sipped her coffee, playing for time. She wanted to reply. 'Everywhere and everything and let's go now!' Instead, trying to appear coy and mysterious, she smiled. 'That would depend on what I was wearing at the time. If I took you to work with me, we'd cover most of the globe in about three weeks!'

'You fly for a living, that must be exciting but don't you miss your family…your boyfriend?'

Rachel could barely contain herself; he was fishing for information on her love life which meant he was definitely interested. She smiled; two could play at that game. 'I miss my friends and there was someone I was close to but we're no longer together … we wanted different things…and you, do you miss someone when you're working here?'

'I wish I could say yes. I am married, but only to my career,' he said, glancing at his watch. 'I'm afraid I must go, I have a conference call scheduled for five. Please, let me walk you to your car.'

At the car he loaded Rachel's Deli groceries into the boot and reaching to lower the hatch, their hands touched momentarily.

'Would you like to …' Pierre hesitated.

'Yes!'

'Pardon?'

'Yes, I will have dinner with you.' Blushing, she added. 'If that's what you were going to ask, I mean.'

Pierre shook his head. 'I was going to ask you if you would like a piece of the camembert I bought from Jean Luc. He gave me a large piece and I will not be able to eat it all, as I return to Paris tomorrow.'

Rachel stared at her feet, wishing she could disappear into the car boot along with her lasagne. 'I see … umm that's very kind of you but I …'

'I'm sorry. I am, how do you say it? Teasing? I am teasing you just a little,' Pierre said, grinning. 'I am going back to Paris tomorrow that part is true but I was going to ask you to have dinner with me tonight? Can you forgive me?'

Rachel took a deep breath and smiled, she'd have to

get her act together or this gorgeous Gallic hunk would think she was a complete idiot.

'I would love to have dinner with you,' she said, glancing at her watch. 'The thing is I'm on standby. If I'm needed for a flight I have to be at Heathrow in two hours, ready to report for duty. We might have to cut short our meal.'

Pierre shrugged. 'Then we will eat quickly.'

Relieved, Rachel said. 'Shall we say eight o'clock in Falaise Square, I can meet you there.'

'Perfect, here is my card in case you are called for a flight. Until then.' He smiled and turned to go.

'What about my number? Shall I write it down for you in case you're held up or anything?' asked Rachel.

Pierre grinned and reached into his jacket pocket. 'I have it here,' he said, showing her the crumpled till receipt she'd given to Jean Luc earlier in the day.

God, now she wanted to die. He knew she had been looking for him; she might as well have DESPERATE tattooed on her forehead. 'Ah ... yes ... I wanted to get in touch to thank you for your recommendations the other day ... your help with the cheese,' she said and knew she was blushing like a baboon's backside. She froze waiting for the wise crack that must surely follow.

'It was nothing,' he said, opening the driver's door for her. 'I am glad we have met in person again, I would have been disappointed with just a phone call.'

Rachel gasped. Was this guy for real? She searched his face for traces of sarcasm and found none. 'Me too,' she said, getting into her car. 'See you later.'

She drove towards the exit, bubbles of anticipation popping deliciously in her stomach. Waiting for a space in the traffic she checked her mirror and saw, to her delight that Pierre was still standing where they'd parted, watching her until she was out of sight.

Chapter 16

On the other side of town, Sarah was clearing away the children's tea when the phone rang. She toyed with the idea of letting it ring; who would be stupid enough to call at 'the witching hour' - the children's tea, baths and the battle over homework? At the last moment curiosity got the better of her and she picked up the phone.

'Hello.'

'Hello. Darling, it's Mum. I know it's short notice but I'm in rather desperate need of your help with Daisy.'

Sarah protested. 'Oh Mum, you know I'm no good with animals!'

'I know you're not a doggy person darling and I wouldn't ask but the poor little sausage needs her medicine every two hours and George is taking me to a very special restaurant tonight.'

Sarah quickly weighed up her options; on the one hand, sorting out the kid's homework and putting all three children to bed, or on the other, dog sitting an ancient Jack Russell with an upset stomach. It was what Dave called a no-brainer.

'OK, what time do you need me?'

'About seven would be perfect. Thank you darling, see you later.'

Jean opened the door in a cloud of *Chanel 5* and as she leant forward to kiss her, Sarah noticed a glow on her mother's cheeks. Whatever her mother and George were up to it was certainly putting a spring in Jean's step.

'Come through darling and I'll show you what you need to do for Daisy.'

Sarah followed her to the kitchen, where the ancient little dog was curled up asleep in her basket.

Jean bent down and gently fondled the dog's ears. 'She needs 2 blue pills at seven thirty and one pink pill at nine.'

There was a loud knock at the front door making all

three of them jump.

'That'll be George!' Jean blushed and rushed to let him in.

Sarah lingered in the kitchen not sure whether she should follow. What was the protocol for meeting your mother's boyfriend? She heard the murmur of low voices and before she had chance to feel more uncomfortable a deep voice boomed from the doorway.

'Hello, you must be Sarah. I've heard so much about you!' And before she could say "have my mother home by midnight", he was shaking her warmly by the hand.

'All good I hope!' she laughed.

'How could it be anything else, it must run in the family, eh Jeannie?' He winked at Jean, who blushed a deep shade of pink.

'Hadn't we better be going? We don't want to lose our table,' Jean said.

'Right as always, Jeannie. Good to meet you Sarah,' he said, helping Jean into her jacket and leading the way out.

Sarah caught her mother's eye and winked. 'Have a good time... Jeannie.'

To her astonishment, Jean winked back and swung out of the kitchen with a sheepish grin on her face.

Sarah made herself a coffee and raided her mother's cake tin, before settling down for a relaxing evening with her all time favourite film, *Gone with the Wind*. By nine o'clock she had fallen in love with Rhett Butler all over again and had to admit that agreeing to look after Daisy had been a smart move. The little dog had been reluctant to take her first batch of medicine, until Sarah remembered she had some chocolate in her handbag. It was just the right consistency to hide the two small pills and when Sarah opened the bottle containing Daisy's nine o'clock pill, the little dog was doing cartwheels in anticipation.

'You've been a very good girl Daisy, well done. Shall we close the blinds now so you can settle down for the night?' asked Sarah, and as she turned to the window, she noticed a faint light in the lane outside the house. It must be those teenagers her mother was always moaning about, smooching in their cars before heading home. Sighing, she drew the blinds; at least someone was having fun, and taking envy, her new best friend with her, she went back into the lounge to watch the rest of the film. Moments later, she heard her mother's key in the front door.

'Hi Mum. Did you have a good time?' she called, without looking up from Rhett Butler's sparkling blue eyes on freeze frame.

Jean came in and sat down, holding her evening shoes in her hand and followed by Daisy, who sniffed at Sarah's handbag, before laying at her mistress's feet.

'Oh, yes darling, we had a marvellous time!' Jean said, alternately rubbing at the pink indents left by her shoes and then, the dog's ears. 'It's so lovely having a reason to wear heels again, my feet are complaining it's been so long.'

Sarah was about to ask her what she had had to eat, when she stopped. There was something strange about Jean's appearance. 'I can't put my finger on it but there's something different about you.'

Jean smiled. 'Oh, I know darling. I can feel it. I'm like a new woman since I met George.'

'Got it!' said Sarah, jumping up from the sofa. 'It's your blouse. It's inside out!'

Jean looked down at her top and gasped. 'Heavens, you're right! To think I went out looking like this, you could have said something earlier Sarah!'

Sarah shook her head as the realisation dawned on her. 'Why would I? It was the right way round before...that was you just now, wasn't it? In the car. Outside in the lane? I saw from the kitchen window.'

Jean pressed her hands into her cheeks. 'I know I should be ashamed, a woman of my age cavorting about like a teenager, but I refuse to be!' She took her hands from her face and grinned. 'And you know Sarah it was such terribly good fun!'

'Mother!' gasped Sarah, pretending to be outraged.

Unabashed, Jean continued. 'To think I wasted all

those years floundering about with your father. It's all about finding your...now what's it called? There was an excellent article about it in last month's *Woman and Home*. It sounds so vulgar, I've given it a name of my own but you'll know what I mean, being of the younger generation. It's all about finding your 'clematis'... sort that one out and you're away!'

Flabbergasted, Sarah stared at Jean open mouthed.

Jean reached out for Sarah's hand. 'Dear, I don't want you to make the same mistakes as I did.'

Sarah felt the blood rush to her cheeks. What could she say? Well, actually Mum now you come to mention it I think mine's got Clematis Wilt, or Powdery Mildew or whatever it was, that her mother always complained her plants seemed to be suffering from. Anyone from Charlie Dimmock to Alan Titchmarsh could tell her what the problem was, horticultural neglect on behalf of her not so green fingered husband! ... No, she couldn't go there, especially with her mother of all people! Instead, she bent to kiss the top of Jean's head. 'I'm glad your Clematis is in good hands Mum and on that note I'll bid you and Daisy goodnight.'

'Goodnight darling. Thank you for taking such good care of Daisy. She seems quite perky now,' Jean said, scooping up the dog and following Sarah into the hall.

Sarah patted the dog's head as it struggled to free itself from Jean's arms. 'See you soon mum, you too Daisy.'

Jean frowned. 'Do you know dear, if I didn't know any better I'd think she was trying to come with you.'

On the way home, Sarah thought about her mother's exciting new love life and as she turned the car onto the main road, she knew loneliness had bunched up on the back seat, to give envy some room.

Chapter 17

While Sarah had been coaxing Daisy to take her first set of pills, Rachel had been preparing for her date with Pierre. Opening the boot to her car, she lifted in her suitcase and laid her uniform on top. As the evening progressed, there would be fewer potential flights she could be called for, and making a final prayer to the airline's Scheduling Gods, Rachel drove into town to meet Pierre.

When she arrived he was already there waiting, and greeting her in the Gallic fashion, kissing each cheek and murmuring 'Bon Soir', into her ear, he set her heart hammering again. Blushing hotly, Rachel dived into her handbag searching for a distraction. 'Do you?' she said holding out an open packet of cigarettes.

Pierre shook his head. 'I gave up a couple of years ago,' he smiled, and reaching inside his pocket, produced a lighter. 'Some habits die hard, no?'

Rachel nodded and took two drags on her cigarette before grinding it into the gutter with her heel. 'I've just gone back to it, silly really. Especially now you're not allowed to smoke anywhere.'

'We have the same law in France, only generally we choose to ignore it,' Pierre said, guiding her towards an Italian restaurant. 'I booked a table. I guessed from your shopping this afternoon, that you were a fan of Italian.'

Having been shown to their table, a waiter handed them a wine list and a menu.

'Just a mineral water please,' said Rachel. 'I'm not allowed to drink alcohol in case I'm flying later.'

Pierre handed back the wine lists. 'Make that two. It is not fair that I should enjoy wine, if you are not able to share in the pleasure.'

There he goes again, thought Rachel; he had a habit of making food and drink sound like an intimate experience. After the waiter had taken their order Pierre leant forward and whispered conspiratorially, 'So, which cheese did you enjoy most?'

'Oh, the Bleu des Causses, it was some of the best I've tasted. You really know your stuff.' Am I only talking about cheese, she wondered.

Pierre shrugged. 'I eat out a lot and have a good memory. It must be one of the pleasures of your job, trying food from all over the world?' he added, snapping a breadstick in two and offering her half.

Rachel took it, delighted at the familiarity of the gesture. 'It is. I guess it's one of the compensations for having a job that rules your life. Take tonight for example, my phone could ring at any moment and I would have to leave. And as for having a social life, forget it! Can you believe, I've lived in Henley for five years and have never been to the Royal Regatta? Perils of the job, I guess.'

Pierre nodded his thanks to the waiter who had brought out their pasta. 'Then, that makes two of us,' he said. 'I have seen the tents on the riverbank and the flags in town. What is it all about?'

'Rowing; or at least that is how it started. Some of the best teams in the world compete here but most of the spectators come for the party. There's music and bars and dancing and a fantastic firework display over the Thames.'

Pierre wound his spaghetti round his fork. 'It sounds like fun. I'd like to see this Royal Regatta for myself, if only I could find someone to show me around.'

Rachel laughed; like his pasta he was reeling her in. 'You never know your luck. You might find some old sculler from the Leander Club who'll take you under his wing!'

'I had someone else in mind. You might know her; she spends half her life above the clouds and the other half, running away from strangers at French markets!'

'I didn't run away, I waited for you but you didn't come back!' she blushed, realising she'd given away any attempt at keeping him guessing. Normally, she kept her cards to her chest but for some reason, with Pierre, she was turning into an open book.

Pierre put down his fork and wiped his mouth with his napkin, as if preparing for a serious announcement. 'I did go back to Jean Luc's stall, after my phone call, but he said you'd gone. That's why I returned to the market today, I couldn't think of any other way of trying to find you.'

Rachel stared at him in amazement. There was no way Josh would have admitted such a thing, it was too vulnerable, too romantic. Flustered, she panicked and made a joke out of it. 'I thought you were there to buy cheese.'

Pierre held up his hand in mock defeat. 'OK, I'm French and never waste an opportunity where food is concerned, but the truth is, I came back to find you.'

Rachel smiled, toying with her lasagne. 'I have a confession of my own. I came back today to look for you too and it wasn't to thank you for the cheese.'

Pierre grinned and clinked his glass against hers. 'I'm deeply flattered. To the cheese, it brought us together.'

'To cheese,' said Rachel, and they both laughed as others in the restaurant turned to stare.

Our first private joke thought Rachel happily. It felt like Christmas and a birthday rolled into one; he liked her and he didn't care that she knew. At last, she began to relax and enjoy herself. 'So tell me, what do you do when you're not staking out French markets looking for wayward trolley dollies?' she asked.

'I have a travel company, Les Places Tranquilles. It's been in my family for years and when my father died I took over. Like your job, it's great if you don't mind living out of a suitcase but that's talking shop isn't?'

'It's hard not to when it's such a big part of your life,' Rachel said, thankful that he would understand the rigours of her job, without being directly connected to the airline industry. 'So, what brings you to Henley? Does your company offer trips to the UK?'

'No, we sell here and I come over once a year to meet with my business partners. They're based in London but I always stay outside the city and travel in, that way I get to see something of the country. Last year I stayed in Oxford and this year I chose Henley…'

He was interrupted by a mobile phone bleeping

beneath their feet.

'Oh no, I don't believe it!' said Rachel reaching into her bag. It was a text from work. 'I'm sorry Pierre, I have to go.' She turned off her phone and threw it into her handbag.

'Where are they sending you?' he asked, signalling for the bill.

'Tel Aviv. It's a short trip and I'll be back on Monday.'

Pierre nodded and paid the bill. 'And I will be back at my desk in Paris. It is a pity that you don't fly short-haul, I could meet you at Charles de Gaulle for lunch.'

The evening brought to an end too early, they walked the short distance to her car in silence. Finally, Rachel spoke. 'I'm so sorry to break up the party. I wish we could have shared some wine and I could have heard more about your work and your life in Paris.'

Reluctantly, she pressed the button on her key fob, unlocking the car and Pierre leaned across to open the driver's door.

'We can do better than that, why don't I show you instead? Would you like to meet me in Paris next week?'

Rachel smiled, relieved that she hadn't blown it by ending their evening prematurely. 'I'd love too. It's been years since I visited Paris,' she said, grinning like the cat that got the crème fraîche. 'Can you email me your address?' Hastily she wrote down her details on a scrap of paper.

Pierre slipped it inside his wallet and handed her a business card. 'I can send a car to the airport to pick you up or to the Gare du Nord, if you go by train,' he offered.

Rachel shook her head and wanting to give the impression of a confident girl about town, she said, 'I'll take the train, and don't bother with the car. I know Paris well and I like the métro.'

'As you wish. Until next week,' Pierre said, catching her face in his hands and kissing each cheek.

It wasn't quite what she was hoping for but with the prospect of a date in the most romantic city in the world, she was prepared to wait.

Later, she sat on the crew bus hugging herself; bursting to tell Sarah her news, but it was already late and Sarah wouldn't be pleased if she woke the kids. So she texted instead, hoping that Sarah had her phone switched on.

In heaven. Met a guy 2die4. Going 2 Paris nxt week! He runs own company, Les Places Tranquilles. Sleep well, luv R x x x

Walking into the crew report building, pulling her suitcase behind her, she felt her handbag vibrate under her arm and flicking open her phone, she saw Sarah's face beaming at her from the mini screen. 'Hi babe, what are you doing still up?'

'I just got back from dog sitting at Mum's and I'm still trying to get over the shock.'

'Don't tell me the old dog snuffed it while you were in charge!'

'Certainly not, Daisy's still alive and kicking. No, let's just say Mum and George are at the steamy windows stage! And before you say anything I know I should be happy for her and I am, it's just that I'm half her age and the closest thing to sex I get, is fantasising over the life guards in the travel mags you give me. You know how it goes, white sand, palm trees and a hot, wet surfer sucking your toes ...'

Balancing her phone on her shoulder, Rachel swiped her ID card into the Cabin Crew tracking system and requested a print off of the crew list for her flight - there were no names she recognised. Trying to do two things at once, and in a hurry, she became flustered. Surely Sarah's love life hadn't gone downhill so soon after the trip to Paris? Her stomach pinched - had the trip been lip service on Dave's part? Was he back playing tonsil hockey with Gemma bloody Jacobs?

Sarah continued. 'I'm glad you rang, as I have a bone to pick with you.'

Rachel almost dropped the phone. Had Sarah found Gemma Jacobs' boarding card in Dave's jacket? Putting two and two together and praying she was wrong, she said, 'Did I get the wrong Barbie for Millie? I can always change it the next time I'm in New York.'

'No, it's Naomi. Apparently, her class were having their first rehearsal for the Maypole dance, which is the headline act at the school fete, and Naomi refused point blank to join in. According to her teacher, Naomi insisted that nice girls didn't do it and she wasn't going to wear a bikini in front of the boys if her life depended on it!'

Rachel almost choked with relief. 'I'm sorry Sarah. Naomi asked me what pole dancing was but she didn't mention the word May, I promise you. I'm afraid she ended up with the nightclub version rather than village green variety!' Smiling, Rachel made her way to the briefing room, where she would meet the rest of the crew. 'I'm sorry babe! Just goes to show what too many trips to Thailand does to you, warps the mind.'

Sarah laughed. 'It's OK. It gave the teachers a giggle. Anyway, the real reason I called you back is Les Places Tranquilles. I thought the name was familiar, so I looked through some back copies of *Condé Nast* and there he was, Pierre Toulon, CEO and owner of Les Places Tranquilles. He's totally gorgeous by the way, and there are photos of all these fantastic boutique hotels on palm fringed beaches.'

Rachel felt her insides flip with excitement and she couldn't help feeling a little smug. After all, she'd found Pierre all by herself - not a Divine Dinner Date in sight! Aware that Sarah was on a downer about men, she decided now was not the best time to enthuse about Pierre, instead she played him down. 'You can't believe everything you read; he probably picks his toenails and farts in bed. Talking of which isn't that where you should be, it's late?'

Sarah snorted. 'Not until I've finished my list - so far I've got to cutlery.'

Shit! Rachel caught her breath. Had the Crouches reached the end of the line? Was Sarah writing a list dividing up their worldly goods - 4 knives for her, 4 knives for him, one and a half children each! 'List?' she asked, nervously.

'Yes. I've got an American crew coming to stay for Regatta. Rupert Fotheringham-Allen talked Dave into it. I only found out when I got home tonight. The crew should have been staying with Rup's girlfriend but he wasn't having any of it and of course Dave agreed, as he'll be away on business and won't be inconvenienced one iota!'

Standing outside the briefing room Rachel sighed, she would have preferred to stay in the country and help Sarah prepare for the rowers. Nothing was going to plan in the Crouch household it seemed. 'You'll be fine, one taste of your cooking and you'll have them eating out of your hand. I've got to go. I'll call you when I get back, bye babe.'

Walking into the briefing room she smiled brightly at the group of strangers, who would, for the next forty-eight hours, become her new best buddies and who, on return to base, she would probably never set eyes on again. Torn as much by the need to stay and she suspected, like most of the people in the room, the need to escape, she sat, only half listening, as the Cabin Service Director ran through the flight details.

Chapter 18

Stepping out of the métro at Lamark Caulaincourt, Rachel felt as though she had stumbled onto the set of a movie. Catching the perfumed aroma of Arabica coffee, she passed a pavement café, slaloming her suitcase between bamboo knotted legs of tables and chairs. Moments later, she paused by a Florist's shop to fetch her bearings and trailed her hand over the velvet heads of red roses, standing in tall displays either side of the entrance. Her senses, already heightened with the anticipation of seeing Pierre again, picked up the smallest detail, and then, following Pierre's instructions, she turned right, making her way along, what appeared to her, a perfect tree lined street.

Elegant white town houses eight storeys high rose up on either side, red geraniums tumbling out from ornate iron balconies and tall shutters closed against the heat of the day. On the way, she passed a boulangerie, a pâtisserie and finally a shop offering 'Escargots Sauvage' and it seemed, little else. It was her signal to turn right again, up a steep incline with steps either side for pedestrians; a ribbon of sky marked the summit. Reluctantly, she began to climb, stopping halfway to pull a bottle of water from her bag and starting to wonder whether she should have accepted Pierre's offer of a lift.

Suddenly a dog ran past, stopping a little further up the hill, for its owner to catch up. Turning round, Rachel saw an old lady pause to catch her breath and then, reaching into her pocket she threw a ball for the dog. Barking impatiently, the dog leapt several feet in the air and caught it mid-bark. Grateful for a reason to linger, Rachel watched as the dog lined himself up with his owner and gently let go of the ball, so that it rolled down the hill directly into the old woman's outstretched hand. The game continued for several minutes and each time the dog was careful to return the ball, so that the old woman did not have to move from her resting place. At last, feeling like Doris Day, Rachel continued her climb. How could she feel any other way she asked herself? Even the dogs in this city were cute and considerate.

Eventually, she found Pierre's house and standing in

the shade of a row of trees opposite, took in the view. It was an end terrace, although unlike any she'd ever seen; three storeys high and covered in ivy, 17 Rue Madeleine was a chateau in miniature. The windows were as large as her patio doors at home and although the ones on the ground floor had metal grilles, there were no shutters to block the view. The edges of elegant curtains, draped just so, and a chandelier were clearly visible. A wide stone balcony encircled the side of the house and disappeared into a forest of greenery at the rear. Rachel hugged herself; the house had romance and good taste stamped all over it.

Suddenly, she was aware that she was being watched. An old man had appeared from nowhere and wanted to know if she was lost. Wishing she could remember more of her school girl French she pointed to herself and gave him a thumbs up. It seemed to reassure him and wishing her 'Bonne journée!' he continued down the street.

Rachel smiled after him and turned to admire Pierre's house a while longer. What she saw made her gasp. Twenty feet away, with her tall size zero back to the window - Pierre's window - was a woman. In what appeared to be Pierre's kitchen, she was putting away groceries. The woman was obviously on very familiar territory.

Blinking back tears Rachel shivered in spite of the hot sun and trying to calm herself she remembered the technique she used to relax anxious flyers; breathe, slowly and deeply, and imagine a tranquil garden...ahhh, there, it was coming to her now, the scent of roses, birds chattering in the trees and on the immaculate lawn ... Pierre rolling naked, over and over with the woman in the window! She shook herself, she had to get a grip, this was the wrong house; the wrong street! Tearing open her bag she pulled out the copy of Pierre's email, containing his address and instructions for using the metro. Trembling she read,

Chère Rachel,
From La Gard du Nord take the métro to Barbès, change lines in the direction of Pigalle, change at Pigalle and take a train to

Lamarck Caulaincourt. As you leave the métro turn right, right again by 'L'Escargot', up a steep hill and after a few minutes you will see the sign for Rue Madeleine. I live at number 17.

If you change your mind about the métro, I can send a car.

À bientôt,

Pierre x

Rachel looked at the house again. There, just above the door, carved within an ornate stone crest, was the number 17. OK, still no reason to panic she told herself, there are hundreds of 17s in Paris. She was in the wrong street. As she fumbled for her 'Plan de Paris' she felt a hand on her arm; it was the old man she'd met earlier, trying to squeeze past on the narrow pavement. He had completed his errand and was clutching a large white box decorated with a curly red ribbon.

'C'est un gateau. Aujourd'hui, c'est l'anniversaire de ma femme,' he explained proudly.

'Monsieur. La Rue … le nom de la rue?'

'Rue Madeleine. C'est bonne?'

Rachel shook her head sadly. 'Non Monsieur, mais merci.' Of course she wasn't in the right place; she should be back at Cygnets' Nest reading 'Naïve & Gullible Weekly.'

'De riens, salut.' The old man smiled and ambled up the street with his cake.

Now what the hell was she supposed to do? Stay and confront the lying bastard? Funny he hadn't mentioned his wife in their plans.

The journey back to La Gare du Nord passed in a blur and she arrived as the next train to London was pulling out. Cursing, she realised that she would have to wait over an hour for the next train. The sights and sounds that had enchanted her earlier, turned her stomach now. She scowled at the couple on an advertising bill board, standing arm in arm, overlooking the city from La Sacré Coeur, they were no longer her and Pierre as she'd imagined arriving at the station but two smug, nameless visitors and the strange smell she'd identified as Gallouise cigarettes and espresso, now tasted foul rather than exotic.

There was only one thing for it ... a drink. A large one. She stumbled into the nearest bar and glancing up from his newspaper; the barman poured a generous slug of brandy into a large balloon shaped glass and pushed it along the counter towards her. Rachel's mouth dropped open in amazement, she'd always thought that kind of thing only happened in films - woman walks into a bar, handbag in one hand and an invisible sign in the other, which only the barman can see, saying 'Some bastard's just ripped my heart out, stamped on it and chucked it out with the potato peelings' - barman pours woman stiff drink. The End.

Smiling her thanks, Rachel perched herself on the high leather bar stool and swallowed a mouthful of brandy, gasping as the alcohol hit her empty stomach. She was about to take a second, when her mobile phone started bleeping. Instantly, she recognised Pierre's telephone number and pressing the red stop key, dropped the phone in her bag. Seconds later, it bleeped again. He'd had the audacity to send her a text.

R u in Paris? Phone me. P xxx

Chapter 19

Climbing the loft ladder for the umpteenth time Sarah wouldn't have been surprised to meet Sherpa Tenzing coming the other way. Storing the kids' clothes and toys in the attic, to clear space for the crew had seemed like a good idea at the time, but that was when she thought that Dave would be around to help. Finally she made her last descent and closing the loft hatch behind her, picked a cobweb from her hair, wiping the sticky mess on her jeans; making an effort with her appearance only to remain invisible, had lost its appeal. With Dave away on business there was no pretence, no having to try only to be disappointed. Slipping into the role of 'Landlady' will suit me perfectly she thought bitterly; making everything clean and comfortable, the omniscient housekeeper keeping everyone happy and with paying guests in the house I can pretend it's my job, rather than the reason for my existence.

'You-who! It's only us,' called a voice from downstairs.

Thank goodness, the cavalry had arrived. Sarah went downstairs and saw boxes of crockery and bundles of bed linen on the kitchen table. 'Thanks Mum, it was kind of you to sort that lot out for me.'

'It was only collecting dust at home,' said Jean, lifting a 'World's Best Dad' mug from the box and giving it a cursory wipe. 'Although why you are going to all this trouble goodness only knows. David must be finding it such an inconvenience.'

'Dave's in New York Mum. I'd hardly call having a queen size bed at the Hilton an inconvenience.'

'Even so, an Englishman's home is his castle and ...'
She was interrupted by Andrew, standing in the door way with two camp beds under each arm.

'Hi Sarah, where do you want these? There's more in the car if you need them.'

'Thanks,' Sarah said, relieved at avoiding a war of words with Jean. 'I need two camp beds in Naomi's room, one in Millie's and one in Harry's.'

Jean sighed heavily and put the 'World's Best Dad' mug in the sink. 'You'll need to rinse the mugs out Sarah, some are dustier than others,' she said, staring pointedly at the mug, as if determined to remind Sarah of her widowhood. 'I'll give Andrew a hand making up the beds.'

Sarah turned her attentions to the dining room which she intended to turn into a mess room for the crew. The plan was to ensure that the crew could be as self-sufficient as possible, especially for breakfast, considering that they would be getting up at 5am for training sessions and she didn't relish a pre-make-up, bobbly nightie encounter with anyone, no matter how bulging the bi-ceps.

She laid out trays of crockery, cereals, a Tupperware containing home-made bread, a kettle and a toaster, and filled an ancient *Frigidaire* (raided from cobwebs at the back of the garage), with milk, yogurt, juice, butter and jam. Finally, daydreaming of lycra clad thighs, she spread out a selection of 'What's On' leaflets, on the dining room table. She'd picked them up from the tourist information centre, hoping that they would provide inspiration for something to do, should the crew get knocked out early on in the competition.

'Penny for them?' asked Andrew, watching her from the doorway.

'Young men in tight sportswear if you must know!' laughed Sarah. 'There has to be some compensation for all this upheaval.'

'And there is that little thing called money,' said Andrew, grabbing her hand. 'Come on, Mum wants to make sure that you are happy with everything upstairs.'

The first door off the landing led to Harry's room and inside the camp bed was neatly made with blue bed sheets and a white candlewick bedspread.

'I thought you'd probably put the Coach in here, so I gave him the best linen,' said Jean, coming out of Naomi's bedroom.

Sarah and Andrew grinned at each other and followed their mother on her 'grand tour' of the newly arranged bedrooms.

'And I thought the young men would appreciate this,' she said, pushing open the door to Millie's room.

Stepping into the room, Sarah felt she'd entered a time warp. On the beds were old bedspreads that had once belonged to her and Andrew - *Duran Duran* with New Romantic sneers on one and *Abba*, with wholesome Scandinavian grins on the other.

'I can't believe you kept those bedspreads!' gasped Sarah, fondly running her hand over Simon Le Bon's frilly shirt.

'Waste not, want not,' said Jean, puffing out her war baby chest. 'I knew they'd come in handy again one day. I didn't have any other trendy bedding, so the beds in Naomi's room are just boring pastels I'm afraid.'

'Don't worry Mum,' laughed Andrew. 'I'm sure the crew won't have heard of *Duran Duran*, and *Abba* is ancient history. Now if you'd drummed up a duvet covered with *Eminem*, we may have had a nasty tussle on our hands!'

'*M & M's*, the confectionary?' asked Jean nonplussed.

'I think it's time for a coffee,' laughed Sarah, closing Millie's door.

Settling on the patio, Jean set about pouring their coffee and wasted no time voicing her concerns.

'I can't understand why you're putting your family through this Sarah. A man's home should be his sanctuary from the world and he shouldn't have to share it with strangers. I don't know how David puts up with your hair brained schemes.'

Andrew put a restraining hand on Sarah's arm but she shook him off. 'No Andrew! Why shouldn't she know?'

'Know what?' asked Jean, at once suspicious.

Sarah glared. 'That your precious 'can do no wrong' son-in-law has got his family into financial crisis, that's what! Do you really think I want my children sleeping on the floor of my bedroom and a house full of strangers just to earn a few extra pounds?'

'I had no idea. How bad is it?' Jean's coffee mug was

half-way to her mouth, where it hung suspended as if part of the question.

'Bad enough,' snapped Sarah.

Andrew flashed Jean a warning look and at last she put down her coffee, saying, 'I wish there was something I could do to help but I've only got my pension ... if I had any savings they would be yours.'

'I know Mum,' Sarah said, her eyes wet with tears. 'I'm sorry I snapped at you and the last thing I want is for you to worry. We got ourselves into this and we'll get ourselves out.'

Looking unconvinced Jean nodded. 'Of course you will, you've always been resourceful in spite of being a bit of a daydreamer. If you need me to look after the children so that you can take on more hours at work, you only need to say.'

'What about Bridge and Tai Chi and golf with George?'

'Oh, the Tai Chi can rot for all I care. I can never empty my mind. I'm always thinking of what needs to be done in the garden and the Bridge bores me senseless!' admitted Jean.

Flabbergasted Sarah said, 'I don't understand, it's been your life since Dad died.'

Jean fussed, wiping imaginary crumbs from the table. 'I had to do something to fill the void and the last thing I wanted to do was to burden you and Andrew. You had your own lives to lead. Anything was better than feeling lonely, even pretending to be a temple in a velour tracksuit. And it hasn't been all bad. After all, playing golf led me to George.'

Sarah saw her mother blush and felt glad that she had found someone who made her happy. It offered, after all, some kind of hope. She squeezed Jean's hand and noticed how fragile the skin was, like crepe paper. 'Oh Mum, don't be embarrassed about George. He's lovely and he obviously thinks the world of you.'

Jean looked up and grinned in spite of herself. 'Yes he does. In fact there's something I need to ask you both ... how would you feel if I was to get married again? George has asked me and I would very much like to say yes but I couldn't do so without your blessing.'

Sarah and Andrew grinned at each other and nodded their blonde heads in unison.

'It's wonderful news Mum. I hope you'll be very happy and as we're playing family confessions, now seems as good a time as any for one of my own,' said Andrew, ignoring Sarah's raised eyebrows, 'The thing is Mum, I've been meaning to tell you for years, probably since you bought me that *Abba* bedspread.'

'Don't tell her it was really the *Bee Gees* you liked, it'll break her heart,' teased Sarah.

Andrew smacked her leg and continued. 'All the time you thought I was in love with Agnetha, it was actually Bjorn.'

'Is he the one with the beard?' asked Jean, sipping her coffee.

Andrew shook his head. 'No that's Benny … come to think of it Bjorn did have one for a while and then he shaved it off…look what I'm trying to tell you is …'

Jean interrupted, waving his words away with her hands. 'I was the same at that age. Always having crushes on the stars of the day. With me it was Marilyn Monroe, I thought she was wonderful.'

Sarah looked at Andrew and raised her eyebrows, as if to say 'What now?' but he only shrugged and grinning, said, 'Maybe next time.'

'What was that?' asked Jean.

'Nothing Mum, it's fine,' said Andrew, draining his coffee mug.

A cacophony of ring tones prevented further confessions and sent mother and son fumbling for their mobiles. Andrew got to his first.

'It's a text from Fotheringham-Allen,' he said, jumping up and punching the air with his fist. 'The investment's going to pay off. I'm sorry Sarah, Mum, I have to cut and run. I need to see the bank as soon as possible about putting in my bid for the farm.'

He kissed the tops of their heads and was gone. As Sarah watched him leave the implications of Rup's text began to sink in. The café was within her grasp, in a few months time she could be whipping up a culinary storm. Should she start sourcing materials right away? Should she go for red and white gingham tablecloths or was that a cliché? What was hip in tablecloths these days? I'll ask Rachel, Sarah thought, she could always be relied upon for spotting the next global trend. And what to do about Dave? Would she have to sneak about behind his back? Going out the door in her 'office' clothes and pulling into a lay-by to don her apron and repeating the whole palaver on the way home. And what if she cut herself slicing salad? Those blue catering plasters were a dead give-away. She'd have to keep a pack of flesh coloured *Elastoplast* in the glove compartment just in case - it was getting complicated - and it hadn't even started!

'That was George on the phone, he's waiting at the house to take me to lunch,' said Jean, dropping her phone into her handbag, 'and this is yours I believe, you left it behind after dog sitting Daisy.' She handed Sarah her *Gone with the Wind* DVD.

'Are you still in love with Rhett Butler?' Jean asked, standing up ready to leave. 'I can still remember how you used to dress up in my old nighties pretending to be Scarlett O'Hara. You always had such imagination. Anyway, I must go darling and break the good news to George. Are you sure you are going to be alright?'

Sarah stood up, and like Scarlett in the closing scene of the movie, she pretended to search the horizon. 'I'll be fine,' she said. 'After all, tomorrow is another day.'

As Jean backed out of the drive, a minibus was waiting to pull in and moments later Sarah's doorbell rang, driving Harry from the lounge and his *Thomas the Tank Engine* DVD.

'Surely that can't be the crew already, Harry,' said Sarah, lifting him onto her hip before she opened the door.

The man on her doorstep smiled and said in a deep southern drawl. 'Hi I'm the coach, Ted Buckner.'

The first thing she noticed was his teeth, white and perfect and shining like a toothpaste advert in his weather beaten face.

'Rhett Butler?' whispered Sarah, having a crinoline moment.

'Excuse me Mam,' smiled the toothpaste teeth. 'Ted Buckner, Baxdale College. I believe you're expecting us?'

'Yes, I am. Your accent, it threw me. I thought your college was in New England,' Sarah said, blushing furiously.

He smiled again making her insides do funny things. 'I was born in Georgia,' he said, by way of an explanation, 'and the last time I looked in my passport, which was not so long ago there was no mention of Mr. Rhett Butler. Sorry to disappoint you, Mam.'

Thinking how Ted couldn't be a disappointment if his life depended on it, Sarah wiped her free hand on her jeans and offered it to him. 'I'm sorry you'll think I'm nuts. Let's start again. I'm Sarah Crouch.'

He shook her hand warmly and flashed a lightening smile. 'Can't I just call you Scarlett?'

Sarah felt something stir around her middle and it wasn't crinoline.

Standing behind Ted, Sarah could see the crew - four giants of men in Baxdale College t-shirts, white with a large red 'B' in the centre and reaching into the mini-bus for a hold-all was a smaller man; the coxswain, dwarfed by his team mates.

'Please come in and I'll give you the grand tour,' Sarah said, showing them through to the mess room.

Suddenly, full of larger than life bodies, the room and all its furniture seemed to shrink like a scene in *Alice in Wonderland* and Sarah felt a moment of panic. All the American houses she'd seen on television were huge in comparison to the average English semi. And now here they were, shining like megawatt human light bulbs with their dazzling teeth and t-shirts, exposing her in her filthy jeans and her poky house. Blushing furiously, Sarah attempted her landlady speech. 'I would like to wish you all a warm welcome and I want you to feel at home, um … here are a couple of spare front door keys so you can come and go as you please … and if there's anything you need, you only have to ask.'

'And you guys, that doesn't include Mrs. Crouch making your peanut butter and jelly sandwiches, you hear?' laughed Ted. 'We're only here for a week and we want to make the right impression, OK?'

'Oh no, I forgot the peanut butter. There's jam…that's jelly isn't it? But I forgot the peanut butter. How could I be so stupid, I'll get some on my way back from school,' said Sarah.

'No need Mam,' smiled Ted. 'Show Mrs. Crouch what's in your backpack Joey.'

Joey grinned sheepishly and unzipped his bag, revealing several jars of peanut butter and dozens of Hershey bars. Relieved, Sarah continued to explain the domestic arrangements, saying, 'Help yourselves to breakfast, everything you need is in the fridge and I'll make sure that you have lots of everything, so you can make snacks whenever you feel like it. This is your room to use how you wish and the computer in the corner has broadband, so feel free to email home.'

Sarah cringed as she spoke. Somehow her voice was no longer hers. Why, in the company of Americans, did she have to sound so terribly English, almost 'To the Manor Born'? She searched their faces for a hint of amusement, but if Ted and the crew had noticed, they kept it hidden.

Pointing to the giants sitting on her sofa, Ted launched into introductions; Tom and Tyler from Pennsylvania, peanut loving Joey was from Washington, Sam was from Virginia and Ryan the coxswain was from New Hampshire. But they all had one thing in common, Ted included; they had muscles to die for and their bedrooms would be just a hop, skip and a jump from hers. Scarlett O'Hara may have slipped quietly back to Tara but Sarah felt every inch a scarlet woman. Suddenly she realized, after the introductions Ted had carried on talking, but she had been so wrapped up in her own thoughts, she hadn't a clue what about, only catching the words 'mountain bike' and 'garage'. Then she heard him say, 'May I?'

'Of course, park it where you like,' she said.

Ted gave her a puzzled look. 'I thought I'd just drop it out of the window,' he said, coming towards her, his hand reaching to some place an inch or so behind her left ear.

Sarah froze, utterly unsure of what he was going to do next, apart from drop his bike out of the window which seemed a bit odd having got it all the way to England in one piece and now he seemed intent on touching her hair. This is just so not funny she thought, maybe that's why Rup had put his foot down; these guys were the 'care in the community' team. Momentarily, she felt Ted's hand touch her hair and then, he uncurled his fingers to show her the spindly harvest spider in his palm. 'It's dead I'm afraid,' he said, prodding the stiff black legs before dropping it through an open window.

Mortified, Sarah put her hand up to her hair. She hadn't looked in the mirror all day and after all the time spent in the attic, there could be a wasp's nest in her hair for all she knew. What must Ted think of her? As she struggled to compose herself, she saw Joey stifle a yawn and decided now was a good time to show them their rooms; the sooner they were busy unpacking, the sooner she could put a comb through her hair and change into a clean t-shirt.

Upstairs, she pushed open the door to where Ted would be sleeping. 'Here's your room,' she said to Ted, 'It's a bit old fashioned but it's cosy.' Then she hurried, to show them the next room. 'There's space for two of you in here,' she said, wishing she'd removed the out-dated bedspreads.

'Wow, that's way cool!' Joey said, whipping out his digital camera and photographing the bed. '*Duran Duran*, they were my mom's favourite. I gotta have this room. Whose gonna be my room-mate?'

Sam from Virginia seemed keen on the idea of having a Swedish blonde on top and nabbed the Abba covered bed. Sarah showed off the final room and if Tom, Tyler and Ryan were disappointed by their conservative bedding, they kept it politely hidden.

Leaving the crew to settle in, she went to collect the girls from school. Before she set off she checked herself in the rear view mirror and combed her hair into a ponytail. Smiling she let her fingers rest for a moment on the spot where the spider had been, until Ted had plucked it gently from her hair.

Chapter 20

Rachel was trembling so much; it took her three attempts to return Pierre's text.

In Paris u cheating, lying ahole. Wtg 4 train bk 2 UK.
R

Seconds later his reply bleeped on to her phone.
Why am I an ahole? P xxx
I saw her. Yr wife! In yr house! R
U saw my sister, Mireille. She's here now waiting 2 mt u. P xxx

Rachel lifted the brandy to her lips and put it down again, punch-drunk. She was shaking and had to grasp the edge of the bar stool to stop herself from falling. Shit! Shit! Shit! How could she face him now? She had little choice and some serious apologising to do, and so for the second time that day she joined the métro bound for chez Pierre.

Walking along Rue Madeleine, her stomach in knots, she remembered the old man from earlier and the birthday cake he'd bought his wife and doubted she'd be able to eat anything EVER again. As she concentrated on keeping her breakfast down, a silver Mercedes purred past, stopping outside Pierre's house. The driver got out, followed by twin boys who ran up the steps and knocked on the front door. It swung open moments later and Pierre appeared, followed by the woman Rachel had seen in the window. Now, seeing them side by side, it was obvious they were related; they shared the same dark hair and wide sensuous mouth.

Suddenly one of the boys pointed at something in the street and the party turned in Rachel's direction. Quickly, she dashed into a doorway, her heart pounding so loudly in her chest she was sure they would hear. She watched Pierre ruffle his nephews' hair and engage them in a mock play fight, until finally Mireille and her husband herded them into the car.

Forcing herself from her hide out and feeling more nauseous with every step, Rachel approached the house. How was she supposed to know the woman was Pierre's sister for goodness sake? He hadn't mentioned having a sister but then she hadn't mentioned she was an only child and had an awful habit of jumping to conclusions! As she knocked on Pierre's door she was sure her chest would burst open and he would find her heart pulsating on his door step, while she expired in a heap on the pavement! She heard his footsteps in the hall and then, just when she thought she would keel over, the door swung open.

'Rachel, ma pauvre petite. How dreadful for you to arrive in Paris and find your boyfriend's wife at home. Please, come in you've had quite a shock,' Pierre said.

'Pierre, I'm so, so sorry. I've been a complete idiot. Can you forgive me?'

He laughed and chucking her under the chin, reached for her suitcase. 'Il y a plus d'un âne a la foire qui s'appelle Martin.'

Rachel frowned and held on fast to her luggage. 'What does that mean? Is it that I have to find a new boyfriend called Martin because if it does, I see your point.'

'Literally, it means there's always more than one donkey called Martin at the fair but translated to make sense, it means don't jump to conclusions because there can be many explanations. The woman you saw could have been my friend, my cleaning lady, my sister or, as you assumed my wife!'

Rachel nodded still trying to ease her suitcase from Pierre's grasp, she said, 'I can see that now…if you want me to go…'

Pierre wrestled the suitcase from her hand and ushered her inside, closing the door behind her. 'Of course, I don't want you to go. Mireille has prepared a meal. She was sorry that she had to leave before meeting you but she had a dinner reservation. I'll show you where you can freshen up.'

Thank goodness he was too much of a gentleman to send her packing to the nearest 'Travel Inn.' By a twist of fate she was being given another chance and there was no way she was going to blow it. She would pull out all the stops, show him that she was a sophisticated woman of the world, strong yet vulnerable, worldly but still willing to learn, sexy not sluttish and most important of all, she would never call him an arsehole *ever* again. It was a tall order, but she was determined to rise to the challenge.

She followed Pierre up the polished oak staircase, stopping on the first floor, where he opened one of the doors. It led into a guest bedroom and in the centre was a Louis XV mahogany bedstead, made up with crisp white linens and a hand embroidered bedspread. At the head end and almost as large as the bed itself, was an oil painting of an eighteenth century gentle-woman dressed in blue silk and a powdered wig. Rachel caught her gaze and instantly knew, that whoever the woman in the painting was, she would never have called a man an arsehole, no matter what he was accused of, real or imaginary. She looked like a woman who could read a man and could recognise a sister when she saw one, and knew all about fairs and donkeys called Martin. Rachel walked over to the bedside table, with its tall vase of white roses and ran her hand over a gold leaved book, offering itself as bedtime reading. It was as if she had ducked under the rope, cordoning off an historic boudoir, in a chateau open to paying visitors. She sighed, half expecting to see a group of Japanese tourists jostling at Pierre's shoulder. 'What a beautiful room.'

Pierre placed her suitcase beside the bed and led her through a side door into the en-suite, where the pale carpet gave way to oak floorboards. At one end of the room a large window draped in white muslin cast a diaphanous light over a central free-standing bath, white and squat like a block of vanilla ice-cream. Rachel was itching to get out her mobile and take a photo to send to Sarah, when she looked up and caught her breath. Above the bath was a vast chandelier, made of thousands of discs of pearlescent shell. It was as if the house was an extension of Pierre himself, oozing effortless charm and good taste.

Pierre turned to leave. 'I'll let you freshen up. I thought we might eat on the terrace. Just come down when you're ready.'

Rachel sat on the edge of the bath and listened to the sound of him whistling, as he made his way downstairs and pinched her arm to convince herself she wasn't dreaming. Jet

144

lag had made her light headed and sleepy, when she was desperate to be wide awake and alert. Unlike many of her crew colleagues, she shied away from drugs designed to combat the exhaustion; many Rachel knew, took Melatonin which was reputed to level out time zones, and others, in their desperation to lock on to GMT when their bodies were still several hours plus or minus, sought dubious combinations from back street pharmacies in down town Mumbai. As it was, even Junior Aspirin upset her stomach, so instead she resorted to cold showers, strong coffee and glucose tablets.

Breaking open a new packet she popped three sweets in her mouth for good measure, set the shower to its coldest setting and shedding her clothes, stepped under the ice cold jets. When she could no longer bear it she got out and towelled dry. With her blood zinging to the surface and temporarily revitalized, she pulled on a pair of black leggings, a mustard coloured silk dress by *Paul Smith Blue Label* and *Christian Louboutin* black satin wedges; all cherished rip-offs from a Hong Kong street market.

Downstairs, Pierre was waiting for her, a glass of wine in his hand. 'Hello again, you look stunning,' he said, handing her a glass of Kir Royale. 'Are you hungry? Everything's ready.'

Rachel followed him through the open French doors onto a terrace, overlooking a mature, densely planted garden and what appeared to be, a vineyard beyond.

'What an amazing garden, it's like an oasis!' she said, breathing in the sweet scent of honeysuckle and roses. 'And down there, beyond the garden, it looks like a vineyard.'

'It is,' Pierre laughed. 'The grapes are harvested every year but the wine is poor. It's a pity but I'm glad it's here, I like to look at something green from my bedroom window.'

Rachel looked towards the house and wondered which one of a dozen windows belonged to his room. She imagined him in the still of the night, standing on one of the balconies looking out across the vines.

'Are you warm enough? We can eat inside if you prefer,' he asked, noticing her shiver.

'No, no I'm fine. I have my pashmina and it's such a beautiful night. I'd like to watch the stars come out.'

'If its stars you want then its stars you shall have,' he smiled, pulling back a chair from the table. 'Please take a seat.'

The table was laid with white linen and in the centre was a square platter filled with canapés, miniature millefeuille of salmon mousse and caviar and open sandwiches the size of postage stamps layered with goats cheese, tapenade and pesto. Pierre filled her wine glass and instantly bubbles of condensation appeared against the pale gold liquid.

'Wow, you didn't mention that your sister was a gourmet cook!' Rachel said, popping a miniature sandwich into her mouth.

Pierre laughed. 'Mireille. A cook? My sister can't boil an egg! But one thing Mireille knows how to do is shop. Our meal came from *Le Nôtre*, it's a gourmet chain.' He took a mouthful of wine and pointed towards the twinkling lights of the city. 'I bet right now there are hundreds of Parisian women passing off *Le Nôtre* creations as their own. I'm not sure many women cook these days.'

'Or know how to,' Rachel said. 'With the exception of my friend Sarah, she cooks the most amazing food. It's how she nurtures her family…and me too I guess. She's always filling my freezer with meals for one.'

As soon as the words were out she wished she could take them back. Bugger, now he'll think I'm a sad lonely woman who eats up another family's leftovers, she thought crossly.

'I eat out with business colleagues and friends but if I am forced to eat alone then I would rather go hungry. A good meal needs good company, no?' Pierre said, raising his glass.

He sooths over the edges like a human comfort blanket, thought Rachel clinking her glass against his. 'I'll drink to that,' she said.

Soon, she found herself regaling him of her favourite places, and the not so favourite. Pierre frowned when she explained that an armed guard was needed to protect the crew in Nigeria.

'It sounds dangerous,' he said, filling her plate with salad nichoise.

Rachel shrugged. 'I guess so but it's not half as dangerous as the oversexed pilots!'

Pierre smiled and topped up her wine. 'Are all men not over-sexed. Or are pilots particularly so?'

'Most of the ones I've met. Who can blame them when they have everything on tap; girls, expenses and fabulous locations. And where are their wives and girlfriends? Turning the other cheek, hundreds of miles away.'

Pierre shook his head in disbelief. 'Surely they know what is going on, they can't be that naïve.'

'No?' laughed Rachel, enjoying her ability to surprise him. 'One of the Ops guys told me recently, how he'd got a call from a pilot's wife, wanting to track her husband down because of a family emergency and he had to tell her that he had no idea where her husband was because he'd retired three years earlier. It turns out that the husband had conned her into thinking he was still flying, trotting off in his uniform and staying away for days on end, when all along he'd been using his travel concessions to visit his Thai girlfriend in Bangkok. It kind of puts you off picking a fly boy for a boyfriend.'

Pierre laughed and then a shadow crossed his face. 'Personal assistants can be just as bad.'

'Really I thought they were souls of discretion.'

Pierre frowned and put down his knife and fork, leaving his salad unfinished. 'Not Claudette. Everything on her résumé was fictitious and her referees turned out to be her cousins. But by the time I had found out, I had fallen in love.' He fell silent and Rachel hoped that it wasn't with regret.

'So what happened? If you didn't mind about the deceit, I mean.'

He smiled and the light returned to his eyes. 'She was an excellent PA.'

Rachel knew he was playing with her now, perhaps he regretted bringing up an old flame, but it made her more curious. 'I wasn't referring to her short hand...you said you loved her…'

Pierre nodded. 'I did, very much. We were together for three years and then it ended. That is life, I have no regret. Coffee?' he said, getting up.

Rachel nodded and although she desperately wanted to know why he was no longer with Claudette, it would have been churlish to ask. When Pierre returned with a tray of coffee and brandy, she asked instead about their plans for the following day.

'I am making a guess that you have seen the main attractions. Is there anywhere you would like to return to or would you like to do something completely different?'

'Something different sounds fun. What did you have in mind?' she asked, gratefully sipping her coffee as her jet-lag had returned and was threatening to engulf her.

'I suggest a picnic in the park with some of the best views of the city and after, dinner at my favourite restaurant. How does that sound?'

'Perfect,' Rachel said, stifling a yawn.

Flying back from Tel Aviv over night had played havoc with her sleep pattern and it was catching up with her. Gently, Pierre took the coffee cup from her hands and replaced it with a glass of brandy. 'Here take this to bed, you're exhausted. We have tomorrow.'

He kissed her, once on each cheek. She breathed in as he came close, catching his scent, a mixture of earth and spice and for a moment she thought he might pick up his own brandy and join her in the guest suite. Instead he wished her good-night and ushered her into the house.

Frustrated but happy Rachel climbed into bed and as she drifted towards sleep, she was sure she saw the woman in the oil painting wink.

Chapter 21

The next morning she woke early. The sun was already warm through the chink in the bedroom curtains and the aroma of coffee and fresh bread beckoned her downstairs. After a quick breakfast on the terrace they headed out for the day.

'Ready? Do you have everything you need?' asked Pierre, swinging open the front door, blasting the cool hallway with humid city heat. Rachel nodded and as she stepped into the sunlight, a voice called out to them from the street. Pierre grinned and raised his hand and Rachel turned to see the old man who had come to her aid the day before. Rachel waved back but was relieved when the old man shuffled off and disappeared inside a house a few doors down.

'That's Jean-Paul. He and his wife François are my neighbours but I think they're trying to adopt me!' Pierre said, shutting the door behind them. 'We have a kind of unspoken agreement. Jean-Paul looks out for my place during the day and I find an excuse to call by with a bottle of cognac or a box of treats from the patisserie for François, it seems to work well.'

They walked the short distance to the cheesemongers and three assistants in long white aprons greeted them, along with the pungent smell of more than 200 types of cheese. Their selection was wrapped as lovingly as fragile china and en route to the station, Pierre bought a baguette and a bag of peaches.

After a short journey on the métro, they stepped from the hot pavement into the lush greenery of the Parc des Buttes des Chaumont. Joggers, taking advantage of the shade flashed past bathed in sweat and lycra, reminding Rachel of her early morning strolls in Central Park, when sleep evaded her and she needed escape from hotel fug. A short way into the park they passed the Restaurant Du Lac, where the sandy path divided into two. The lower path offered tempting deep shade from an arc of mature trees but Pierre pulled her hand in the opposite direction.

'I have a surprise for you,' he said, placing his hand

over her eyes and leading her to a clearing. 'Voila! The Temple of Love!' Pierre removed his hand and squinting against the bright sunshine, Rachel saw an elderly Chinese woman practicing Tai Chi.

'Umm, it's supposed to be very calming … I'm not sure I could …' she muttered, assuming he was referring to the position the old lady had got herself in to. Rachel hoped he didn't intend for them to join in, she was hardly dressed for it, in skin tight Capri pants and kitten heels.

Pierre laughed, reading her thoughts. 'No, not the old woman. There, look!'

Rachel looked beyond the woman who looked less crouching tiger and more upturned turtle and saw a magnificent Corinthian temple, rising out of a giant granite precipice.

'It's beautiful,' she said, her brow creasing into a frown. 'But we don't have to go up there do we? I hate heights.'

'But you work in the sky,' Pierre said, shaking his head in amazement. 'We won't go up there if you don't want to, although the view is spectacular.' He pointed to the horizon. 'Do you see the building to the left in the far distance?'

Following the direction of his outstretched hand she saw a shimmering, silver shape like a sultan's palace. 'Le Sacré Coeur. It looks like a mirage floating above the city.'

Pierre nodded. 'Yes, I've often thought that. I like the change in perspective from up here, it helps me to think, look at things from a different angle. Do you not find the same when you are flying, looking down on the world in miniature?'

'I try not to think about things too much,' Rachel said. 'Trolley dollies run on automatic pilot most of the time, just like the skippers up front. I thought everyone knew that! Come on, you're being far too serious for this time of day,' she said, grabbing his arm. 'Ask me again on a full stomach and I might be able to conjure up a deep thought or two! Show me some more of this lovely place.'

They followed the path through a tunnel of leafy shade and found themselves by a lake, slate green and edged by willows. In the distance Rachel was sure she could hear thunder but looking up through the canopy, the sky was blue and cloudless. As they ventured further along the path the noise became deafening and Rachel realized it was coming from a cave, its entrance partially obscured by overhanging vines and creepers.

'It's all man-made. This park used to be one of the city's rubbish dumps,' Pierre shouted above the din. 'Look up there.'

Huge grey stalactites hung from the roof of the cave and a waterfall exploded through a gash in the rock face, plummeting into a dark pool at their feet. To her despair, Rachel realised that to continue their walk they would have to negotiate stepping stones, dangerously edged with slippery green algae. Pierre stepped easily on to the middle stone and beckoned her across.

'In these shoes?' Rachel yelled over the roar. 'You promised me a sedate walk in the park not pot-holing in heels!'

'I thought you were a woman of the world. It's only a few stepping stones or are you a coward?' he shouted back, holding out his hand.

She took a wary step onto the first stone and surprised herself at remaining upright. Then, taking his out stretched arm, she stepped hesitantly towards him, the smooth sole of her shoe landing on a patch of slime, sliding her towards him faster than either of them had anticipated. Laughing at her squeal of surprise, Pierre caught her around the waist with his free arm and clutching her to his chest, he said, 'Maybe you were right, I think I'd better hold onto you from now on!'

With their bodies pressed together Rachel could feel his warm breath on her face. 'I think,' she whispered to his shirt buttons, 'that I'd like nothing more.'

He saw her lips move but couldn't hear her above the waterfall. Hesitating for a moment, unsure how to unwrap her without letting her fall, he released one arm, raising her chin so that he could see all of her face. 'Pardon?' he mouthed, keeping his face close.

She opened her mouth to reply but no words came, surely this was the moment, she closed her eyes in anticipation … suddenly a brilliant white flash snapped them apart like a lightning bolt. A Japanese tourist, digitalizing the memory of the magical cave in a single click, had broken the spell. Flustered and blinking, they followed the stream out of the cave, into the midday sun.

Watching the pigeons bathing their twisted toes in the water and picking at their feathers, like old ladies in dusty hats on a day trip to Brighton, Rachel said, 'That water looks tempting.'

'I know the perfect place and you don't have to share with the birds!' said Pierre, grabbing her hand.

They settled in a hollow at the edge of the lake and Rachel dangled her feet in the cool water, while Pierre set out their picnic.

'This brie is so good!' she said, tearing off a hunk of golden baguette and dipping it into the creamy cheese, oozing from its greaseproof wrapping.

Pierre grinned. 'I think the ride in my rucksack ripened it to perfection.'

Rachel smiled as she watched him un-wrap the rest of their picnic. He was worth millions of Euros and could afford to eat at Michelin starred restaurants morning, noon and night but he seemed just as comfortable eating on the grass and flicking his crumbs to the birds. She liked the fact that he had nothing to prove, unlike Josh who'd always seemed to be boasting about the fancy places his job took him to and which five star hotel suite he preferred most. Pierre sensed her watching him and asked, 'I'm curious, what made you take up a flying career when you're so afraid of heights?'

'It seems an odd choice doesn't it, but back then I would have done anything to put distance between myself and my parents. Mum had me late in life and so I ended up an only child. Dad was ten years older than mum and between them I don't think they knew what to do with me, I was either suffocated or ignored …' she paused mid-flow, assailed by memories. 'As soon as I turned eighteen I applied to be Cabin Crew and the rest, as they say is ancient history.'

'And your parents now …'

'They died within a year of each other, my dad first, following a complication after heart surgery and mum … I don't think she could bear to be without him. We'd made our peace by the end but I think we all wished there had been a brother or sister, it would have made things less intense.'

'It probably would have helped,' agreed Pierre, handing her a bottle of mineral water. 'I can always rely on my sister to bring me back down to earth. I may run a global business and employ hundreds of people but to Mireille I'm just the little brother who put worms in her bed.'

Rachel laughed trying to imagine him grubbing around in the soil. 'Ugh, that's disgusting! What a horrible brother you were.'

'Of course, it's in the job description but we've always supported each other too. My father wanted Mireille to join the company but I knew that she'd set her heart on becoming a nurse, so I worked on him until he gave in. So, you see I wasn't all bad.'

Leaning over, he tucked a stray strand of hair behind her ear and for a moment let his hand linger on her face. In a transient, almost paternal moment of tenderness, she saw how she had spent half her life trying to escape her parents and the other half trying to replace them and in doing so, had been prepared to be anything and everything to everybody; the sexy girl about town bending to every boyfriend's whim, the laugh-a- minute friend always ready to party even when she was dead on her feet and the tart with the cart, smiling sweetly at businessmen with octopus hands, and all along it had been to avoid what she dreaded most, being alone.

She shivered involuntarily in spite of the hot sun, when suddenly a scream pierced the air and shaken from her thoughts, she turned to see a middle-aged women in a pencil skirt running down the hill towards the lake screaming, 'Philippe! Non, Philippe pas d'en l'eau!'

The woman sped past, disappearing behind a bush at the water's edge. Ready to dive in and save the drowning boy, Rachel leapt to her feet.

'Wait!' Pierre said, grabbing her arm as she was about to plunge into the lake.

'No, I'm a strong swimmer and I know CPR from my medical training. Let me go!' Rachel said, trying to shake him off.

Pierre held on fast. 'No, look!' he said, pointing to the bushes. The pencil skirted woman pushed her way through the undergrowth and Philippe followed at her heels. Rachel stared in amazement, as the woman clipped a lead to Philippe's collar and led the immaculately groomed Afghan away in disgrace.

Pierre laughed. 'I've seen them before. The dog does it to her every time. He never goes in the water; he just hides behind the bushes to tease her. You would have gone in if I hadn't held onto you, wouldn't you? I take back what I said in the cave. There is nothing cowardly about you.'

Rachel stepped back from the water's edge, laughing. 'I'm just glad I didn't have to give mouth to mouth to a smelly dog!'

'Would you rather give mouth to mouth to a smelly Frenchman?' he asked, wrapping his arms around her waist.

She had accused him of being an adulterer, called him an arsehole on their second date, consumed by jet-lag she'd yawned through their first proper meal together *and* he knew she had a fridge full of meals for one, and yet he didn't care. He even thought she was brave. 'If it's this smelly Frenchman then most definitely,' she said, pulling his face towards her.

Rachel dipped her shoulders under the bath foam and dialled Sarah's number on her mobile. It rang several times and then she heard a click, followed by Sarah's voice.

'I said one biscuit Naomi … sorry … hello.'

'Hi babe, it's me. Guess where I'm calling you from?'

'OK, you can have two biscuits if you take Harry with

you so I can speak to Auntie Rachel in peace. Sorry, I can concentrate now…let me guess, you're on the top of the Eiffel Tower?'

'No, you know I've no head for heights! I'm soaking in a lavender scented bath, with a glass of champagne on the side.'

'And did Pierre get the tap end?'

'No such luck! He's in his study making business calls. He's a real gentleman. He's the first man I've been with since the age of seventeen who hasn't tried to jump my bones by the second date!'

'Next you're going to tell me he's interested in your beautiful mind!' laughed Sarah.

'Don't worry, I've already told him he'll have to dig deep on that front. It's hard to explain Sarah, he makes me feel looked after and he wants to know what I think about everything.'

'He sounds wonderful … a bit too wonderful. Are you sure he's not gay? I mean, you were having fantasies about Andrew until I put you straight.'

'No way! I know my gay-dar has been a bit off kilter recently but Pierre's a woman's man believe me. He's just waiting for the perfect moment that's all and I have to tell you I can't wait. We spent most of the day snogging in the park like teenagers and eating a picnic out of his rucksack. How cool is that? For a CEO he's very grounded. Anyway, enough about me and my sensational love life. Did you manage to get everything organised in time for the rowers?'

'Just. Mum and Andrew helped get the house ready, which was a mixed blessing as Mum kept going on about how I shouldn't expect my poor darling husband to turn his home into a B & B just to earn a few extra pounds and then I snapped and told her it was because of Dave that we're in this mess!'

And she doesn't know the half of it, thought Rachel, imagine if she knew about Dave's adulterous flit to the Big Apple. 'How did she take the news that her favourite son-in-law has fallen from grace?'

'Once she got over the shock she said she would do whatever she could to help and thankfully, it was eclipsed by Andrew's good news. It looks as though the investment with Rup is going to pay off. My head's bursting with ideas for the café. To tell you the truth, I can't wait to chuck in my job and get started.'

Rachel couldn't remember the last time she'd heard such enthusiasm in Sarah's voice. It was such a relief that things were finally on the up. 'Congratulations! I'm so happy for you,' she said, raising her champagne glass to the phone. She glanced at her watch lying next to the soap dish. 'Sorry babe I've got to go and get ready for dinner. Love you lots and enjoy your gorgeous rowers. Don't forget there's no rule against looking, even for married women!'

Sarah laughed. 'Who said anything about looking! I've got an extra large tube of *Deep Heat* ready and waiting to be rubbed into sore muscles, landlady's prerogative! We'll compare notes when you get back.'

Chapter 22

Sarah tucked the children into their sleeping bags and pulled her bedroom door close. Ted and the crew hadn't yet returned home from the day's rowing and she guessed they had decided to have dinner in town. Apart from a brief good morning as they crossed in the hallway, Sarah on her way out to do the school run and the crew on their way in for breakfast after their early morning training session, she hadn't clapped eyes on them all day.

On the landing she passed Ted's room and hesitated, catching a glimpse of blue bed linen. The pull was irresistible and unable to stop herself she pushed open the door, a tingle of excitement running along her spine. Suddenly, this room, so familiar, had become uncharted territory, exciting and out of bounds. What was she looking for, a sign that he was married or involved with someone? Had he brought her photograph with him and placed it by his bed? She glanced at the bedside cabinet - no clues there - only a wash bag and next to it, a wristwatch with a wide black leather strap. Picking it up, she slipped it over her wrist, where it lay in a Ted shaped circle, until slowly, as if it were a fragile thing, she pushed it along her arm until it fitted tight. Suddenly, from downstairs, she heard the sound of the front door opening. Hurriedly, she returned the watch and left the room. Downstairs, Ted greeted her in the hall.

'Hi, Mrs. Crouch. Me and the guys wanted to thank you for the breakfast. The blackberry jelly and the bread were out of this world. Did you make them yourself?'

Sarah nodded and glanced at her arm, half expecting to see an impression of his watch on her skin. 'Please call me Sarah, everyone does. Have you had anything to eat, can I make you something?'

'No thank you, Mam ... sorry, Sarah. We've just had ourselves a pub meal of steak and kidney pie and the guys are going to watch some T.V. and get an early night.'

An early night, thought Sarah, wasn't that what they had last night? They slept almost as many hours as Harry!

She'd put it down to jet-lag but it looked as though early nights were going to be routine. 'Oh, I see. I was going to ask you if you'd like to have a glass of wine,' she said, hoping he couldn't hear the disappointment in her voice.

'I'd like that very much.' Ted smiled and Sarah's stomach did a back flip.

'Shall we take our drinks outside?' she asked, taking out a bottle of wine from the fridge.

Ted nodded and picking up two glasses from the draining board, followed Sarah outside. They sat for a few moments sipping their wine and enjoying the warmth of the evening sunshine, while Sarah struggled to think of something to say. All day she'd imagined herself entertaining him with witty stories and now she was struck dumb. Try getting the other person to talk about themselves, wasn't that the advice she was always reading in the advice columns? So, taking a deep breath she asked Ted how he had become a coach.

'Evolution I guess. I started rowing at school, won my first Royal Regatta at the age of twenty, representing my college in Georgia and carried on competing until my bones complained and that's when I became a coach.'

'Is that hard? Watching from the sidelines, after competing I mean?'

Ted shrugged. 'No, it's just different. As a coach I'm competing for my team to be the best and we're half way to proving it,' he said proudly, raising his glass towards the mess room where the crew were watching T.V. 'These guys are some of the best I've coached. Our track record automatically qualifies us for the Regatta, so we don't have to do time trials with the other teams.'

'I'll have to be on my best behaviour if I'm landlady to one of the top teams,' laughed Sarah, topping up their wine.

'You sure will, no mistaking the Coach for deceased Hollywood actors for a start or I might have to start calling you Elsa Craddock.'

'Who on earth is Elsa Craddock?'

'Vivien Leigh, and I'm guessing she's a heroine of yours. She played Elsa Craddock in *A Yank at Oxford*. It's about an American college boy who ends up rowing for Oxford, and Elsa is one of the kind English ladies who help him settle in. They say it was the role that landed her the lead in *Gone with the Wind.* So, if you promise not to call me Rhett, I promise not to call you Elsa. Do we have a deal?' he grinned, flashing his perfect teeth.

Sarah laughed and clinked his glass. 'Deal,' she said, hoping Ted was over his jet-lag and wouldn't be having anymore early nights.

Ted topped up Sarah's wine. 'Now it's my turn to ask you a question. What made you decide to become a Regatta Landlady? Is this your first time?'

'Oh no, is it that obvious?' Sarah cringed, her face reddening. 'The truth is I'm doing it out of necessity ... don't get me wrong it's lovely to have you here. But the reason behind it is financial. We've not had this house very long and we're a little over stretched.'

Ted nodded. 'Makes sense, can't see many folks turning their homes over to a whole bunch of strangers just for the fun of it. And what about the Regatta, are you a fan living so close?'

Sarah sipped her wine and wished she'd had time to do some homework. 'Umm, to be honest I don't know much about it. I guess it's always struck me as something for the privileged few.'

'It used to be. Before the second world war anyone who did a menial job, or should I say menial in the eyes of the rule makers, wasn't allowed to compete.'

Unimpressed, Sarah said, 'That's what I mean, common all garden carpenters or bus drivers need not apply. How snobbish can you get?' It was on the tip of her tongue to say how such a rule would have appealed to Dave. Mixing with the 'right' people and keeping out, what he saw as the 'riff-raff' was precisely why he had wanted to move to the famous Regatta town in the first place.

Sarah shivered and pulled her cardigan around her shoulders. Dave's snobbery drove her to distraction, but was it a good enough excuse for enjoying wine with a handsome stranger? What would she say next for heaven's sake - 'My husband doesn't understand me'? Tempting though it was; it was a path she had no intention of going down and finishing her wine she said, 'It's getting late. Shall we go in?'

Ted stood up. 'Sure. I'd better get some shut-eye, it's day one of racing tomorrow. Thank you for the wine and the conversation. Do you think you might come down and watch us row tomorrow? We're due to race at four o'clock.'

'Yes, I'll bring the children down after school,' she said, gathering up their glasses. As a Regatta Landlady I should at least have half a clue as to what it's all about she told herself, and involving the children made going to meet Ted straight and above board…didn't it?

'Great. Goodnight then, Scarlett,' Ted said, disappearing through the back door.

Sarah called after him. 'Hey, I thought we had a deal.'

Ted turned round, grinning. 'Sure we did. I agreed not to call you Elsa. I didn't say anything about not calling you Scarlett. Anyway it suits you better, your man's away and you're doing what you can to save your home, just like Scarlett fighting to save Tara.'

Sarah laughed. 'That's just the kind of double crossing thing Rhett Butler would have done. Well, two can play at that game. I'm reneging on our deal, from now on I'll call you Rhett whether you like it or not.'

As she put the wine back in the fridge she smiled to herself. Rachel wasn't the only one who could have a little fun, and as for the fact that the guy she was flirting with, was someone other than Dave - she felt more like Rhett than Scarlett - because, frankly, she didn't give a damn.

Chapter 23

Rachel climbed out of the bath and smiling to herself, dressed for dinner. Sarah wasn't exactly out of the woods, but at last she'd found a path that would lead her out of the misery of the last few weeks. Dabbing perfume on her pulse points and for good measure, adding a drop to her cleavage, she went downstairs and saw that Pierre was waiting for her in the lounge, absorbed in a glossy car magazine. Dressed in a linen suit and open necked shirt he looked fashionably undone and sexy, his long legs stretched out on the coffee table. Sensing her presence, he looked up and flashed a smile that made her tingle.

'You look radiant,' he said, reaching up to kiss the inside of her wrist, sending delicious shivers across the tiny hairs at the back of her neck. He got up, slipping his feet into a pair of loafers and jangled his keys. 'The car's outside. I've got the roof down, I hope that's OK?'

They cut through the back streets and for a short distance, joined the chaotic traffic on the Champs Elysée, before turning down a quiet side street and pulling up outside an elegant cream terrace. A dark green canopy hung above the entrance, embossed with the restaurant's name in curly gold script and on either side of the door, stood a tall tapered wooden planter topped with a pert green ball of closely cropped privet. It made a subtle statement compared to the glitz of the Champs Elysée.

Pierre handed the door man his car keys and led Rachel inside, where they were shown to an intimate booth for two. The waiter pulled out the table and Rachel slid onto the suede banquette before the table was pushed back into place, barricading her in. Pierre sat in the chair opposite.

'It's so that you don't try to escape,' he laughed, noticing her expression of surprise.

Rachel grinned. 'I have no intention of going anywhere!' she said, admiring the understated luxury of the room.

Having made their selection from the menu, the waiter

disappeared with their order and was replaced by the Sommelier, dressed in a long black apron decorated with a badge of gold grapes.

Pierre winked at Rachel. 'Is there anything in particular you would like to try?' he asked, offering her the wine list and gently stroking the inside of her calf with his foot.

Stifling a giggle, Rachel shook her head and motioning that he should choose, she listened as he selected different wines for each course and discussed their merits with the Sommelier, who nodded his satisfaction at Pierre's choices.

'How do you like the restaurant?' Pierre asked after the Sommelier left with their order.

'It's wonderful. How did you come to know so much about wine?'

'Through the Sommeliers at my hotels and restaurants like this one, but mainly, as you would expect, by drinking it!' he grinned and raised his glass. 'You could say it is one of my passions.'

Through their first course of asparagus mousse garnished with smoky morille mushrooms Rachel tried hard not to think about what his other passions might be, and Pierre explained how he hoped to move to the South of France and own his own vineyard, but first he wanted to find the right buyer for Les Places Tranquilles.

For a moment Rachel allowed herself the pleasure of imagining him walking along a powder white tropical beach, until eventually she said, 'Won't you miss visiting all those exotic places?'

Pierre shook his head. 'I can always take a holiday if I miss it too much and besides, I'm getting old,' he said, pointing to the sprinkling of silver at his temples. 'Airports and travel don't interest me anymore. I want to wake up in the morning and know which country I am in. Who knows I might even get a dog. With the right company I'd be happy to stay in just one place.' He smiled. 'What about you? Do you plan to fly forever?'

'Oh, that I had a choice,' Rachel said, taking a sip of her wine and smiling at the waiter as he placed her main course discreetly in front of her. 'I love my job, I mean who wouldn't? Patting orphan elephants in Kenya, drinking gin slings at Raffles...' she paused, uncertain whether she dare say the words out loud, 'sometimes it can be very lonely.'

'You are surrounded by people but all of them strangers, yes?' Pierre asked gently.

Rachel nodded, amazed at how he always managed to get to the heart of the matter. Others would have argued that with a life so full of people, she couldn't possibly feel lonely. 'Perils of the job,' she said. 'We fly with different crews on every flight and passengers assume we know each other because we're all chatting and laughing and getting on together, but it's a façade. We form these instant, intense friendships to keep ourselves sane but then as soon as we're back at base it's all over and there's a good chance we'll never see one another again! But hey, it's the only thing I know how to do and it pays well, so...'

'Faute de grives, on mange des merles.' Pierre said, and seeing Rachel frown, translated it into English. 'Loosely translated it means, lack of thrushes, one eats blackbirds.'

Rachel laughed. 'In English we would say beggars can't be choosers. You French are always thinking of your stomachs, even in your proverbs.'

Pierre grinned and raised his hands in mock surrender. 'Guilty as charged. But how can you blame us?' he said, gesturing at the pretty desserts that had been laid in front of them.

'It's like a work of art,' Rachel agreed, turning her plate to admire tiny wild strawberries sandwiched between delicate caramel discs, topped with a cloud of ice-cream and a pink sugar triangle.

'So Rachel, tell me, if your bush was full of the thrush what would you do?' asked Pierre.

Lost in translation was beginning to take on new meaning, thought Rachel trying desperately not to guffaw a mouthful of tiny strawberries onto the tablecloth.

'What is it? Have I said something amusing,' he asked.

'Not really, it's just the idiosyncrasies of language,' she grinned. 'So… what would I do if I had lots of thrushes? Well, I've always thought I'd like to run my own business. Lots of cabin crew go onto run guesthouses and bars; it seems to suit their personalities.'

'And what about you? Are you ready to clip your wings?'

Is he testing me? Rachel asked herself, very much hoping that he was. Flying was not supposed to have been a long-term plan and she had no intention of packing reading glasses and HRT patches in her cabin bag, but she knew that unless she did something about it soon, it would be too late. 'Yes, if I found the right person I'd be ready to put down my roots,' she said, relishing the thought of confining her *Samsonite* to the loft, once and for all.

'Café, monsieur, madam?' asked the waiter, hovering at Pierre's shoulder.

Pierre looked directly at Rachel. 'Non, merci. I think we will take coffee at home.'

Rachel grinned, the way he said 'we' and 'home' sounded as hooked up as candy floss on a stick.

'Another brandy?'

Rachel nodded, enjoying the warm glow the first one had given her. Sipping her drink, she wriggled her bare toes in the soft cream rug beneath her feet. Gorgeous but impractical, it will have to go when we have kids, she thought to herself.

'You're smiling, tell me what you're thinking,' Pierre asked, tracing the outline of her lips with his finger.

'Nothing really, just how the brandy is making me all warm and sleepy,' she said.

Pierre smiled and taking her glass, placed it on the coffee table. He kissed her, slowly at first tracing the line from her lips, along the curve of her jaw and the side of her neck, ending in the soft hollow of her collar bone. Then he raised his head, searching her face and in answer Rachel began to undo his shirt, kissing each newly revealed triangle of skin, button by button. Sliding her hands around his back, she felt his muscles twitch in anticipation and easing his fingers under the straps of her dress, Pierre slipped the thin ribbons of silk from her shoulders. Suddenly, a frantic knocking from the direction of the front door echoed down the hall, startling them both.

'Ignore it,' Pierre said, circling her waist with his hands and kissing her throat.

The knocking grew more insistent. Pulling on his shirt, Pierre went to investigate. Re-assembling her clothes, Rachel strained to listen to the rapid dialogue taking place in the hall. The other voice was deep and agitated, another man. Moments later Pierre re-appeared buttoning his shirt, his face ashen.

'It's Jean-Paul. My neighbour, the man you spoke to in the street. His wife is very sick, heart attack or stroke, I don't know which,' he said, reaching out to stroke her cheek. 'I'm sorry Rachel, but I have to go with him in the ambulance, he has no one else.'

'Of course,' said Rachel, leaping to her feet. 'Is there anything I can do? Anyone I can call for them?'

'No, there is no-one, they have no family ... no kids.' He shrugged sadly. 'I'm sorry I have to go. Help yourself to whatever you need and I'll be back as soon as I can.' He grabbed his wallet and phone from the coffee table and was gone.

Chapter 24

Rachel couldn't remember where she was when she woke up. It was a familiar feeling, she'd lost count of the number of times she'd woken up in yet another anonymous hotel and had to phone reception to find out where she was. Glancing round the room for clues, she caught the gaze of the woman, in the oil painting above her head and memories of the previous evening flooded back. The house was silent and wrapping herself in her pashmina, she crept downstairs. She passed the open door way to the lounge and saw their glasses from the night before and the dents in the cushions where Pierre had kissed her and where she'd decided that if she was going to put down roots, they would definitely be in French soil.

She pushed open the kitchen door and her heart jumped in her chest. Pierre was slumped at the table fast asleep, a half-empty brandy glass inches from his head. Silently she searched the kitchen for things to make coffee and while it was brewing she watched Pierre sleeping, until eventually the aroma of coffee bought him to his senses. He sat up, rubbing his eyes and when he saw her there, smiling at him, her face full of concern, he pulled her onto his lap. 'I'm sorry if I gave you a shock by you finding me here,' he said. 'I got back just after five and couldn't sleep … or so I thought.'

Rachel stroked the hair back from his face. 'You look shattered. Can I make you some breakfast? How is François?'

He shook his head. 'It was a stroke, a small one, but enough to terrify Jean-Paul. She won't be allowed to leave hospital for several days and he's refusing to leave her side.'

'There must be someone we can call for them, so Jean-Paul can rest or take a shower,' Rachel said, remembering how kind the old man had been to her.

Pierre sipped his coffee and holding his face over the steam, closed his bloodshot eyes for a moment. 'No, they have no-one. Claudette used to joke that we would end up like them, a little old couple rattling around in this big house.'

'Didn't Claudette want children?' asked Rachel quietly.

'Yes she did, that's why it ended; I didn't,' Pierre said, his words punching the air from Rachel's lungs. 'At the beginning she said she wanted a career, to help me build up the business but it was another lie. Deep down, Claudette wanted a family and thought she could make me change my mind.'

'And she didn't?' asked Rachel, her voice cracking.

Pierre shook his head and lifted her off his lap. 'I'm going to take a shower and wake myself up, then we can decide what to do today,' he said and heading for the door, he added, 'Help yourself to anything, I'm sure there's everything you need.'

When he'd gone, Rachel fled upstairs to pack. Why now? Why Pierre? There should be rules, she decided, blindly pulling on her clothes from the night before and throwing the rest of her things into her suitcase; rules that let you find out the really important stuff before you fell for a guy, rules that made it OK to say 'I'm crazy about you but before this goes any further, can I just check that you want kids?'

Dragging her suitcase downstairs, through the hall and out onto the street, she made her way to the station. She pushed her way onto the métro, where the passengers, used to shrugging off drunks and drug addicts, took little notice of the sobbing woman sharing their carriage, more troubled by her annoying suitcase knocking their ankles, than her obvious despair. Somehow she made it on to the *Eurostar* and fell into a fitful sleep, nearly missing her connecting train to Henley. Normally she would have walked the short distance from the station to home but feeling wrung out, she hailed a taxi.

Lifting her case into the boot, the driver noticed her tear stained face, asked if she was OK.

'I'll be fine,' she sniffed into a soggy tissue, wishing he hadn't started her off again by being kind. 'I just need to get home that's all.'

'Alright love, let's get going then shall we?' he said, turning on the radio in an attempt to lighten the mood. He was about to turn out of the station forecourt, when a Mercedes cut him off at break neck speed.

'Crazy bastard,' he shouted, shaking his fist. 'Excuse my French love but he nearly took my wing off!'

Rachel nodded and stared out of the window with bleary eyes. 'It's OK. I know him and he is a bastard,' she said, recognising the car's private number plate, 'but he's not crazy, Rupert Fotheringham-Allen knows exactly what he's doing.'

Chapter 25

Imagining the look on his wife's face when he presented her with the eternity ring, Rup dumped the Merc on the drive. His PA had chosen it along with a handful of other treats, nothing too lavish, just a decent hamper with lots of bubbly. Opening the front door of the house, he bounded up the stairs two at a time. He planned to take Carolyn out in the boat, make her feel like she was the only woman in his world and within moments she would fall in to his arms, all thoughts of divorcing him pushed from her head. As he approached their bedroom he heard a muffled moan - Digby snoring he thought - the old Labrador was entering his autumn days and often slept the day away, curled up on the rug by Rup's bed.

Pushing open the door he was disappointed to find the rug empty. Across the room something reflected in the mirrored wardrobe caught his eye. He crossed the floor, adjusting the angle of the door to catch more of it and was rewarded by the reflection of his wife's bottom, rhythmically rising and falling, atop the tanned lap of her personal trainer.

Rup stumbled silently from the room and half running, half falling, threw himself down the stairs, his heart pounding in his chest as he struggled for breath. Desperate for air, he fell against the front door and catapulted head first into a giant hamper, being carried up the front steps by a delivery boy. Youth being on his side, the boy was the first to get to his feet.

'So, so sorry sir,' the boy stammered. 'Bottoms Up!'

'What did you say?' hissed Rup, wiping spittle from his lips with the back of his hand.

'Bottoms Up, sir!' The boy repeated, his acne ridden cheeks flushing in embarrassment.

In one leap Rup grabbed the boy's collar and slammed him against the wall. 'What the fuck do you mean Bottoms Up? Is that some kind of sick joke you spotty little prick!'

The boy too terrified to speak pointed frantically at the label on the forgotten hamper.

'Bottoms Up!

Instantly, Rup loosened his grip on the boy, who looked as though he was about to cry and reaching into his wallet shoved a wad of notes into the boy's hand. 'Clear off! And don't mention this to anyone, or I'll personally see to it that you never deliver another hamper to anyone ever again!'

The boy scrambled back down the steps and muttering, 'Fucking psycho,' under his breath, threw himself into his van.

As the little white van skidded out of the drive, Rup shook his fist and forcing his way into the hamper, yanked out a bottle of *Bollinger*. Once open, he gulped at it like a new born and as the alcohol fizzed its way to his brain the image of his wife's bobbing bottom began to blur, so that he barely noticed his mobile phone vibrating in his trouser pocket. It was only when the tiny rectangle of electronics began to nudge its way to his groin that he realized he had a call.

Hoping it was Lucy requesting a good seeing to, he pulled the phone from his pocket. Whoever it was had rung off and he didn't recognise their number. Not that it mattered; he knew very well who had called. They wouldn't leave him alone; the number was always different; they liked to cover their tracks, but it was always the same international dialling code, 07... Russia. He tossed the tiny *Nokia* as far as it would go, until it landed with a satisfying splash and was obligingly swallowed by Father Thames.

'Oi! Watch it mate! You nearly hit me,' yelled the skipper of a passing pleasure boat.

Rup shook the champagne bottle menacingly and shouted back a mouthful of obscenities, which were instantly swallowed by the booming pop music coming from the boat's sound system. The skipper laughed and raised a glass of *Pimms*. 'Sorry mate, can't hear you.' Then giving Rup the bird, he accelerated away, his female passengers clinging to their cocktails and squealing with excitement.

Lucky bastard cursed Rup to himself; it should be me

heading off to the Regatta, at the helm of the Slipper Launch, with Lucy and her girly friends. The reality he knew was that his life was splitting apart like a cheap condom, spilling its consequences in an embarrassing and inconvenient mess.

Chapter 26

On the other side of town, Sarah was on her way to fetch the girls from school. It was stifling under the cloudless sky, heat pounded off the playground. When the children finally appeared, they were flush cheeked and keen to escape their stuffy classrooms. Inside the car it was blisteringly hot and airless and Sarah wondered whether she should take the children home, or to the Regatta as planned; but because she had promised Ted, and because it was always cooler by the river even if it was purely the physiological effect of being near to by water, she set off for the Regatta.

At the riverbank the girls dashed ahead and Sarah followed, pushing Harry's pushchair through a tide of blazers; striped, plain, outrageous and conservative and above, bobbing like milliner's flotsam, hats of all kinds. All of the men, it seemed, preferred to wear their blazers undone. On the college boys, who could have buttoned up their jackets with room to spare, it looked rebellious and cool but as Sarah looked at the older men, with their spreading middle-aged mid-riffs, she wondered if they were jealous, counting the years since the edges of their jackets had met in the centre. Apart from the blazers and hats, everyone had something in common; pretty coloured badges hanging from their lapels, as if they'd come straight from Sports Day. The badges appeared to influence entry to several giant marquees and being not just badgeless, but clueless, Sarah approached a young security guard.

'Hi, I wonder if you can help me? Everyone here appears to be wearing a badge and I don't know what they mean or whether I need one,' she explained, feeling like it was her first day at big school and everyone knew where the tech block was except her.

The guard from 'Ealing Security' smiled, pleased to have someone to talk to. 'The answer to your question is yes and no, it's up to you. It depends what you want to do.'

Sarah stared at him nonplussed; she hadn't been expecting a multiple choice. How many options could there be for goodness sake? Option one - stand on the river bank and watch the rowing, option two - duh! … stand on the river bank and watch the rowing!

Noticing her bemused expression the security guard explained. 'First you've got the Stewards' Enclosure. That really is the dog's wotsits that is and you can get your *Pimms* and your champagne and there's a bandstand. That's where it's really kicking off.'

'Sounds good,' said Sarah, thinking how nice a cool glass of bubbly would go down while she watched Ted's boys do their stuff. 'How do I get a badge for that one?' '

The guard smiled enjoying his little game. 'You can't. Unless you're a Steward, Member of the Stewards or a guest, and you wouldn't be allowed in anyway, not dressed like that.'

Sarah looked down at her nondescript black trousers and slightly off white blouse; her office clothes. He had a point; she wasn't exactly looking her best. She began to mumble excuses about having come directly from work, when the guard began to laugh.

'There's nothing wrong with your clothes, darlin', you look lovely, it's just that you're wearing trousers and you can't see; they've got rules. Ladies have to wear dresses or skirts and none of them micro minis neither, your skirt has to be over your knees,' he paused, looking down at Harry who gave him a gummy grin. 'I don't think they let pushchairs in there neither.'

Then he leant forward, as if about to divulge a great secret. 'I wouldn't bother myself; they won't even let you use your phone or your iPod or nothing in there. You're better off going in the Regatta Enclosure, bit farther down river and for that you just buy a badge.'

'But what about my trousers?'

'Only problem will be if you take'em off,' he smirked. 'You can wear what you like in there darlin' and it's got a good view from the grandstand, not like Wembley or nothing. Or you can walk past the end of the tents and see the rest of the course for gratis, no badges or nothing.'

'Right thanks, you've been very helpful,' said Sarah, feeling grateful that she wouldn't have to spend the rest of the afternoon badged up like she'd come second in the egg and spoon race.

She walked along the back of the boat tents and noticed that the fields on the other side of the path had been turned into temporary car parks and in between the cars people were having picnics. They weren't the cheese and pickle, thermos flask type of picnics she was used to; these picnics were in a league of their own - elaborate, outdoor feasts held under gazebos and on tables decorated with vases of flowers, ice buckets and silver candelabra with cream tapered candles. Watching platters of quails eggs and smoked salmon being passed around, Sarah began to get the feeling that there was a lot more to the Regatta than a bunch of fit men messing about in boats.

At last, she spied the end of the marquees and an unobstructed view of the river. Keeping her eyes open for Ted, she joined the throng on the tow path leading towards Temple Island, which marked the start of the Regatta course.

It was one minute to four and two boats, one she recognized as Ted's crew, were lined up at the start, waiting for the Umpire's signal. The oarsmen's skintight rowing vests left little to the imagination and their pumped up muscles were worthy of any Mr. Universe thought Sarah, taking a photograph on her mobile and forwarding it to Rachel.

She waited for what she hoped would be an instant, smutty response but the phone remained silent. Disappointed she dropped the phone into her handbag; if Rachel was somewhere in mid-air her phone would be switched off, but at least she would have something attractive to drool over, when she finally came back down to earth.

Suddenly the boats sprang forward, a blur of red and white blades slicing through the water.

'It's our boys! Give them a cheer kids,' she said, waving frantically at the Baxdale team and screaming encouragement.

'Mum! Pack it in, cheering is *so* lame,' said Naomi,

grabbing onto Sarah's flailing arms.

Nearby a group of young men wearing the opposite team's colours, were shouting words of encouragement but the rest of the crowd appeared to agree with Naomi and rather than cheering on the crews, were intent on hitting the bars or the marquees offering corporate hospitality.

'Hey Mum, those people look like goldfish!' giggled Millie, pointing to the marquees.

Sarah turned to look. Millie had a point; with their clear plastic sides the tents looked like giant aquariums, allowing those on the inside being wined and dined to maintain the façade of watching the rowing, while getting off their faces on someone else's expense account.

And still, there was no sign of Ted. Sarah wondered if he had decided to watch the race from the Stewards' Enclosure, meaning he was firmly out of bounds. As if I need reminding she thought, pushing Harry's pushchair along the towpath, in the direction of home.

Back at the house, Millie raced to be first inside, desperate not to miss a moment of children's T.V. and as she pushed open the front door, the morning's post skidded along the polished wooden floor.

'Look Mummy, it's a postcard from Daddy,' she squealed, waving a small rectangle of Manhattan sky-line under Sarah's nose. 'He says he's missing us lots and sends you a great big kiss! And there's another letter just for you and Daddy.'

Sarah ignored the postcard and with her heart pounding, opened the envelope marked with a Building Society logo. Was it a response to the letter she'd sent after her visit to 'Debts 'R' Us'? Had following Margery's advice done the trick or would the first line read, 'Dear Home Owner - Not! Ha! Ha! Nice try … now send us the keys stupid!' With relief, she read how they had been pleased to receive her letter and had accepted her proposal. Margery's words of wisdom had been right after all.

Unfortunately, there was still no word from the credit card companies. Perhaps they're still trying to work out a euphemism for County Court Judgment thought Sarah, as she got on with making the children's tea.

Later, when Ted and the crew got back from the river she was more than ready for a glass of wine.

'So Scarlett, is Tara to be saved?' he asked, pouring them both a glass and following her out to the garden.

Sarah shrugged and sipped her wine. 'Who can say? I haven't had to pawn the family jewels just yet.'

Ted reached inside the neck of his t-shirt and pulled out a silver pendant on a chain. From her visit to the Regatta, she recognized the shape of the pendant; it was the blade of an oar.

'I'd let you have this but it's only of sentimental value. I bought it here in Henley after I won my first race. I don't know why I still wear it ... a lucky talisman I guess.'

Sarah wanted to reach out and touch it - was it for luck or to touch something he kept close, she wasn't sure. Instead, she played with the stem of her glass. 'And has it worked?' she asked. 'Has it bought you good luck?'

'In rowing, sure.' He tucked the chain inside his shirt and shrugged. 'As for the rest, who can say? I managed to screw up my marriage which didn't feel so lucky at the time.'

'What happened?' Sarah asked and then instantly regretted it as a shadow crossed his face. 'Please forget I said that, it's none of my business.'

'Hey, it's OK it was a long time ago. I lived for rowing and fitted my marriage around it, when it should have been the other way around,' he said, staring into the mid-distance and then something caught his eye. 'What's with the sleeping bags on the clothes line? Is someone going camping?'

Relieved at the change of subject Sarah explained. 'The girls are going on Brownie camp at the weekend and I've got to make up their bedding rolls. They're supposed to be small and neat but I can't even get the silly things back in their bags.'

'I'd be happy to do it for you. I used to go camping all the time as a kid. I can make a bed roll in my sleep.'

Sarah accepted his offer and trying not to think of how exactly he might make a bed roll, she went to fetch the rest of the girls' camping gear. When she returned Ted had already taken the sleeping bags off the line. 'I took the children to the Regatta this afternoon,' she said brightly, keen to keep off wives and husbands, even if they were exes.

Ted grinned. 'And was it as snobby and privileged as you thought?'

'Yes and no. With all the badges and blazers and rules about where you can and can't go it's kind of like a public school, but you can ignore all that and just enjoy the rowing and being by the river.'

Ted nodded and smoothing out the fabric of one of the sleeping bags rolled it into a tight bundle. 'I'm sorry I missed you, it can get real busy down there sometimes. It's so different from Maine; the only people we see when we're out rowing are the lobstermen. Hold up the sack and I'll ease the first sleeping bag in.'

Together they wrestled the sleeping bag inside, while Sarah struggled to make the link between sea crustaceans and rowing. 'Lobstermen?' she asked, puzzled. 'What are Lobstermen doing on a river? I thought you only got lobsters from the sea.'

'The New Meadows river may as well be the sea,' he laughed, rolling up the second sleeping bag. 'It's only five miles east of the Atlantic; if we're lucky we have porpoises swimming right beside the boat. Sometimes I think I have the best job in the world; getting out on that river, the sun on your face, the ozone on your tongue…it's like a little piece of heaven on earth.'

Sarah held out the second sack. He made it sound so open and free, a place where you could breathe. She was suddenly aware how she held a tightness in her chest, as if her ribs were a permanently clenched fist. How long had she been holding her breath? Seconds, it had to be, so why then did it feel like years? And what was she waiting for; something to end or something to begin?

In a moment, she lost her concentration and the

sleeping bag, only half in the sack began to spill out and grabbing for it at the same time as Ted, she caught his hand instead. Instantly, she was struck by the rough callouses on his fingers.

'Like elephant hide aren't they?' he grinned, gently letting go of her hand and showing her his upturned palms. 'Rowers hands, I'm afraid. First we get the blisters, then we spray them with this magic called 'New Skin', then we get callouses, then we don't hurt anymore.'

Above his left palm, Sarah noticed a strap of black leather. He was wearing the wristwatch, the one she'd secretly tried on the day before. Remembering the softness of the leather and the cool metal clock face against her skin, she thought suddenly how his hands would feel on her and the maleness of him, until her head began to swim.

'Are you OK, you've gone quiet,' Ted asked, gently touching her arm. 'Shall we have another attempt at this sleeping bag?'

'Yes, sorry,' she said, holding out the bag for a second time. 'I was thinking how different it is here, from your life in Maine. We're so hemmed in, all racing about trying to hold down a job, look after the children, fend off the mortgage company … sometimes I think I don't breathe out at all.'

'Sounds like you've been sucked into the rat race,' said Ted, pushing the sleeping bag into its sack, his forearms brushing against her fingers, making her skin tingle. 'What would you do if you could get out?'

'Run my own café. The thing is I keep wondering if I can really do it, if I've got the courage…'

Ted pulled the string closure on the camping sacks and tied them in a double bow. 'You're a fighter, you'll find a way. Why else would you have a crazy bunch of yanks to stay? You're more like Scarlett O'Hara than you realise and she never gave up did she?'

He was right she thought, she needed to make plans. With or without the café she couldn't continue holding her breath, waiting for permission to live her life. Signing up for a couple of evening courses couldn't hurt and it would show everyone, Dave included that she meant business. 'Yes, you're right I can't be defeated before I've even begun,' she said, feeling more confident than she had in a long time. 'I'm going to put my name down for a Cordon Bleu evening course.'

'That's the spirit,' said Ted, approvingly. 'I feel bad about not seeing you at the river today, I was watching from the finish line and I missed you. Do you think I could persuade you to give me another chance? If you call my cell, I could meet you and if you want to see fighting spirit in action, watching a close race is hard to beat.'

Sarah nodded, in the interests of her potential new business she owed it to herself to seek a little inspiration, didn't she? After all, Dave was always going on corporate training days; telling her that 'coaching' was the key to running a successful business and boy, could she do with some 'coaching'.

'Well? Can I persuade you?' asked Ted, gathering up the sleeping bags.

Sarah blushed furiously as if he had been reading her thoughts. 'OK, you've twisted my arm. I guess I could force myself to spend another hour by the river, watching handsome young men in lycra,' she said, draining her wine glass. 'It's a hard job but someone's got to do it.'

'Hey, less about the young men what about the old Coaches?' said Ted, pretending to be insulted.

'Oh, they're not so bad either,' laughed Sarah, picking up their glasses delighted that he was flirting with her. 'I'm going to bed. All that river air has gone straight to my head.'

Upstairs in her en-suite Sarah opened the bathroom cabinet. She was sure she had a bottle of nail varnish somewhere, from a birthday or two ago. At last she found it, hidden behind a tub of nappy rash cream. Sending shards of brittle red flakes onto the floor, she twisted open the lid and then, with the utmost care, turned each toenail into a perfect miniature sunrise.

Chapter 27

The next morning Sarah woke early, her thin cotton nightdress sticking to her like a shroud and the children, a sheen of perspiration coving their sleeping faces, had wriggled free of their duvets. Apart from the children's gentle snores the house was silent. Relieved that Ted and the crew had already left for the river, Sarah crept downstairs, keen to make a start on the chores before the children woke and began to demand her attention. As she neared the bottom of the stairs, she caught sight of herself in the hall mirror. Usually she rushed past, mirrors and shop windows had long since lost their appeal but this time, recognizing something different, she stopped to stare. In her reflection she saw a younger, sexier version of herself; her cheeks were soft from sleep and her hair fell in damp tendrils about her face. If only there was some way of making it last she thought, at least until the school run.

Suddenly the door to the dining room swung open and out stepped one of the crew, she recognized as Joey, the peanut butter enthusiast. He mumbled his excuses and avoiding eye contact, scooted out the front door. Then the rest of the team followed and like Joey, mumbled an embarrassed excuse me, as if it were their fault she had been caught semi-naked, and made a dash for the door.

Sarah hesitated, the crew had left the front door open expecting Ted to follow, and sunlight filled the narrow hall, illuminating her nakedness beneath her nightdress. She reached for the banister - she could make the middle stairs perhaps - but her legs, suddenly brazen, refused to move. She heard the sound of a chair scraping on the floor, being pushed back from the breakfast table and before she had a chance to change her mind; Ted was there, standing in the hall. She watched his mouth open and a pulse track across his temple as he took the sight of her in; from her fuzzy bed-head hair down to her toes, red and shiny like forbidden fruit. Then, keeping his eyes lowered he made for the front door.

Suddenly she knew, all those years of practicing in front of the mirror, wearing her mother's old nighties and swooning over handsome Hollywood hunks had been for this very moment. Tucking a loose tendril behind her ear she smiled. 'See you later, Ted.'

Sarah pulled up at the school gates. 'Off you go girls. Have a good day. See you at 3.30.'

'Aren't you coming in with us?' asked Naomi, hardly believing her luck.

Sarah shook her head. 'No, the bell will go in a minute and I'm sure you don't want to hang around with me.'

Nodding enthusiastically, the girls slid from the car and disappeared into the tide of blue and white gingham, swirling through the school gates. Relieved they hadn't insisted that she see them into the playground, Sarah drove off. Her posh summer dress would have raised eyebrows at the school gates and she felt self-conscious enough as it was. Even if she had no hope of entering the Stewards' Enclosure, at least today she would look the part. She parked the car and tottering on unfamiliar heels and keeping one hand on the brim of her hat to stop the breeze from taking it, she pushed Harry's pushchair towards the Regatta.

On the bridge over the Thames, she paused for a moment to look at the boat tents, striped blue and white and laid out with miles of racking like a gargantuan left luggage office and on the floating pontoons, boats as thin as toothpicks waiting to be lifted into the water. She continued on, past the Leander Club with its flag, sporting a fat bottomed pink hippopotamus, floating prettily in the breeze. Ted had explained that the club had chosen the hippo as their emblem because in African legend it represented the king of the river; but Sarah couldn't help think, that considering the width of the boats an animal with a smaller backside, like a gazelle or a meerkat might have been more appropriate.

At the boat tents, rowers, tall, toned and beautiful were coming and going through the tent flaps, reminding Sarah of models on the cat walk. She hovered uncertainly, only hours ago Ted had seen her half-naked and now fully dressed in an outfit bought for a cousin's wedding the previous summer, she felt more conspicuous than ever, wanting more than anything, to go home and hide. What had she been thinking? She didn't flaunt herself and flirt with men she hardly knew, or with those she did if it came to that. She wasn't that sort of a woman, she was a wife and a mother who hid herself in fleeces and jeans and who could pass by a thousand building sites without the risk of a wolf whistle or a 'give us a smile love'

In one moment of madness she'd dragged the good name of the Regatta Landladies into the gutter. What would the Regatta rules have to say about that? No doubt she'd be strapped to a chair and plunged into the Thames like a medieval witch. If she drowned she would be declared innocent and would be allowed to remain on the register of Regatta Landladies, if she survived she would be found guilty as charged and would be struck off forever more!

Before she had chance to make a run for it, Ted's head appeared through the tent flap. 'I was just coming out to look for you. I'm glad you're here, you're just in time.' He smiled, peeling back the heavy white canvas. 'Come through here, I think we can get you into the Umpire's launch for our race. I've spoken to the official and one of the press spaces is free, the guy's gone into town to grab some breakfast.'

'Oh ... I wanted to say about this morning I'm ...'

Hurrying her through the tent Ted interrupted. 'Hey, it's me who should be apologizing. I'm sorry that we woke you ... right here we are, just sign in with this guy and we'll get you in the boat.'

Trembling Sarah signed her name on the register. He hadn't made any reference to her stunt in the hallway. She wondered if he'd even noticed. She didn't know how to feel - relieved or disappointed. Trying to regain her composure, she said, 'I'd love to go in the boat Ted but what about Harry?'

'No problem. I've spoken to the girls on our women's team and they are happy to mind him for you.' He smiled and ushered her towards a group of athletic, sun kissed girls. 'It's only for a few minutes and it will take their minds off their nerves for their race this afternoon.'

Sarah left Harry to be cooed over by the Baxdale women's team and smiled to herself when he didn't give her a backward glance. Like mother like son she thought, those Americans could charm the birds from the trees.

'Here we are, watch your step,' said Ted, helping her into the Umpire's Launch.

As she settled comfortably among the polished wood and brass, Ted leant forward and whispered in her ear. 'These boats have got rules I'm afraid, no shouting or cheering. If you have to talk it's got to be in a whisper OK?'

She nodded, suddenly feeling out of her depth especially as Ted was making no move to join her. 'Aren't you coming with us?' she asked, wishing she'd stayed at home.

Ted shook his head. 'No. I can't see the race as well from behind. I'll watch from the Stewards' Enclosure and meet you in the Rower's tent at the end. By the way, have you seen the name of this boat? It reminds me of you.'

Sarah was about to reply when Ted put his finger to his lips and gestured at the Umpire, there was to be no more talking. The Launch began to reverse from the pontoon and there was nothing she could do, except watch Ted as he disappeared into the crowd.

The Baxdale boat and their competitor were already lined up at the start and as the Umpire's Launch glided sedately downstream to join them, she glanced over the side to read the boat's name and found only bare, polished wood. Tempting though it was, she daren't risk launching herself to the other side of the boat, for fear of ending up in the river or heaven forbid, causing the whole damn thing to capsize. Besides there was no guarantee that she'd like what she'd see anyway. People called their boats all kinds of names and this one could be called 'Daft Cow' for all she knew.

Suddenly, she realized that the Launch was turning in a wide circle, to face up river towards the finish line. In front, she could see fluorescent orange starter markers and the competing boats were being held in their starting positions by two men, lying prostrate on floating pontoons. The Baxdale team, dressed in matching vests, red and white and emblazoned with a giant B, reminded her of American cheerleaders she'd seen on T.V. To take her mind off a list of potentially unflattering names for the Umpire's Launch, she tried to make eye contact with Joey, but he was oblivious, his face taut with tension and adrenaline, all thoughts of peanuts forgotten.

Suddenly, the Umpire stood up and anticipation rippled across the water. 'Baxdale and Lomont. When I see that you are straight and ready I will start you like this,' he said, waving a red flag. He paused and on the riverbank, a hush fell across the spectators. 'Attention. Go!'

Sarah watched as the oars ploughed through the water, propelling the boats from zero to race speed. Seconds later, the crews settled into a rhythm with all the oarsmen in sync and the boats accelerating smoothly through the water with every stroke. As they passed the three quarter mark the tension grew and the coxswains were screaming their lungs out for the oarsmen, whose muscles were twitching and pulsing with every stroke, to use full power.

As they headed into the final sprint Sarah saw something in their expressions change; their faces became blank and their eyes unfocused as if in a trance. Ryan, the Baxdale coxswain, was yelling at them, desperate to pierce through their hypnotic state and draw out the fight, unleashing months of training, and at last, with one almighty effort he guided them to the finish line, half a length ahead of the other boat. Hoarse with emotion he screamed, 'On the paddle!' and the crew threw themselves forward in exhaustion.

Sarah felt drained from watching and was glad, that back at the landing stage, Ted was waiting to help her out of the boat. He was grinning from ear to ear. 'We did it Sarah, we won! It was a barnburner of a race but we won. We're through to the semi-finals.'

For a moment, she thought he might kiss her but protocol demanded no show of emotion. Even the racing commentator, announcing the results of the last race over the loud speaker, spoke in an even unemotional tone, as if a stiff upper lip was a pre-requisite of the job.

'I'm sorry I can't escort you out. I've got to see the guys,' Ted said, offering her his hand.

'Of course, say well done from me,' said Sarah, stepping onto the pontoon.

Still holding her hand, he said, ' I have to take a rain-check on your company this evening and tomorrow I'm afraid, I'm having dinner with a bunch of other Coaches, it's kind of tradition.'

Sarah squirmed - like some desperate housewife she'd over-stepped the mark and now he was going to avoid her like the plague. Trying to hide her disappointment, she smiled as if this was the best news she'd had all day. 'I didn't expect...I mean I don't expect you to spend your evenings with me, it's not what you're here to do.'

'No,' said Ted shaking his head in a meaningful way. 'But when I accepted the invitations to dinner, I hadn't known how much I would enjoy spending evenings with my landlady.'

Feeling the blood rush to her cheeks she let go of his hand, in case he should feel the perspiration on her palm.

Ted grinned. 'I've turned them down for Saturday night; I thought maybe we could watch the Regatta fireworks together.'

'I'd like that, very much,' she said and watched him go to congratulate his team. As she turned to leave she remembered that she still didn't know the name of the Umpire's Launch. Holding her breath in anticipation, she walked the few paces along the landing stage to the stern of the boat, where, in curly black script she read the name – 'Enchantress'.

She read it again, twice, just to be sure - Ted thought of her as an 'Enchantress' - not 'Finder of Lego', 'Ironer of Shirts' or 'Peeler of Spuds'. She smiled and turned her face to the sun. 'Enchantress' had a much nicer ring to it and if Ted believed it, then perhaps she could too.

Chapter 28

On Saturday morning, Sarah awoke with the beginnings of a smile twitching at the corners of her mouth. She'd missed her nightly chats with Ted, forced to be content with snatched smiles and brief hellos, swiftly followed by 'see you laters,' as he came and went with the crew. She glanced at the bedside clock; Ted would have left for the river hours ago. With the Baxdale team through to the semi-finals, his mind would be on one thing only, until the race was over. She was glad, it would give her time sort out the children and decide what she was going to wear (if only more cousins had decided to get married last summer).

Naomi and Millie's beds were empty and she could hear them pottering about in the kitchen. Scooping Harry out of his sleeping bag and onto her hip she went downstairs. In the kitchen Millie was devouring a bowl of cereal and Naomi was busy filling water bottles. Both girls were dressed in their Brownie uniforms and their kitbags were stacked by the back door.

'I can see you two are ready for camp. How come you're never this prepared for school?' asked Sarah, taking their packed lunches from the fridge and squeezing them into the top of Millie's rucksack.

Naomi sighed and raised her eyes to the ceiling. 'Duh, Mum! We don't have camp fires and marshmallows at school do we?'

Sarah grinned in spite of herself. 'No, I guess not.'

Through the kitchen window she saw a car pull onto the drive. 'Your lift's here,' she said, bundling the girls and their bags through the door, trying to hug and kiss them as they dodged away, in case their friends could see from the car. In the rush, a see through wash bag fell from Naomi's rucksack; it was full of *Molton Brown* miniature toiletries.

'Where did you get these from?' asked Sarah, squeezing it back into Naomi's bag.

'Auntie Rachel gave them to me when she looked after us, when you and Daddy went to Paris. She said a girl doesn't need to let standards slip just because she's sleeping in a field!'

'Quite right too,' said Sarah, closing the car door on their smiling faces. As she walked back to the house she tried to remember when she'd last spoken to Rachel. There had been a brief text after Rachel got back from Paris but nothing since and she hadn't responded to the sexy photos of the rowers Sarah had sent her from the Regatta. It didn't make sense. If Rachel was around why hadn't she come to goggle at the crew and if she was away, why hadn't she asked her to look after Biggles? Back inside, she tried Rachel's home number and then her mobile and got no answer on either. Instinctively, she knew something was wrong.

Quickly, she threw on her jeans and bundled Harry into the car. Minutes later she turned into Rachel's street and parking behind Rachel's car, noticed that its shiny black paintwork was littered with pollen and dead insects and a grey-green bird turd had baked to a hard crust on the windscreen; Rachel hadn't been out for days.

Pulling a fist full of mail and free newspapers from Rachel's letter box, Sarah rang the door bell several times.

Nothing.

Crouching down, Sarah peered between the gaps in the bamboo blind which shielded the basement kitchen from the glances of passer-bys. She could see the wall mounted television flickering with life, but no-one appeared to be watching. With a sick feeling in the pit of her stomach, she fumbled for Rachel's front door key and let herself in.

She smelt the basement before she reached it, a pungent combination of litter tray and cigarettes. Sarah shuddered with relief, at least it meant that Rachel and, she supposed with a grimace, the bad tempered cat were still alive.

'Rachel, it's me,' she called out, pushing open the kitchen door and holding tight onto Harry's hand. Having found Rachel alive and kicking the last thing she wanted to do was give her a heart attack. A disembodied hand waved from behind the sofa shaking fag ash onto the once pristine ivory cover. Lifting Harry onto her hip Sarah picked her way past discarded newspapers, take-out cartons and a heaving litter tray.

From the sofa, Rachel looked up with half focused eyes, before pushing an empty *Bacardi Breezer* onto the floor and brushing off piles of ash, leaving smoke trails on the cushion. 'Take a seat, good to see you,' she said.

'What in the name of God happened to you?' gasped Sarah.

Rachel was dressed in one of Josh's old golfing t-shirts, stained with what Sarah guessed to be chicken tikka massala and red wine.

'Men!' said Rachel, her voice rasped with nicotine. She tucked a strand of greasy hair behind her ear and drew heavily on her cigarette. 'Men have happened to me!'

'But men have 'happened' to you before,' said Sarah, clearing a space on the floor for Harry and flicking on a children's T.V. channel, 'and you've never been like this before!'

'That was before I met Pierre…' Rachel stared into the distance, scratching at an angry spot on her chin. 'It was different with him…I was different with him.'

Her voice was slurred and Sarah guessed that the *Breezer* had qualified as breakfast. Had the visit to Paris turned out to be nothing more than wham, bam, merci madam? she wondered and trying to sound sympathetic, she said, 'It didn't work out then? Just a bit of a fling.'

'Hardly,' mumbled Rachel, her cigarette hanging off her bottom lip like an unfortunate growth. 'We didn't even get that far, not that we didn't want to. It's just that François had a heart attack or a stroke or something and Pierre had to go with her to the hospital.'

Sarah gasped. 'François? I see now why it didn't work out. Pierre's into threesomes….very *Jules et Jim*. That's the French for you, I guess.'

Rachel stared at her blankly. 'What the hell are you banging on about Sarah? François is in her eighties!'

'Ughhhh! That's disgusting! I'm sorry, I'm not ageist

or anything but that's like having sex with your granny!'

'François didn't have sex, she had a stroke!'

'Was she the one watching then?'

Rachel groaned and ground out her cigarette in an overflowing ash tray. 'No! No-one was watching anybody! François is Pierre's neighbour. Pierre and I were just … you know when Jean-Paul, François' husband bangs on the door to say she needs to go to hospital.'

'So you didn't sleep with him?'

'No, and I know it would have been perfect,' Rachel said, rooting under the coffee table for the *Bacardi* bottle.

Sarah took it from her before she could tip the last dregs into her mouth. 'I still don't understand why you're so upset, it was just sex. Why can't you invite him over for a few days and pick up where you left off?'

Rachel shook her head. 'There's no point, it's over,' she paused as tears began to spill onto her cheeks. 'Pierre doesn't want children.' She buried her face in her hands, as great heaving sobs racked her chest, sending streams of snot from her nose.

For a moment Sarah was stunned, Rachel had lived with Josh for two years and hadn't shed a single tear when he left and yet this French guy had reduced her to a gibbering wreck in a matter of days. 'Oh my poor baby,' she said, pulling Rachel into her arms. 'You've really gone and done it this time haven't you?' Stroking Rachel's hair, she murmured soothing words until her sobbing subsided into sharp little hiccups and sniffs. 'So, what are you going to do?' she asked when Rachel pulled away, blowing her nose into a soggy tissue.

Rachel shrugged. 'I can't see Pierre again, it would be too painful but after that I'm all out of ideas.'

Sarah couldn't think of anything either, but in desperation she said, 'I know something that might cheer you up. There's a football crowds worth of eye candy down at the river right now.' She raised her hand as Rachel began to protest. 'Don't get me wrong, I'm not suggesting you go and pull yourself a rower but putting on a bit of lipstick and getting out of this fug might make you feel more human.'

Rachel sniffed and lit another cigarette. 'I can't, officially I'm off sick and the airline will have its spies out. If I get caught out of my sick bed I'll be sacked.'

Sarah searched her handbag for a clean tissue and handed it to Rachel. 'I think you're being paranoid. How on earth will they know?'

'They'll know, believe me. A couple of years ago, one of the bosses was watching Wimbledon on T.V. and recognized a trolley dolly in the crowd. She was supposed to be home in bed with gastroenteritis, not singing with Cliff Richard on centre court. She was sacked on the spot and they've kept their eye on the social calendar ever since.'

'Wow, talk about Big Brother! But surely you'll be alright at Regatta; it's hardly in the same league as Wimbledon. I'm sure it's not televised so as long as you don't do an interview on Regatta Radio, no one will know you were there.'

Rachel considered for a moment. She was sick of daytime television and smelling of rum and take-away curry had begun to lose its charm. 'Do you really think it'll be alright?'

Sarah nodded enthusiastically. 'I know so. Why don't you pop upstairs and have a nice hot shower? I'll clear up down here and have a fresh pot of coffee ready. Then you can decide, OK?'

Rachel smiled weakly and dragged herself upstairs.

The reversal of roles felt deeply unsettling to Sarah. Rachel was the strong one, always telling her what to do, sorting out her problems and now the tables were turned. Grabbing a bin liner from under the sink she began clearing up. She was aching to tell Rachel about Ted and how her stomach flipped over and made her catch her breath every time he walked into the room; how she found any excuse to touch him when she talked and how for the first time in years she felt sexy and interesting and ...

'What's a girl got to do to get a coffee around here?' Rachel asked, appearing fresh from her shower wrapped in a fluffy dressing gown, her hair whipped up into a towelling turban. 'You were away with the fairies, penny for them?' she asked, taking the mug of steaming coffee from Sarah's hand.

'Oh, was I? I was just wondering how the girls were getting on at Brownie camp,' Sarah said, a tell-tale blush creeping across her cheeks.

'Sarah Crouch, you couldn't lie to save your life! What were you really thinking about?' pressed Rachel, sipping her coffee.

Sarah buried her face in her hands. 'Is it that obvious? I try and squash it down but every time I think of him, I feel like I'm lighting up like a Christmas tree!'

Rachel put her coffee down. 'Him?'

'Ted, the American coach. We've become ... friends.'

'Umm, bet you don't light up like a Christmas tree when you think of me and I've been your friend for donkey's years!' Rachel teased. 'Are you sure he's just a friend?'

'I would never be unfaithful to Dave,' said Sarah indignantly, pouring herself a coffee.

'Bet you're tempted though. What's good for the gander is good for the goose I say!' said Rachel, slapping a hand over her mouth as soon as the words were out.

Sarah jumped sloshing coffee onto the work surface, Rachel's words rekindling a fear she'd carried around like a grumbling appendix since returning from Paris. 'What did you say? What is good for ganders exactly?' she asked, her cheeks burning.

Rachel waved her hand dismissively. 'You know ganders ... men I mean, like to look, so er, should we.'

Sarah pressed her. 'That's all? That's all you meant? You would tell me if you knew something was going on wouldn't you? We don't keep secrets from each other do we?'

Rachel turned her back on Sarah and ran her coffee mug under the tap, playing for time. 'I'm sure Dave loves you to bits,' she said, with more conviction than she felt. Turning around, she thread her arm through Sarah's and tried to concentrate through a fug of nicotine, alcohol and her own disappointments. She didn't trust herself not to say anything stupid and damage Sarah's marriage beyond repair.

What she needed was for Sarah to leave and let her wallow in her own misery, but Sarah, standing there with her hands on her hips, would be hard to budge, so for once she decided to back down. 'It's against my better judgment but if it makes you happy I'll go wander by the river for a while, OK? I'd better go and get ready.'

Sarah nodded but she was still churning over what Rachel had said about geese and ganders. She couldn't shake the feeling that Rachel knew more than she was letting on. Had Dave been following his animal instincts? With Ted leaving for the States in two days time, would she be able to resist her own? More to the point why the hell should she if Dave was playing away? Unravelling herself from Rachel, she picked up Harry, hugging him to her like a comfort blanket and made for the door. 'I've got to go," she said, even though she had no reason to hurry away. 'I'm really sorry about Pierre, call me if you need to chat won't you?'

Rachel shook her head. 'Don't worry about me. I'm going to forget about men once and for all and to prove it I shall go to the Regatta and the only thing I shall be admiring will be the fashion!'

Sarah spent the rest of the morning in a morose mood, fussing around the house and playing half-heartedly with Harry. The high point of her afternoon was supposed to have been watching Ted's team compete in the semi-finals, but in the end Harry had decided it was the time to enter 'the terrible twos' and after a temper tantrum from hell, both he and Sarah were too exhausted to make the trek to the river. Eventually, Harry had fallen into a restless sleep and Sarah had listened to the race on the radio. The result was not what she had been hoping for - Baxdale college the outright favourites - lost by a length.

Sarah hung the dress she'd planned to wear for her evening with Ted back in the wardrobe; not for a moment did she imagine that he would want to indulge in the festive atmosphere of the Regatta fireworks, so soon after his team losing. Preparing for an evening of her own company, she changed into her old jeans and t-shirt and tried to tell herself it was for the best; that whatever this thing with Ted was, it had been nipped in the bud. In less than 48 hours, Ted would be back in the States and Dave would be home. As she set to work ironing a pile of Dave's shirts, she was reminded she could not escape real life forever. All the same, it was hard not to feel short changed.

Chapter 29

'Hey watch out, that's my foot you clumsy idiot!' Rachel said, as a bone crushing size 12 ground her sandal clad size 5 into the grass.

The owner of the offending foot swung around and began to apologise profusely.

'Andrew! What an earth are you doing here?' she gasped, rubbing her foot briskly to numb the pain. 'I didn't know the Regatta was your scene. And why on earth are you still wearing gardening clothes? You won't get anywhere near the Stewards' Enclosure dressed like that!'

Andrew looked down at his desert boots and mud smeared shorts and shrugged. 'My clothes don't matter; I'm not here for the Regatta.'

'Oh? Now let me think why else you could be at the river? Fishing? No, it can't be that, you've got no tackle. Sorry, that was very Carry on Camping wasn't it?' she said, in an attempt to make him smile.

His face didn't crack and as he still looked concerned she tried to reassure him. 'Please stop worrying about my foot. Once you've had a loaded cabin trolley run over you half a dozen times your toes get quite tough!'

'For God's sake Rachel, I'm not worried about your bloody foot, OK!' he snapped.

'Thanks a bunch!' she said, taken back by his uncharacteristic display of bad temper.

Crestfallen, Andrew stared at the ground. 'Sorry Rachel, that didn't come out right. Of course I am sorry about your foot, only I'm a bit distracted...'

I'm not surprised, thought Rachel with all this toned male flesh around and Andrew just out of the closet, it must be driving him crazy. 'I know what you mean,' she grinned, cocking her head towards the big, strong boys plying their way up the Regatta course, 'sex on legs most of them!'

Andrew blushed a deep crimson. 'Umm, to be honest I hadn't noticed, although I'm sure you're right.' He lifted his head briefly in the direction of the river. 'Actually Rachel, I'm in deep trouble. I think I may have made the biggest mistake of my life.'

All at once the colour drained from his face and his cheeks turned an ashen grey; a startling contrast to the dark tan of his arms and legs. Concerned that he was about to keel over, Rachel dragged him towards the nearest catering marquee and as there were no free chairs she appealed to a friendly looking group. 'I'm sorry, my friend's a diabetic and I need to get some food into him. If he doesn't sit down he'll fall down. Can I have a chair?'

One look at Andrew's face was enough to convince them of her story and one of the men shot up from his seat and pushing Andrew onto it. 'There you go mate, you need it more than I do.'

Andrew nodded his thanks, staring vacantly into the distance. Andrew's rescuer grabbed Rachel's arm. 'You'd better hurry up and get him some food before he goes off into one of those coma things. We were just off but we'll wait with him until you get back.'

'Thanks. I'll be as quick as I can,' she said, disappearing into the marquee. Ten minutes later, she emerged with a tray of food and two pints of beer.

'He hasn't said a word since you left. Do you want us to get the St. Johns over?' asked Andrew's guardian.

'No, no he'll be fine once I get this sandwich into him. Thanks ever so much for looking after him, you've been really kind.'

'Anytime, perhaps I'll bump into you later?' he winked.

His friend tugged his sleeve. 'Come on Sir Galahad or we'll miss the next race!'

Rachel pushed a beer and a plate of food towards Andrew. 'Get a mouthful of this and then you can tell me what's going on!'

Andrew nodded and downed his beer in one hit, and then putting down his glass, cradled his heads in his hands. 'You're going to think I'm a total dickhead.'

Rachel placed a hand on his arm. It was almost a relief

that he needed her help, it distracted her from the gut wrenching twist she felt, every time she thought of Pierre. 'No I won't and whatever you've done or not done we can deal with it, two heads are always better than one. There's never been a problem that Sarah and I haven't been able to fix by getting our heads together and thrashing things out. I'll just pretend you're Sarah and we'll have this thing done and dusted and put to bed before the last race!'

Andrew looked up with a hang-dog expression. 'I very much doubt it…I've lost my grandfather's inheritance, every sodding penny! All of my savings, ISAs the lot…the bastard's run off with the whole fucking lot!'

'Who?'

'Rupert Fotheringham-Allen!'

'I don't understand it, Rup's loaded. Why the hell would he run off with your money?'

'Because I gave it to him, that's why.'

Rachel shook her head. Could it be that Rup was a closet homosexual and he and Andrew had had some torrid affair? 'Since when did you start giving money away?' she asked.

'Since I caught him shagging his latest piece of arse in the summerhouse. To get me to keep my mouth shut he offered to invest my inheritance in overseas property and gave me his word that he'd make me my fortune. The bastard gave me his personal guarantee! That turned out to be worth a crock of shit didn't it?'

'I still don't get it. He may be an arsehole in his private life but he must know his stuff when it comes to business. How else would he own that mansion by the river? I would have thought, that having Rup look after your money was quite a good decision on your part,' said Rachel, taking a swig of beer and giving him a look of encouragement.

'It probably would have been until he got greedy and started playing with the big boys!'

'What do you mean big boys? He's a main player in this town that's for sure.'

Andrew shook his head and drained the last dregs of

his beer. 'No, Rup was never in their league. Complete bastard I grant you, but the Russian mafia's a different league all together.'

Rachel choked on her beer. 'Did you say Russian mafia?'

Andrew nodded; his expression grim. 'Rup promised me my money by today. He knew I had to sign the papers for Water Meadows first thing Monday. So, when the money wasn't forthcoming I tried getting in touch but there was no one at his house and his mobile was switched off. I thought he'd be here, so I came looking for him and found his mate Nigel. He didn't want to tell me anything but when I explained why I was looking for Rup, he took pity on me and spilled the beans.'

Rachel took a bite from her beef and horseradish sandwich and tried not to think of dismembered animals. 'This isn't going to involve horses heads is it? Only I can't stand cruelty to animals and I could never understand why they had to take it out on horses anyway.'

Andrew shook his head, reaching for his beer glass and putting it down again because it was empty. Rachel pushed her own across the table.

'Thanks,' he said gulping a mouthful before he continued. 'No, no dismembered horses. Only Rup abandoning his car at the tennis club as a decoy before persuading Nigel to give him lift to Ashford and legging it to France!'

'What a bastard! He must have known what that money meant to you ...'

'He knew everything, the farm, my plans for developing the place and now it's finished. He's destroyed me.'

'I find there's only one thing to do when dreams go down the sewer,' said Rachel, forcing an image of Pierre's face from her mind.

'Please don't tell me to find some learning in all of this. If ever lay my eyes on Fotheringham-Allen again, I'll kill him!'

Rachel nodded her head in agreement. 'You could sell tickets; he's shafted enough people around here one way or another,' she said, crunching their empty plastic pint glasses inside each other. 'I am going to get these glasses refilled and you and I are going to forget our troubles, courtesy of several pints of 'Hooray Henley'.'

Rachel couldn't remember how they got back to Cygnets' Nest several hours later, nor how they negotiated the burglar alarm and most disconcertingly of all, how they found themselves sprawled across her unmade bed.

Chapter 30

Rup boarded the Paris bound *Eurostar* with a puckering fear that he was being followed. His latest project on the Black Sea resort of Varna had gone tits up in a big way and with it the patience of his investors, half of whom it now appeared were members of the Russian mafia. Yet he saw no irony in his plight, having always regarded himself as an opportunist, rather than a villain exploiting cash hungry States - whether for their land or their women.

Taking his seat in the First Class compartment, he was in no mood for a chat. The sight of an old school tie would have been a comfort, but the faces of his travelling companions were hidden by their broadsheets. Rup took a fountain pen from his pocket, a *Mont Blanc*, examined it briefly, screwing the lid on then off again as if checking the mechanism, then slid it past the opening of his trouser pocket and onto the floor of the carriage; affording him the excuse of checking out his neighbours' lower halves.

'Mr. Independent's' ankles were white and delicately boned, almost feminine but for the hair standing proud, curly black punctuation marks between turn-up and sock, and on the socks, embroidered an inch below the elastic, the distinctive castellated shield of Wentworth golf club. Adjacent, coquettishly crossed sat the legs of 'Mr. Times', in a classic *Paul Smith* pinstripe, blue-black.

Having discovered no indications that either man hailed east of Berlin, Rup raised his head above the table and quaffing a mouthful of champagne, turned in his seat to observe the other passengers. A battalion of carbon suited clones were tapping feverishly into laptops, while the rest, like his neighbours, sought anonymity behind their newspapers. Although desperate to learn their identities, he couldn't repeat his trick with the pen, or risk being thrown off the train for lewd behaviour.

He jumped suddenly as the doors at the end of the carriage opened, cracking his knees on the table and sloshing champagne into his lap. It was the catering staff bringing brunch and when the trolley reached his seat, the attendant placed a generously filled plate in front of him.

'Rather more caviar than usual sir, seems extra was ordered for this train. And vodka shots, they're new today. Looks like you picked the right train, sir. *From Russia with Love,* I reckon.' The attendant winked and pushed his trolley on, to the row behind.

Rup's mouth had gone to chalk. What the hell was that? A sick joke? A coded message from his very own Dr. No? He shuddered, recalling the voicemail the Russians had left on his mobile; he was to pay back their investment with interest by midnight or find himself face down in the Thames by breakfast.

Inside, he berated himself. Why in God's name hadn't he flown to Paris instead of taking the blasted train? As his chest tightened, he reminded himself that being tossed out of an emergency exit at 37,000 feet by a mafia mobster, ending his days as unidentifiable debris spread over the Sussex Downs, made the train the more attractive option.

Never the less, the caviar and the vodka were sure signs that 'The Boss-ski' were on to him. The bastards had bugged his phone, discovering his plans to cut and run and now they were on this very train, waiting for the opportunity to strike. Sweat trickled down his back and as he wiped away the beads of perspiration threatening to run into his eyes, his hands felt detached from the rest of him, ice cold and clammy. He hadn't felt this terrified since Peregrine Tattington, a rampant homosexual even at the tender age of fourteen, had cornered him in the showers after Rugger. He'd been a sitting duck then, but he wasn't going to make the same mistake twice. Leaping to his feet, he sent a glass of champagne crashing into the laps of his neighbours, who lowered their newspapers and glared.

'So sorry old chaps! Urgent call!' Rup said, nodding in the direction of the toilets.

'I think you've missed the boat,' scowled 'Mr. Times', pointing at the wet patch at the front of Rupert's trousers, 'old chap!'

Rupert pulled his overnight bag protectively over his crotch. 'I spilt champagne earlier on...'

'You seem to be making rather a habit of it old boy. Perhaps you, or should I say we, would all be a safer and no doubt a great deal drier, if you were to purchase a juice carton and straw from the buffet car!' 'Mr. Times' shook his head and disappeared behind his champagne spattered newspaper.

Rup stormed into the adjoining carriage, glaring at its occupants as he lurched from seat to seat, like the drunks on the Underground he despised and secretly feared. Nauseous and out of breath, he took refuge in the lobby between carriages.

Suddenly and without warning the train plunged into the Channel tunnel and his body responded, adrenaline scoring through his veins like cocaine, his senses cutting like razor wire. All at once, he became aware of the billions of gallons of salt water only metres above his head and he choked, spitting foul metallic tasting saliva onto his sleeve. If I was them I'd go for the kill now, get it over quickly and lob the useless body into the darkness he thought, slowly becoming mesmerized by the flick, flick, flick of the tunnel's emergency lights. Then, with a sickening twist in his guts he remembered that he was the intended préy and began to shiver violently.

Despite the fact that he hadn't entered a place of worship since his wedding day three years earlier, he offered up a plea bargain to an unnamed deity. 'If you let me get out of this, I'll give it all up; the fast cars, the women, the bent deals, all of it,' he gasped, falling against a toilet door, which gave way beneath him as a hand reached for his neck, dragging him backwards.

His muscles cramping with fatigue and his back stinging hotly with sweat, he squeezed his eyes shut, refusing to eyeball his murderer and take the image of the killer to his grave. Desperately he sought a more comforting image - the face of Digby, his chocolate brown Lab - and like his dog during his annual check-up, he began to whimper. He wished now, that he'd been more sympathetic to the old dog, instead of shouting at him to pull himself together and stop whining like a bitch.

The hand moved suddenly from his neck, shoving him roughly onto the toilet. Rupert was close to tears. His assassin was going to punish him; beat him senseless before tossing him onto the tracks, to be dismembered by the next train.

A sharp voice snapped him from his morbid thoughts. 'Rupert, will you open your eyes!'

He must be hallucinating, he was sure he had heard a female voice. He'd read about this sort of thing; in your last moments one often had flashbacks or imagined the faces of loved ones and it was entirely appropriate that he should conjure up a woman; there had been enough of them over the years. He braced himself for the blow that must surely come and when none came, he felt his body slacken, temporarily relieved. And in that moment, like a mountaineer surrendering to hyperthermia, he gave in to the deliciousness of letting go and feeling the strength drain from his body, pitched forward against his captor's thighs.

Silky fabric enveloped his face and a vaguely familiar scent filled his nostrils. He hadn't been hallucinating after all; the Russians were using female assassins. Very clever he told himself, he hadn't seen that one coming. He'd been on the look-out for a hairy arsed, Slavic butcher, built like a brick shit house. Feeling hard done by, he imagined the news of his death in the tabloids - 'Ex Public School Rugby Champion Slain by a ...Girl!' How his Henley chums would smirk, girls were for one thing and one thing only! Tatty Tattington would get off on it for weeks, giving eager journalists the inside scoop on their 'sexy showers.' The sheer indignity of being bumped off by a woman; it was more than he could take and he began to moan softly.

'Rupert! Stop that silly noise and sit up!'

'Nanny Price!' he gasped, immediately sitting bolt upright as years of nursery discipline came flooding back. The Russians had got to his old nanny, warping her mind and turning her into a psychotic killer. He did a quick calculation; the old girl had to be over eighty!

The hand snatched a shock of his hair and yanked his head upright. 'Rup. Get a grip, look at me!' the voice demanded.

Rupert opened his eyes. 'Fuck me!' He gaped at his assailant. 'Lucy!'

Lucy rolled her eyes. 'Not here Rup it's like, so unromantic!'

'No, I didn't mean fuck me, I meant FUCK ME! As in what the fuck are you doing here? I was expecting...'

Lucy interrupted him, making a shape with her fingers, youth speak he could not interpret. 'Like random! Honestly Rup, I can't believe you'd shag your nanny!'

Rup stared at her, wishing she wouldn't use such language; it made him feel old. Then he shook himself; what did he care? He wasn't about to be smashed to a pulp by brutal, Bolshevik fists.

'Nanny Price.' He shuddered. 'I can assure you Lucy I never had salacious thoughts about Nanny Price,' he paused, a private smile spreading across his face, 'well maybe once but that was just a pubescent ...' he stopped himself going further. 'Christ Lucy, I shouldn't be sitting here discussing the wanking habits of twelve year old boys. I am in mortal danger, I am a wanted man!'

'Shhhhh!' Lucy said, placing her hand over his mouth. 'I know.'

'How an earth ...?' he mumbled into her fingers, which he noticed, smelt curiously of *Play-Doh*.

'I waited for you but when you didn't show, I drove over to your house and let myself in with our secret key. I found a note addressed to you and I know I shouldn't have read it Rup, but I thought it might be like, important,' she said, blinking rapidly, her iridescent pink eye shadow sparkling like fairy dust. 'It was from Carolyn; she wants a divorce.' She paused, scrutinizing his face for signs of emotion over the news of his wife's departure.

'Please, go on,' he said, moving her hand from his mouth and giving her 'Mood Ring' a squeeze of encouragement. He was intrigued as to how she'd figured it all out. She had a body that could make grown men cry and had proved a willing bit of skirt when the need arose but he'd never for one moment thought she had brains as well.

Relieved at his lack of concern regarding the demise of his marriage, Lucy continued. 'In your study I found *The Yellow Pages* open on your desk and someone had ringed 'Penny's Pet Palace'. I rang them pretending to be Carolyn and they said Digby was OK but like, a six month stay was a long time for a dog to be in kennels.'

At the mention of his dog, Rup felt a knot form in his throat and he changed the subject quickly. 'But how did you know I would be on this train?'

'I texted your secretary asking for your itinerary … she thought I was Carolyn.' Under her childlike freckles, Lucy flushed with the idea of being mistaken for Rup's wife.

Rup lowered his voice, suddenly remembering his predicament. 'The Russians. How did you know about them?'

'Oh, that was like, so freaky. I saw this creepy black car coming up the drive,' she said, her smooth brow puckering. 'I still haven't worked out how they got through the security gates. God, it's like, so hot in here,' she paused and began searching fruitlessly for a window.

'For Christ sake Lucy, do get on with it!' Rup snapped and seeing her angelic blue eyes fill with tears, regretted his short temper instantly. He ripped off a handful of toilet paper and mopped the sweat from his face. 'I'm just feeling a little tense right now,' he explained.

Lucy nodded sympathetically. 'I was the same with my A'Levels; I was like totally wasted, I got through like gallons of *Impulse*. As I was saying, the car freaked me out, so I raced to the kitchen and grabbed Mrs. Hancock's apron and a can of polish.'

Rup shook his head in disbelief. 'I'm sorry Lucy, you've lost me. How was polishing the family silver going to help? What were you planning to do? Buff the living shine out of them?'

'God Rup, you can be like so naïve sometimes. They wouldn't tell me anything if they guessed I was your girlfriend, would they?'

'Ummm, smart thinking,' Rup agreed, beginning to realise that he may have seriously underestimated her.

'That's what I thought!' she said proudly. 'I opened the door to this really creepy guy. He kept asking me where you were and when I was expecting you back. He sounded like the waiters in 'Bar None' on the High Street, so I guessed he wasn't local.' Leaning forward she slipped Rup's hand inside her blouse. 'And he kept his hand inside his pocket like this the whole time; I swear he had a gun!'

For the first time since the age of sixteen, Rup fought the urge to fornicate and reluctantly removed his hand from her breast. 'You didn't let slip about my travel plans did you?' A gruesome image of a mafia psycho forcing himself on her tender flesh flashed through his mind. 'Tell me they didn't touch you!'

'No way, that would make me a total loser,' said Lucy, making another shape with her fingers to emphasise her point. 'I acted like my nan, she used to clean for people up the road. We talked about my bedding plants, what with the hosepipe ban and everything and I asked him if they had hosepipe bans in Romania, course now I know I should have said Russia. Then I told him *Dr. Zhivago* was like my all time favourite film, which took real acting cos' it like so isn't!'

'My God, Lucy,' he interrupted. 'You stood on my doorstep discussing Omar bloody Sharif with a Russian hit man. Next you'll be telling me you invited him in for tea!'

Lucy worked her lower lip. 'I did, but when I told him I could only do pop tarts he said he wasn't hungry.'

Speechless, Rup shook his head in disbelief. Either the girl had balls of steel or she was completely mad!

'Don't look at me like that Rup! It was all part of my plan. It's called a double bluff. I've seen it on TV. And before he left, I told him how mean you were putting Digby in kennels but you hadn't any choice, seeing as you were going on an around the world sailing trip.' She paused and rolled a strand of hair between her thumb and forefinger. 'Like a Gap year, but for like, older people.'

Rup stared at her in awe as the brilliance of her plan became clear. 'They'll be searching the marinas on the south coast...oh Lucy, you clever, magnificent girl!' He crushed his face into her abdomen, pulling her to him in a fierce embrace. 'But what made you follow me?' he asked, looking up, his brow furrowing with concern as he grasped the full implications of what she'd done. 'You must know how much danger I'm in....and that means you are too.'

Lucy made a dismissive gesture with her hands. 'This is way more fun than college. And now Carolyn's gone we can be together! Lovers on the run; like...'

'Bonnie and Clyde?' he guessed.

Lucy looked at him blankly. 'Who? I was going to say Thelma and Louise.'

Suddenly, Rup was aware of sunlight flooding the cubicle, from the gap beneath the door. Breaking free of the tunnel the train began to pick up speed, and with it, Rup felt a sense of release. Like the train, after the terrifying darkness, he too had been thrust into light and he felt grateful beyond words to have been given a second chance. He took Lucy's hand, the mood ring was turquoise; it meant faith she'd told him once. That his redeemer was female felt more to him than poetic justice, and again needing to offer up words, to a force he knew to be greater than himself, he said, 'Thank you, Lucy.'

Chapter 31

Sarah finished the ironing and placed the iron on the kitchen window sill to cool. Opening the fridge, she stared at the contents trying to convince herself she was hungry.

'How long will it take you to get ready?' said a voice from the doorway.

Sarah jumped, dropping a punnet of tomatoes which spilled across the floor, landing at Ted's feet. 'You scared me. I didn't hear you come in.' She looked down at her old jeans. 'I thought you wouldn't want to go … after what happened this afternoon.'

Ted stooped and picked up the tomatoes. 'Are you kidding? Why turn a bad day into an awful one? Besides, I've been looking forward to it.'

'Oh, so have I,' said Sarah with such enthusiasm that Ted began to laugh.

'I sure hope the fireworks live up to your expectations, I'd hate for you to be disappointed. It's a warm evening; I thought we could walk down to the river.'

Ten minutes later, Sarah had changed into the dress she had originally planned to wear, applied make-up, bundled Harry into his pushchair and was ready to go. As they walked in the direction of the river, Ted told her that the crew had gone into town to drown their sorrows.

'Will they be OK?' asked Sarah, thinking alcohol and a fast flowing river could prove a dangerous cocktail for disappointed young men.

Ted shrugged. 'They're grown men Sarah and besides, what don't kill you can only make you stronger.'

Sarah nodded and wondered; when Regatta was over and inevitably life had returned to normal, how often she would repeat those words. As they got closer to the river, the air rang with music and laughter and clinking glasses. Decked with flower garlands and fairy lights, boats were moored stern to bow, so close you could step from one party to another and never risk getting your feet wet. And on the riverbank dozens of gazebos lined the towpath, with landlubbers determined to join the party.

'Hey look there's Elvis!' said Ted, pointing to a river cruiser decked out like a Vegas stage, where five 'Elvis's' in white satin jumpsuits were miming to a booming soundtrack. The lead 'Elvis' had charge of a microphone and was calling for the crowd to join in his next song. 'Come on you know the one! It's for all you star crossed lovers out there - *Love me Tender.*' He started to sway, his satin thighs quivering, and 'The King's' voice began to drift across the water.

Grinning Ted offered Sarah his hand. 'Are you dancing?'

Embarrassed, she giggled. Dancing on the tow path was crazy, what if someone who knew her saw, but the 'King' had a point - it was now or never and tomorrow would definitely be too late.

'Are you asking?' she said, offering her hand.

'I'm asking,' Ted said and before she could change her mind, he was swirling her around, twisting her, this way and that.

'I didn't know you could dance,' laughed Sarah, catching the smiling faces of onlookers.

Ted only grinned and swept her backwards into his arms. 'If I had known this was the way to impress you, I'd have asked before.'

Meanwhile 'Elvis' was crooning his way to the second chorus, his words reminding Sarah, that after tomorrow, she didn't know when she and Ted would meet again. In an instant she let go of Ted's hand. What the hell was she doing? Larking about like some love-sick GI Bride; what if someone recognized her, how would she explain herself to Dave? Gripping the handles of Harry's pushchair she said, 'I didn't apply the brake, anything could have happened.'

'But it didn't, did it?' said Ted, suddenly serious. 'Sarah, you've done nothing wrong. We were only dancing.'

'We should move nearer to the bridge for a better view of the fireworks,' she said, swinging Harry's pushchair away from the river.

It was growing late, coloured ribbons of tangerine and

indigo criss-crossed the sky and small boats, lit with storm lanterns, bobbed above the dark water like fire flies. The sunset was beautiful, romantic even, but not to Sarah. The end of another day meant only one thing and to make matters worse, 'Elvis' had rubbed salt in the wound; time with Ted was running out. Suddenly, the crowd around her breathed a collective sigh, as if sympathizing, but it was only their reaction to a streak of light shooting through the night sky, signalling the start of the firework display. Sarah watched as showers of purple, green and silver light turned the river shimmering metallic and when the crowd breathed out she caught it as a cool breeze around her bare shoulders.

Noticing her shiver Ted took off his jacket. 'It sure cools quickly when the sun goes down. Take this, you're cold.'

He laid the jacket around her shoulders and feeling the weight of his arm across her back, she held her breath. For a moment she felt him hesitate and she moved a fraction closer, still staring straight ahead as if concentrating on the fireworks. Ted moved his arm, but only to find a more comfortable position, his fingers folding around the curve of her shoulder.

The firework display was reaching its climax, washing the night sky a brilliant white, capturing everything beneath like a photographer's flash light and Sarah had the feeling that if she held her breath, the two of them could stay there, suspended forever. Did Ted feel the same, she wondered? He seemed reluctant to leave, holding her to him as the crowd swarmed past, going home. Finally, when they were alone again Ted let go of her and the place where his arm had been felt cold. Shivering, Sarah reached into the basket under the pushchair and found a blanket, which she used to wrap around Harry. As she fussed over it, carefully tucking in the edges she heard Ted say, 'I know I shouldn't be saying this to another man's wife, but you look beautiful tonight.'

Sarah felt her knees turn to mush and she gripped Harry's pushchair for support, unable to speak. When she straightened up, Ted reached for the handles of the pushchair. 'I'm sorry, that was out of line. I've embarrassed you. I'm a sad old man taking advantage of the dark. We should go,' he said, his voice gruff.

They walked home in silence and when they arrived Ted lifted Harry from his pushchair and carried him upstairs. On the landing, Ted passed him into Sarah's outstretched arms and gently eased off Harry's *Thomas the Tank Engine* trainers. Sarah smiled, touched that Ted knew what to do without being asked and went to put Harry to bed.

As she had tucked Harry in, she panicked - it was late, she was in her bedroom, it made sense to go straight to bed - but she hadn't said goodnight to Ted. She couldn't leave things as they were, with him thinking that he'd over stepped the mark, but then if she went back out on the landing - they were the only two adults in the house - did it imply that something would happen, that one compliment might lead to...Oh God, why did this have to happen? She jumped, hearing a soft knock at the door - please don't let him come in, please let him come in, please don't ... she leapt around the foot of the bed, propelling herself through the door.

Ted jumped back in surprise. 'I wanted to say goodnight and thank you for a great evening and to say I'm sorry about earlier,' he said, turning to go into his bedroom.

Standing just feet away, it was all she could do not to follow him inside and offer herself to him on the candlewick bedspread. 'What you said, about me being beautiful I wasn't embarrassed ... I was flattered.'

In less than a moment Ted reappeared in his doorway, a look of relief on his face. 'Good. I would never want to make you unhappy ... I guess this is goodnight.'

'Yes, I guess it is. Goodnight then,' Sarah said, but neither made a move. 'Tomorrow it's our ... I mean it's your last day. If you're not doing anything ...'

Ted jumped in, grinning widely. 'I'm not. What did you have in mind?'

'A picnic by the river. We can sit in the sun and talk and ...'

Ted interrupted again as if suddenly keen to end the conversation. 'Sounds great, see you in the morning,' he said, stepping into his room and gently closing the door behind him.

Panic over, Sarah went to bed but not to sleep. She lay watching the hours click by on the clock radio and, resigning herself to insomnia, switched on her bedside light, turning the lamp away from Harry so as not to disturb him. Taking out a notebook and pen from her bedside cabinet, she began to write a list. On one side of the paper were the positive things in her life; the children, running the new café at Water Meadows with Andrew, Ted, Dave coming home, and on the opposite side were the negatives; debt, Ted leaving and Dave coming home. Then she put a line through debt and wrote it again under the positive column - it wasn't that being in debt was a good thing, more that she had taken steps to turn it around and was allowing herself to be optimistic. As for putting Dave on both lists, it was ridiculous she knew, but it summed up how she felt about him, which was, she didn't know how she felt, so she switched him to a new column in the middle, marked pending. And Ted appearing on the negative list, that could be easily fixed if he didn't have to leave, which she knew was also ridiculous - he had a life to lead in the States, training future American champions for next year's Regatta.

That's when it hit her, how she would turn the negative into a positive - a cast iron guarantee that she would see Ted again. Ted and the crew would return to Henley next year and it would make perfect sense for him to stay with her; they could simply pick up where they had left off. Although, quite where that was, she wasn't sure either, but it was a start and convincing herself that a handful of summer days spent with Ted could stave off a year of loneliness, she finally drifted off to sleep.

Chapter 32

The morning after her drinking session with Andrew, Rachel awoke slowly, as bits of her body raced to be the first to get their pain signals to her brain. The knobbly bone at the top of her spine felt bruised and jarred, even against the soft mattress; her eyes were squashed in their sockets as if vicious fingers had poked at them during the night and her jaw felt slack and jowly. Gradually, she began to re-surface, discovering her right hand was sandwiched between Andrew's thighs, and as she tried to release it, she'd lost all sensation below the elbow. Raising her right knee off the mattress she nudged his thigh backwards, giving her fingers the space to escape. Andrew moaned and swung his arm over her, so that it rested in the hollow of her waist, pinning her to the bed. And then, as if his arm suddenly sensed contact with the female form and sent a screaming 'Houston, we have a problem' message to his brain, his eyes flew open.

'Hi,' Rachel said, trying to ignore that his gaze had drifted down to her nipples.

'Hi,' he replied in a strangled whisper.

They continued to stare at each other, trying to make sense of things.

'I ... last night ...,' Andrew mumbled, reaching for the crumpled sheet at the foot of the bed.

'I know, we were both very drunk.' Rachel kneaded the back of her neck trying to ease the pressure in her brain, which felt like it was fighting a hod load of bricks for leg room. 'I'm going to take a shower,' she said, picking her robe off the floor. 'Help yourself to what you need, there's another bathroom off the landing. I think there's some paracetamol in the medical cabinet.'

As she stepped under the jets of hot water, fuzzy edged memories filled her head; Andrew fondling her nipples, her kissing the hollow below his Adam's apple and surreal dreams of Rup talking like Marlon Brando in *The Godfather* and rowers dressed in dinner jackets, using violin cases instead of oars. Her brain was addled and she couldn't remember whether they had actually got around to having sex and Andrew seemed just as embarrassed and confused as she was. Wrapping herself in her towelling dressing gown she decided it would be better to let sleeping dogs lie and act as if nothing had happened (because maybe, just maybe, nothing had).

When she got downstairs Andrew was hovering in the hall and by the furtive way he was shuffling from foot to foot, it was obvious that he was keen to be leaving.

'I'd better be off. Look about last night ... I'm sorry about ... the bed thing. God knows how much beer I sank, the whole night is just a blur,' he said, staring at the Victorian floor tiles so as not to catch her eye.

'It's OK. We were both very drunk and let's face it, if anyone needed a drink you did.'

Andrew opened the front door and winced as sunshine flooded the hall. 'And now I have the mother of all hangovers, when what I really need is a clear head to work out what I'm going to do with the rest of my life!' He shrugged and seemed uncertain whether to step into the sunlight or remain in the dull gloom of the hallway. 'And thanks for taking me under your wing last night. I think I might have thrown myself from the bridge if I hadn't bumped into you.'

'Which you did quite literally if I remember, I have a bruise to prove it!' said Rachel, sticking out a foot from beneath her dressing gown.

Immediately concerned, Andrew bent down to look. 'Looks OK, perhaps a little mark just here,' he said, gently rubbing the top of her foot with his thumb.

'Oh, for goodness sake, stand up you big softie! I'm teasing you, my foot is fine!' Rachel said, pulling on his t-shirt and he stood up quickly, almost sending her flying.

Andrew grabbed her arm before she fell. 'Steady! You're a bit light on your feet this morning. You'd better go and have some breakfast. I've made some coffee and I put a couple of croissants in the oven to warm for you.'

Josh had never warmed croissants for her and come to think of it, she could count on one hand the number of times he'd made her a coffee. Andrew was thoughtful, generous, good-looking and had muscles to die for. There was only one other man as perfect, and putting aside thoughts of Pierre, she pulled Andrew into a hug. 'Sarah's very lucky to have a brother like you,' Rachel said and let him go, pushing him gently towards the front door. Andrew smiled a watery smile and left.

Drawn by the aroma of coffee, Rachel went downstairs to the kitchen and as she was taking the croissants out of the oven, she heard a knock at the front door. Going to answer it, she noticed Andrew's wallet on the hall table. He must have realised it was missing and had returned to collect it.

'Here it is Andrew ... Pierre!' she gasped, hastily dropping the wallet in her dressing gown pocket, hoping he hadn't spotted it and realised she'd been expecting someone else. 'I was about to have breakfast. Would you like a coffee?' she asked, in what she hoped wasn't a too hopeful a voice.

Pierre nodded and followed her downstairs to the kitchen, where he sat at the table, watching Rachel pour two mugs of coffee, using both hands to steady the pot.

Just having him in the same room made her tingle, nothing in her feelings towards him had changed. It was so bloody unfair; of all the men in her life, they either wanted her and no babies, or babies and not her. She wanted to scream, rant and rave, but to whom? There was no one to blame. It wasn't Pierre's fault that he didn't want children and it wasn't hers that she'd fallen head over heels in love with him. Loading her coffee with sugar, she wondered what he was doing there. The hastily written note she'd left behind in the guest room would have made her feelings clear.

'You don't take sugar?' Pierre said, finally finding his voice.

Sitting down opposite him she snapped. 'I've just started to OK and you didn't come here on a social visit from the Diabetes Society, so what say we forget my sugar intake and cut to the chase!'

'You're still upset...'

214

'Of course I'm upset. You got my note? ...' *Don't cry, don't cry, you never cry.* She got up from the table and moved to the door. She needed a diversion or she'd bawl and he'd comfort her, and then she'd have no hope of standing her ground. 'There's no point to this Pierre. I'm sorry, I really am, like it said in the note, I want a family, 2.4 kids, a shaggy dog and roses round the door. Please ... I think it's better if you go.'

'All I ask is that you hear me out. Then if you still want me to go, I'll go. I promise. OK?'

Rachel nodded but stayed in her position near the door.

'I need to tell you about Claudette. Since you left Paris my life has turned upside down...,' he said, his dark eyes turning darker still.

Rachel thought she was going to throw up; suddenly she knew what was important; it was having Pierre in her life, with or without a baby but it was too late, he had come to tell her that he was getting back with Claudette. Unable to stop herself, she began to cry.

'It's not the end of the world,' Pierre said, leaping from his chair and pulling her close.

Rachel sniffed, dabbing at her nose with her sleeve. 'No? It just feels like it, that's all!'

'Here, take my handkerchief and please, stop crying. I hate to see you so unhappy.'

Rachel blew her nose loudly and blinked at him through blood shot eyes. A snotty nose, no makeup, hair still wet from the shower and a spot on her chin the size of Wales, was not how she'd imagined she would look, when she discovered for the first time, she was completely and vulnerably in love. Wiping her eyes, she said, 'I'm not unhappy. I've finally realized something really important. I don't care that you don't want kids because it's you I want, all along it's been you from the first time I saw you in the market. Please don't go back to Claudette; you know you can't trust her.'

Suddenly he was kissing her. 'Forget Claudette,' he

said against her cheek.

It was all too much; the hangover, seeing Pierre again and what he was doing with his tongue; she felt her legs give way. The kitchen table broke her fall but as she gave herself up to Pierre's kisses, shifting her weight into more comfortable position, her backside skidded against something soft and buttery - she was sitting slap bang in the middle of a plate of croissants. She was about to protest but as Pierre slipped her dressing gown from her shoulders, she forgot about the flaky pastry sticking to her bum and concentrated instead, on something just as French and delicious, making its way down her front.

Later, Pierre picked a crumb of croissant from her hair. 'I have never felt like this about anyone, but I need to tell you about Claudette and me.'

Rachel felt the ground shift again and prepared herself, for what exactly she did not know, but if it involved Pierre's ex it wouldn't be good. She was too familiar with the words 'you're a lovely girl but I can't leave my wife / girlfriend / mother,' to feel optimistic.

Pierre continued. 'You know the reason we broke up was over children, she wanted them and I didn't. All along she'd been hoping I would change my mind.'

'And you didn't?' asked Rachel.

'No, not then, but years later I did. Only now I wonder if I'm too old, do you think your kids would mind having an older dad?'

'My kids?' she asked, and slowly the penny dropped. 'Do you mean our kids?'

Pierre nodded and kissed the tip of her nose. 'That's if it's still alright with you?'

Grinning, Rachel hugged him but as he bent to kiss her again, her mobile phone began to vibrate across the kitchen table. 'Sorry,' she said, grabbing the handset before it launched itself onto the slate floor. 'I'll get rid of them.'

'Them' turned out to be a text message from Andrew

asking her to call him. Her heart began to thump. What if he wanted to discuss last night? Or even worse call round for his wallet! How could she explain it to Pierre? She hit the phone's reply option. Thankfully, it clicked onto Andrew's voicemail and she left a message that she hoped would put him off for a few hours. 'It's Rachel. Don't worry about your wallet, I found it on the patio this morning. It must have fallen out of your pocket when you were doing the garden. I'm going out later so I'll pop it in a plastic bag and leave it under the tub of pink geraniums for you.' She pressed send and then the off button. 'The gardener. Great guy but always forgetting things.' Nothing important, only his wallet and the fact that he's gay she thought, snapping the phone shut.

'So, where are we going?' asked Pierre, nuzzling her shoulder.

Confused Rachel asked, 'Going?'

'On your message, you said you were going out.'

Rachel laughed. 'We're not going anywhere,' she said, taking him by the hand and leading him upstairs. 'But no one else needs to know do they?'

Chapter 33

Harry sat up, rubbing the sleep from his eyes. Sarah had been awake for hours, too excited about the picnic with Ted to sleep, and pulled him onto her lap. Stroking Harry's blonde curls from his clammy forehead, she sang *The Teddy Bear's Picnic*, softly into his ear.

'Picnic,' repeated Harry, clambering off her lap, to retrieve his truck from under her dressing table.

'Yes darling, a picnic for you, me and Ted,' she smiled, hugging herself at the thought.

Harry beamed at her, pushed his truck into his empty sleeping bag and dived in behind it, wiggling his body down to the foot end making high pitched siren noises.

'OK. I'll leave you to play cars while I jump in the shower,' laughed Sarah, knowing that he would play happily in his polyester cocoon until breakfast.

In the shower, she applied a generous squeeze of Dead Sea exfoliant onto a sponge and scrubbed herself until she was pink and shiny, and after shampooing her hair, she massaged in a coconut oil conditioner Rachel had bought her, saying it was flying off the shelves in New York in spite of its thirty dollar price tag. She was thinking that nothing was too good for a day out with Ted, when a loud bang sent her hurtling from the shower - Harry had pulled something over or worse, decided to play Spiderman off the tallboy.

'Harry, are you OK?'she yelled, skidding into the bedroom.

He was exactly where she had left him. Although by now he had turned himself around and was driving his truck back and forth over his pillow. The banging started again and grabbing her dressing gown from the bed she went to investigate. Perhaps one of the rowers had left something behind and had forgotten their key.

'Andrew!' she gasped, pulling open the front door. 'What an earth are you doing here at this time of the morning?' She paused, noticing a pair of small white trainers sticking out from beneath her privet hedge. 'Looks like the

cox had one too many real ales last night. I can hear him
snoring, so I think we'll leave him to sleep it off don't you?'
she laughed.

Not answering, Andrew pushed past her and she
caught the stale smell of beer and cigarettes on his clothes. He
looked grey and old beyond his years.

'Andrew, what's happened, you look dreadful?'

'At least something makes sense, I feel like crap and I
look like crap,' he said, running his fingers through his
tangled hair.

'Come through to the kitchen,' she said, taking his
arm. 'You look like you could use a coffee.'

Sarah switched on the kettle and took Dave's extra
strong Columbian ground coffee out of the fridge. 'Can I
leave you to make it whilst I get this gunk out of my hair and
bring Harry down?' she asked, pushing back a gloopy strand
of hair from her forehead.

'Sorry I got you out of the shower … I … I didn't
know where else to go.' He shrugged sadly and stared at his
feet.

Sarah showered quickly and threw on a pair of shorts
and a t-shirt. Harry followed her downstairs and climbed onto
on Andrew's lap. Still towel drying her hair, she poured hot
water into the cafetière. 'I thought I left you to make the
coffee,' she laughed, playfully clipping Andrew's shoulder.

'Sorry Sarah. I'm so useless I can't even make coffee
now. You may as well throw me on my own compost heap
and leave me there to rot!'

'Hey, come on that's not my brother speaking,' she
smiled kindly and pushed a steaming mug towards him. 'Have
you had any breakfast? You look green around the gills.'

He shook his head and lifted Harry off his lap. 'Do
you mind if we go outside? My head's swimming and I feel
sick.'

Sarah nodded. 'Take Harry with you and he can play
in his sandpit. I'll be out in a minute after I've made you some
toast,' she said, her stomach twisting in knots of anxiety.
Moments later, she followed him outside and laid a breakfast

tray on the patio table.

'I think you had better sit down Sarah. What I have to say affects you too,' said Andrew.

Sarah pushed a plate of toast towards him. 'This sounds ominous.'

Andrew continued. 'I'm sorry Sarah. If I had known any of this was going to happen I wouldn't have dragged you into it. It's all down to that bastard Fotheringham-Allen.'

'I don't understand. What has he got to do with me?' she asked.

'Everything I'm afraid. I don't really know how to tell you this Sarah but our dream … the farm, your café, us working together.' He paused, tears brimming in his bloodshot eyes. 'I'm sorry Sarah, it's over.'

Sarah put her mug down sharply, slopping coffee onto the table. 'But I've handed my notice in at work. You said it was a dead cert, you said Rup guaranteed it.'

Andrew put his head in his hands, rubbing furiously at his temples. 'I know I did and it was. At least until he ran off with my money. He's legged it Sarah. I've got nothing left.'

Sarah felt tears well up behind her eyes, hot and stinging. It was so unfair, just as things were picking up they'd been done over, by Rupert Fotheringham-Allen of all people. She'd always known he couldn't be trusted around other men's wives but not once had she imagined that he was a common thief. She shook her head, dumbfounded. 'I don't understand. He's loaded.'

Andrew interrupted her. 'It's complicated and there's no comfort in the detail believe me.' He swallowed a mouthful of coffee, wincing as it burnt his tongue. 'Do you think they'll give you your job back? Perhaps if you explain, you know about the situation, the money problems at home.'

Sarah shook her head, tears brimming. 'No, they've already found my replacement. She's been shadowing me all week learning the job …' She stopped in her tracks unable to bear the look of guilt on his face. 'Don't worry,' she added quickly. 'I can easily find another job and I've got some holiday pay owing to me so that'll tie me over in the meantime. Please eat some toast, you'll feel better.' She picked up her coffee stared unseeing into the steam, trying to avoid picturing Dave's face, when she announced that she was now officially unemployed.

Andrew drained his coffee, wishing that he had something stronger to supply the Dutch courage he needed, to deliver his second piece of news. 'Sarah … there's something else …'

Andrew looked close to tears, what the hell could be worse that losing every penny to a devious bastard like Rupert Fotheringham-Allen? Sarah's head hurt and she put down her mug. 'Andrew you're really scaring me now,' she said, clutching his arm. 'You're ill aren't you? Or is it Mum? Does one of you have …?'

'No.' He rubbed her hand to reassure her. 'It's Rachel. I met her at the Regatta last night.'

'Rachel's ill. Oh my God, why didn't she tell me? I thought she looked dreadful because of what happened in Paris …'

'Sarah will you just shut up and listen. Nobody is ill, OK? I … Rachel and me, we slept together last night.'

Sarah stared at him, her mouth opening and closing like a goldfish. 'But you're gay.'

Andrew shook his head and tore a piece of toast in two. 'Exactly. I'm gay, nothing's changed.'

Incredulous, Sarah stared. 'I'm sorry Andrew, but I think you'll find that sleeping with a woman is a hetro-sexual activity!'

'Well, in our case it was just a pissed out of our skulls, human comfort activity!'

Sarah shook her head disbelievingly. 'I don't know who you're trying to convince but I wouldn't put that to a jury if I were you. I don't know what a gay guy is supposed to do to drown his sorrows, although I'm sure that sleeping with a gorgeous stewardess isn't one of them. And talking of stewardesses how is Rachel with all of this?'

Andrew shrugged. 'Embarrassed, wishing it had never happened, we both are. The thing is Sarah, when I say that I slept with Rachel, that's the only thing I know for sure that I did.'

'You mean you can't actually remember having sex?' asked Sarah, feeling a perverse twist of satisfaction; Rachel liked to give the impression she was something of an expert between the sheets and yet, here was Andrew not even able to remember it.

'No, not exactly. I mean, I woke up with her hand around my balls and we were completely naked but what could I say? Morning Rachel, did we make mad passionate love last night, only I can't remember?'

'There's an easy way to find out,' said Sarah, reaching for his mobile phone.

Andrew leapt from his chair, grabbing the phone off the table. 'No! It was a stupid drunken mistake and it ends here and now. Promise me you'll say nothing to Rachel. I shouldn't have told you, it's just that so much has happened in the last twenty-four hours ...'

She cut him off. 'It's OK, I won't say anything if you don't want me to.' She stood up and began to gather their breakfast things onto the tray. 'So what, you had a drunken fumble because your head was in a mess. Forget about it, OK?'

'Thank you,' he said, hugging her.

'So, what now?' She caught the warning look on his face, 'about the other business I mean, surely what Rup did is illegal?'

'Yes, it probably is, but by the time it goes through the courts I'll have lost the farm anyway. I'll have to call the agent in the morning and tell him the deal's off.'

'I'm sorry Andrew.'

He sighed and kissed the top of her head. 'Me too.'

She watched him go, head down, his hands stuffed deep in his pockets and without his customary wave. And he hadn't said goodbye to Harry.

As she watched Harry build a tower with his building blocks and smash it over, she thought how bright the future had looked barely an hour ago and now, with one swoop of his arrogant, manicured fist, Rup had smashed it to smithereens. God help him if he ever showed his face in Henley again, she thought, throwing Andrew's half eaten toast onto the lawn; she'd have to be held down!

Chapter 34

Hearing the soft flip flop of bicycle tyres coming from the side of the house, Sarah's hand flew to her mouth wiping off imaginary crumbs. Ted was back from his morning ride. Damn! No chance to apply make-up or to blow dry her hair - which felt like a ton weight on account of Rachel's expensive New York conditioner.

'Hey,' he called, leaning his bike against the wall. 'How are you this morning?' He walked across the lawn, stopping to pick up one of Harry's building blocks from the grass. 'There you go little fella.' He sat down opposite Sarah and took off his bicycle helmet. 'You look like you lost a dollar and found a dime, anything I can do to help?'

Sarah shook her head. It was spinning with images; Rachel drunk and depressed, and Andrew, eyes dulled by defeat, and all of it made worse by her own well intentioned, but disastrous meddling. If only she hadn't persuaded Rachel to go to the Regatta, she would never have met Andrew and gone back to her place for drunken sex. They were never going to be a couple and now they'd probably go out of their way to avoid being friends, something they both needed more than ever. 'No, I don't think so,' she said, determined not to sour a single moment of their time together. 'It'll blow over and after all, we're wasting valuable picnic time.'

'OK, as long as you're sure. I'll grab a shower and what say we head off straight away? I have everything we need right here,' he smiled, tapping his rucksack. 'I called in at the Deli on the high street, so there's nothing for you to do except enjoy the ride!' Ted got up and went inside.

Brushing the sand from his knees, Sarah carried Harry into the house, and as she passed the bathroom, she could hear Ted taking his shower. She stopped for a moment and liked to imagine the scene inside; the beads of silver water spilling from Ted's eyelashes onto his chest, then his stomach, to lie in a secret pool in the hollow of his naval. The sound of cascading water stopped abruptly and she sped downstairs, giggling like a teenager.

Minutes later, when Ted appeared dressed in blue shorts and a white polo shirt, her heart was still hammering but she had managed to strap Harry into his bicycle seat and was ready to go. Ted lifted Sarah's small rucksack off her shoulders, slipped it inside his own and they set off, with Ted slowing his regular cycling pace so that Sarah could keep up. Quickly, she became mesmerized by the rhythmic turning of his legs and the subtle wiggle in his backside and she was almost disappointed when the river appeared in view and they were forced to dismount, to wheel their bikes through the long grass of the water meadow. They leant their bikes against a willow tree and Sarah lifted Harry from his seat, exchanging his helmet for a sun hat.

'Come on little fella, let's you and me go see if we can catch some water bugs,' Ted said, leading Harry down to the narrow silt beach at the water's edge. Sarah watched them with a tug of guilt; she couldn't remember the last time she'd seen Dave play with his son. After a while, she lay back in the grass, picking out the irregular shapes of blue through the delicate green canopy, until even that felt too much like hard work, and she dozed off.

When she awoke a while later, her t-shirt was sticking to her back and pushing herself up on her elbows, she saw that Harry was pink cheeked under his sunhat and she called out to Ted. 'I think Harry had better come out of the sun.'

Ted raised his hand, scooping Harry up with one hand and Harry's tiny blue sandals in the other. 'He had a paddle,' he said, sitting Harry on a picnic blanket in the deepest part of the shade.

'Don't you mean you had a paddle? Your shorts are soaked,' laughed Sarah, handing Harry a juice carton and a breadstick, which he promptly ignored and lay down to sleep.

Grinning, Ted went back to the beach and appeared to be fishing something from the river and moments later, he came back, carrying a bottle of champagne. 'I couldn't resist. Paddling and sparkling wine, I'm a pushover for both,' he said, popping the cork and pouring it into two plastic tumblers he'd retrieved from his rucksack.

Sarah accepted a glass and took a sip. 'It's delicious and the food looks great,' she said, eyeing the picnic Ted was spreading before her on the rug. 'You have gone to town.'

'It's my way of saying thank you. Coming back to Henley has made me realise how much I like it. I've been thinking about a sabbatical for some time, I'd like the opportunity to coach here.'

'Wouldn't you miss the porpoises and the ozone?' teased Sarah. 'In Henley you'd have to make do with Moorhens.'

Ted smiled and offered her a piece of asparagus tart. 'And driving on the left, and warm beer. What is it with the British and warm beer?'

'It didn't bother Ryan, by the look of him under the hedge this morning!'

Ted laughed and topped up their champagne glasses. 'You can't blame him for getting his dollar's worth, he won't be back here again in a hurry.'

His words brought her up short and she coughed, bubbles in her champagne catching in her throat. 'I don't understand. He told me he doesn't graduate until next July, won't he be coming back to crew again next year? It seems a shame to waste all that talent and experience on one Regatta.'

Ted shrugged. 'No choice I'm afraid. The US athletic conference, they're the guys who make the rules, maintain that a school can only compete once every three years.'

'But if the team doesn't come to Regatta then ... neither does the coach.'

Having lost her appetite, Sarah put down her glass. Her plan of having Ted come to stay next summer was in tatters. She knew she had no right to be angry at Ted, he didn't make the rules and he hadn't broken any - maybe that was her problem she thought, maybe all along she'd wanted him to. Would she have made different choices if she had known she might never see him again?

Ted looked up, hearing the catch in her voice. 'Them's the rules,' he said, reaching out and, very gently straightening a strand of her hair that had come loose from her pony-tail.

Sarah held her breath, aware of nothing but him, his eyes sparkling like sunlight on water, his smile and the warm scent of his skin. 'Lemons,' she said and then blushed when she realised she'd spoken out loud.

'Lemons?' asked Ted, pretending to search his rucksack. 'I don't have lemons but I think I've got strawberries here somewhere.'

Sarah played with the fringe of the picnic rug, not looking at him. 'You, you smell of lemons … and the sea.'

Ted laughed. 'I haven't been near the ocean for a week. And how about you? What does a Regatta Landlady smell like?' he teased, leaning towards her.

He was close, almost touching and she was aware of his breath, could feel it on her skin. As for herself, she was barely breathing and even so, she could detect the coconut smell the conditioner had left on her hair. Smelling like Rum Baba did not automatically strike her as attractive but maybe Ted would think it was exotic, tropical even.

'*OMO*,' he said finally.

'*OMO*?' asked Sarah with a feeling of dread, whatever *OMO* was; it didn't sound exotic or remotely tropical.

Ted grinned. 'It's a washing powder.'

Crushed, Sarah felt her cheeks burn. She couldn't escape the domestic mantle - no matter how much expensive hair product she used - it was so ingrained, it oozed from her pores.

'It's one of my favourite smells,' Ted said. 'It says home.'

Sarah pulled a face as if to say that it wasn't a good thing.

'It doesn't necessarily mean where you live, it can mean where you feel good and where you feel at home,' smiled Ted.

'Of course,' she sniffed. 'You must be missing the porpoises.'

'I haven't missed them or anything at all from back home,' said Ted, batting at a wasp that had appeared from nowhere, attracted by the picnic, and crushing it under his shoe. He looked at its body, now a crumble of black and yellow pieces and shrugged. 'I've tried to stop feeling the way I do. I tried staying away as much as I could, even when I didn't have to.'

Sarah looked up, puzzled. 'Stay away from what?'

Ted shook his head. 'Not what; whom. I tried to stay away from you. I didn't have to go to dinner with the other coaches, it was an excuse. I couldn't sleep at night for thinking of you lying a few feet away in the next room. If I had stayed around ...' He shrugged and his words faded.

Sarah stared at her lap, unsure what to say or do. It was a moment she hadn't dare hope for, that he felt attracted to her too, but now what? They couldn't go on as before, things had changed, something implicit had become explicit. 'I have feelings for you too,' she said. 'I didn't invite them, they just happened and I don't feel lonely anymore.'

He kissed her then, showing her it was the same way with him.

Some time later, deep in her consciousness she became aware that they were being watched. Harry had woken up and was pressing a small sticky hand on her leg. 'Mama, Harry drink.'

Ted let her go, quickly, as if she scalded him and staggering onto her knees, she fumbled in her bag for a carton of juice. It was buried beneath a bundle of papers, and as she pushed them aside the names on one of the envelopes caught her eye; Mr. and Mrs. David Crouch. Somehow, in the midst of everything she'd allowed herself to forget that tomorrow, Dave would be arriving home from the States, just as Ted was leaving - they would almost be able to shake hands mid-Atlantic - except of course that they wouldn't, especially now.

Chapter 35

Later, back at the house, Ted excused himself, having promised to spend his last evening with his crew. He left in a hurry, long before the pubs started serving evening meals and moments later, Naomi and Millie arrived home from Brownie camp. Relieved to have a distraction, Sarah asked them about their weekend, but they were both mute with exhaustion and asked to go to bed.

As she unpacked their crusty kitbags she reflected on what had happened at the river, or at least, what she had wanted to happen. If Harry hadn't woken up would she and Ted have made love? She knew she had wanted to more than anything and it shocked her. How could she have come so close to being unfaithful to Dave? Had Ted sensed how badly she needed to be touched, brought back to life from the shadow of herself? Staring at her reflection in the washing machine's window, it was as if she had discovered a photo of her younger, prettier self in the bottom of a drawer amongst the paper clips, receipts, fluff and string.

She knew it was being with Ted that had changed her, made her feel alive again, but within hours he would be gone, back to his life, the one that didn't include her. And what of her life then? A husband who she suspected didn't want her, her dream of running the café over, still saddled with debt and, to top it all, no job.

Suddenly, the washing machine kicked into life, sending streams of soapy water against the glass and tumbling the Brownie uniforms over and over into a sludge of brown and yellow. Through it, Sarah watched her reflection disappear.

Then, from somewhere outside she heard a crunch of gravel followed by a loud rap on the front door. Her heart missed a beat, Ted had come back to spend his last hours with her. Taking a deep breath, she went into the hall and opened the front door.

'Hi, darling. Sorry I had to knock. I left my keys in the hotel room.' Dave squeezed past, pulling his suitcase behind him. He kissed her cheek and her stomach churned, as she caught the smell of whisky on his breath, and remembered another scent - lemons and ozone.

'Don't look pleased to see me, will you?' he said, noticing the look of disappointment on her face. 'We finished the project ahead of schedule so I thought I'd surprise you.'

Sarah followed him into the kitchen where he opened the lid of the biscuit barrel and wolfed down a digestive in two bites. 'Christ I'm starving, the airline food doesn't get any better. Where are the kids?'

Sarah forced a smile onto her face. 'In bed. The girls just got back from Brownie camp. They haven't slept all weekend. You'll have to catch up with them tomorrow.'

Catching the edge in her voice, he looked at her, seeing her properly for the first time. Her eyes were brighter than he remembered and she was wearing her hair down; it fell onto her shoulders, which were freckled and sun-kissed, exposed in a strappy top he didn't recognise.

'I've missed you,' he said, brushing back her hair and kissing the side of her throat. 'You know Sarah, being in New York was the best thing I could have done. The distance made me realise what an arrogant pig I've been. I got us into the financial mess and all I did when you tried to sort it out, was ignore you.'

That's putting it mildly. She opened her mouth to speak and he stopped her. 'No, don't make excuses for me Sarah. You've had to take in Yanks to make ends meet and I haven't been here to help you!'

Thank God.

'Where are they anyway? I expected to come home and find a house full of muscle men.'

Sarah shrugged. 'Tonight is their last night. They've gone to town for a meal.'

Ted's gone too.

Dave fumbled inside his jacket pocket and pushed a small black velvet box towards her. 'The thing is ... I owe you an apology. And before you say anything I didn't get us into more debt by buying you this. I sold my grandfather's watch to a dealer in Manhattan and it more than paid for what's inside.'

Sarah pressed the tiny gold button on the front of the box and the lid flipped open, revealing a gold band studded with four diamonds, princess cut.

Dave prodded it with his finger. 'It's an eternity ring. I know I've got a lot of making up to do.'

You can say that again.

'The financial stuff won't be solved overnight but this time I'll work with you, not against you,' he said earnestly, taking her hands in his. 'And the farm business, you going in with Andrew. I want you to know you've got my whole hearted support.'

That balloon burst hours ago.

She swallowed hard trying to quell the queasiness in her stomach and struggled to find the right words. 'I'm glad you've had chance to think but the thing is …' she paused, swallowing back tears.

'Me too, let's see if the ring fits shall we?' he said, plucking it from the box and pushing it up her ring finger, where it fought for space against her engagement ring. 'Umm it's a bit of a squash isn't it?' He frowned, forcing the ring on even harder until she squealed in pain.

'Stop!' she gasped, easing it off followed by her engagement ring and finally, her thin gold wedding band. Blinking back tears, she stared at the pale indents on her finger. 'I … there's something I need to tell you about the farm. Andrew …'

She was interrupted when the back door swung open and Andrew walked in, brandishing a bottle of champagne.

Immediately Dave jumped up and began searching among the kitchen cupboards for glasses. 'Ah, Andrew, it's you. We were just discussing the farm. Come to christen the deal have you?'

Behind him Andrew pulled a quizzical 'what have you told him face?' at Sarah, who mouthed back 'nothing' and placed her finger across her lips to indicate that was how it should remain.

'I can't find the right glasses. I'll just grab some from the dining room. I won't be a minute,' said Dave, disappearing out the door.

In a moment, Andrew had crossed the room and raised Sarah off her feet. 'It's all OK Sarah. Everything's going to be OK. I've got the money.'

Sarah pushed against his chest so that he had to let her down. 'I don't understand, you said that Rupert Fotheringham-Allen had run off with the money.'

'I've been trying to get you on your mobile all day,' said Andrew.

Sarah blushed. Her phone had been switched off. 'I've been down at the river. Must have been in a black spot. Anyway, that doesn't matter. How have we gone from deal off to deal on again in less than twelve hours?'

'I got a text from Rup after he'd made it to France, telling me he'd deposited the money in my bank account. Seems he wasn't quite such a bastard after all.'

Sarah gripped his arms, unsteady on her feet. 'You're going to get the farm?' Because if you lose it again I really don't think I'll be able to …' her words dissolved into floods of tears.

'Here we are. I knew we had some decent glasses somewhere. Took me awhile to find them under all the crew's stuff,' said Dave reappearing. He set about pouring the champagne. 'Here you are Sarah get a glass of this in you and you'll soon feel better. I expect it's overwhelming, eh?'

Understatement of the bloody year she thought, knocking back the alcohol as if her life depended on it.

Andrew pressed a piece of kitchen towel into her hand. 'And you'll never guess what Rup has asked me to do?' he said.

'Have his babies?' she asked, helping herself to more champagne.

Andrew grinned and rubbed her back. 'Nope, he wants me to look after his place for him while he's away. His wife has run off and he doesn't want to leave the place empty, in case of squatters. He left me a set of keys and alarm codes in my shed at the end of his garden!'

'He's got an indoor pool and a Jacuzzi … you lucky sod,' said Dave topping up their glasses.

'And a billiards room, a home cinema and ten bedrooms,' laughed Andrew clinking his glass against Dave's. 'And as I can only sleep in one of them I'd like you all to move in with me. Rup will be gone for months and if you move in, you can rent this place out and solve your money problems.'

Sarah watched Dave's face, bracing herself for his reaction to the news that Andrew was aware of their financial difficulties. She held her breath, as he frowned and put down his glass.

'We would be glad to,' he said finally, offering Andrew his hand. 'That's if it's alright with you Sarah.'

Stunned by the turn of events Sarah nodded, unable to speak. While Dave and Andrew congratulated themselves on their good fortune, Sarah tried to imagine moving the family for the second time in six months and as she struggled to remember just how many packing cases they'd needed last time, she became aware of a soft tapping on the back door. She called for whoever it was to come in and when Ted stepped into the kitchen, her stomach flipped - he'd come back after all. She watched, as the significance of a new man at her table flickered across his face.

'Ted, this is my husband Dave and my brother Andrew,' she said, watching as they shook hands.

Dave was grinning from ear to ear. 'We're having a little celebration aren't we, darling,' he said, squeezing Sarah's shoulder. 'Will you join us in a glass of bubbly?'

'No, thank you kindly. I apologise for interrupting your evening. I came back for...' Ted hesitated, catching Sarah's eye.

He's trying to think of an excuse she thought, suddenly finding it hard to breathe.

'Did Joey forget his anti-histamine again?' she asked at last, getting up from her chair. 'I think I've seen it somewhere, I'll help you look. You don't want to be late for your dinner reservation.' Heart pounding, she followed Ted into the hall.

'You came back,' she whispered.

'I shouldn't have … your husband …'

Sarah slid her hands around his neck and kissed him. 'I can't bear it,' she said against his lips. 'I can't bear that you have to go.'

'I have to,' Ted said, his voice cracking. 'I shook hands with your husband for Christ sake.' Gently he pushed her away. 'I'm sorry, Sarah we can't do this. I can't take you away from your family.'

Suddenly, Andrew's head appeared around the kitchen door. 'Have you got any crisps Sarah, I'm ...' he stopped mid-sentence as they sprang apart.

'Oh, er … thanks for finding the meds,' mumbled Ted, before making his escape past Andrew's gaping stare.

Sarah glared at Andrew daring him to speak. 'I know what you're thinking and before you say anything I haven't been unfaithful to David. Ted and I … we …' she faltered, 'actually it doesn't matter, he'll be back in States this time tomorrow, OK?'

Andrew shrugged. 'Hey, I'm the last person to judge, I'm the gay drunk who sleeps with women remember. Or at least I think I am!'

'Come on you two, I thought all the best parties ended up in the kitchen. What are you two doing gossiping in the hall?' asked Dave, appearing at the kitchen doorway.

Andrew squeezed Sarah's hand and gave her a knowing look. 'I'd better be going, I'm sure you two have a lot of catching up to do.'

When they were alone Dave finished the champagne, regaling Sarah of his adventures in Manhattan, before finally complaining of jet-lag, and retreating to bed. Making excuses of having to clear up, Sarah stayed downstairs and shut herself in the study. Her mobile phone was on the desk and she remembered Andrew's comment about not being able to reach her all day. Checking her messages she saw that she had three missed calls from Andrew and two texts from Rachel.

Rachel...shit! In the midst of Dave's homecoming, Andrew's announcement and kissing Ted, she'd forgotten Rachel. How was she coping after her one night stand with Andrew? With a feeling of dread she opened Rachel's text.

Hi Sarah. Great News! Pierre wants kids. Hurray, it's LOVE! xxx

No mention of Andrew, but then why would there be? she thought snapping the phone shut. Rachel had got her happy ending, pity was, there wasn't more to go round.

Chapter 36

When Sarah awoke several hours later, it was with the disorientated nauseous feeling of finding yourself not where you expect to be; she had fallen asleep in the study, her head on the desk. A noise in the hall had disturbed her and guessing it was Ted and the crew coming back from their night out, she opened the study door. The hall was empty, but a red tail light reflected in the glass panel of the front door caught her eye and she could see the hazy reflection of a mini-bus backing on to the drive. The noise hadn't been the crew on their way back from the restaurant; it had been the sound of them leaving for the airport. She must have been asleep for hours. Through the narrow panel of opaque glass she watched them load their suitcases onto the bus and climb on board, one by one, until only Ted was left. She saw him hesitate and look back at the house.

All fingers and thumbs, she fumbled for the latch and wrenched the door open, but it jarred, refusing to open more than an inch. The door chain! Dave had fixed the door chain across before going to bed. Slamming the door shut again, she released the chain and flung the door open, at the exact moment the mini-bus pulled out of the drive.

Dave, woken by the noise appeared suddenly at her shoulder. 'What the hell's going on? I thought someone was breaking in!'

'It's Ted. I mean it's the crew ... they've gone,' she said, pushing past him and going into the kitchen, where she stood in the dark, her head spinning.

Dave followed her and switched on the light. 'Look they've left us some presents,' he said, pointing to a bundle of college sweatshirts and base-ball caps on the kitchen table. 'And there's a note addressed to you.'

Trying not to look too eager, Sarah tore open the envelope.

'Do they want to come again next year?' asked Dave, putting on a Baxdale base-ball cap. 'It's easy money if you ask me. What does the note say?'

Reluctantly, Sarah read it out. 'Dear Sarah. Thank you so much for everything. I'm sure that your hospitality helped us reach the semi-finals! The sweatshirts are for your family but I'm afraid I didn't have enough for everyone so I've left you one of mine. You'll know the one; it has COACH in big letters right across the back. I'll never forget our time in Henley. Yours ever, Ted.'

It was discrete - the perfect thank you note from house guest to landlady - gut wrenchingly disappointing. It revealed nothing, only the Coach playing by the rules.

'Here's your shirt, *Coach*!' Dave said and as he tossed Ted's carefully folded shirt across the table, a piece of silver jewellery slipped out from between the folds. 'Looks like the Coach left you something else,' he said, picking it up and dropping the chain into Sarah's hand. It was Ted's pendant.

Her fingers curled around it, crushing the cold metal into her palm, and to no one in particular she said, 'What am I supposed to do now?'

Assuming she meant getting the house straight, Dave said, 'Leave everything until the morning. You have a lie in. I'll see to it, everything will soon be back to normal.'

'Dave,' she paused so that he was forced to look at her. 'I can't do normal. Things have to change, *we* have to change.'

He stared at her, his eyes moving from her face to her hand clenched around the pendant and finally, he understood. 'Did he...did you...?' he struggled to find the words.

'No,' said Sarah, taking her favourite cookbook off the shelf above the hob and gently placing Ted's pendant amongst the pages. 'No, I didn't sleep with him if that's what you mean.'

She watched his facial muscles relax. What was he thinking? That she didn't have it in her or that no other guy would ever fancy her enough to try it on? Suddenly, she was consumed by the desire to shock him, hurt him even. Just because he'd ignored her for months he needn't think she was invisible to all men. Defiant she said, 'Not that I didn't want to.'

'I couldn't blame you if you had,' he said, taking off the baseball cap. 'I know I've been a crap husband these last few months.'

She opened her mouth to agree but the look of genuine sadness in his eyes stopped her and he seized his opportunity, saying, 'I promise I'll do anything to make it up to you, just tell me what I can do.'

Sarah sighed, all energy drained from her. 'Treat me like a woman. It's still me behind the supermarket trolley and all the domestic stuff. I haven't disappeared, not quite anyway…and the café, working with Andrew, I'll need your support, more help with the children.' And even as she said the words, she wasn't sure that it was enough.

Tentatively he took her hand, not sure if she would allow it. 'I know I took you for granted and it stops here, right now. I can work from home a couple of days a week so I can do the school run. And the over-spending ...'

Sarah raised her eyebrows.

'Sorry, *my* over spending, keeping up with the Jones, that stops too.'

She nodded but he saw that her gaze had shifted to the sweatshirts on the table.

'And the Coach. This thing with…Ted wasn't it? Is it over?'

Sarah shrugged. 'I was lonely … and he was kind. I soaked it up like a sponge,' she said, almost to herself and she saw him wince. 'Ted's gone and he's not coming back.'

She knew she hadn't answered his question but it was the only truthful one she could give.

Chapter 37

Outside the GP's surgery a volunteer from the local church was handing out leaflets. Rachel tried to scoot past unseen but the woman, practised in her role, managed to press a flyer into her hand. It was an invitation to Harvest Festival the following Sunday. As she waited in the GP's reception, Rachel squashed it into her handbag - anything involving food was off limits. Ten minutes later, the silver-haired doctor stuck his head around the swing door. 'Rachel Ryder.'

Rachel chucked a pre-historic copy of *Woman's Own* on the coffee table and followed him down the narrow corridor to his surgery.

'Take a seat Rachel,' he smiled, shuffling some papers on his desk for good measure before turning to give her his full bedside manner. 'And how are we today?'

'We ... I mean ... I'm not sure really. I feel awful, totally exhausted, even more than usual. I've lost my appetite and I keep getting these sharp pains low down in my stomach.'

The doctor nodded. 'All right, slip off your skirt and jump up on the couch so I can feel your tummy.' Discreetly he turned away, to fiddle importantly with his computer mouse.

Rachel unzipped her skirt and prayed that she would be able to get it back on again, getting into it earlier that morning she'd broken into a sweat. She lay on the couch and crossed her fingers that whatever the trouble was, it wouldn't mean an internal.

'Right, I'll just warm up my hands,' said the doctor and laughing at his own joke washed his hands in the tiny white basin in the corner of the room.

Rachel stared blindly at a poster about the dangers of childhood obesity while he gently pressed her abdomen.

'OK, slip your things back on,' he said returning to his computer.

Her heart thumping, Rachel squeezed herself back into her skirt and joined him at his desk.

'When did you last have your period?' he asked, peering at her, over half moon spectacles.

'That's difficult to say, as you know with the flying and everything, my cycle is erratic to say the least.' Her brow furrowed as she tried to remember. 'I think it was towards the end of June, around the 24th. I've had a bit of spotting since. I don't take much notice of it really. It's topsy turvy.'

He nodded flicking open a tented desk calendar. 'It's certainly well documented that flying can effect a woman's menstrual cycle. I have to ask the question because I believe that you are pregnant.'

Rachel sat in stupefied silence as he slid transparent rulers across the calendar.

'According to when you had your last period and by the feel of your abdomen you are almost three months pregnant. This little ready reckoner tells me that your expected date of delivery is April 1st, which means you conceived around the weekend of July 7th. Congratulations my dear, it looks as though we can cancel that referral to the fertility clinic doesn't it? And don't worry about those niggly pains, that's just your ligaments loosening up to support the baby.'

'Baby...' Rachel said under her breath. 'And the dates, how can you be so sure about the dates?'

'I'd bet a year's salary on it. Women can only conceive on a handful of days in a month and fourteen days on from the start of your last period, which is when you would have been most fertile, is July 7th. Now why does that date ring a bell?' he paused, tapping his fountain pen on his chin. 'Ah yes, that's Regatta weekend isn't it? You'd be amazed the number of conceptions around high days and holidays. And a baby due on April Fool's Day ... well the Regatta can make fools out of most people, especially when they've had a *Pimms* or three!' he chuckled, filling out a pink form and handing it to her. 'Give this in at reception and they'll book you in with the practice mid-wife for your ante-natal appointments.'

Rachel thought back to the Regatta Finals weekend

and flushed darkly. She could only nod and gathering up her things, shut the door behind her with a soft click. As she walked down the corridor towards reception, she recalled the moment when she and Pierre had tumbled into her bed, the covers still creased from where she had slept with Andrew only hours before. She reached the front desk and pushed her pink form past that name plaque, announcing that Barbara was today's receptionist.

Barbara smiled over her computer. 'Congratulations love, you'll receive a list of appointments in the post next week, OK?'

'That's no good. I always have to plan appointments. I fly you see.' Rachel rustled in her handbag for her work roster and then stopped bringing her hand to her mouth. 'What am I saying? ... I'll be grounded as of today.'

'That's lovely dear. You'll be able to have a nice rest before the baby.'

Rachel frowned. 'But if I stop flying everyone will know won't they?'

Barbara gave her a quizzical look and passed her a 'So You're Pregnant - What to Expect' leaflet. 'Everyone will know soon enough love,' she said, pointing to Rachel's midriff.

Rachel clutched the edge of the counter, waves of nausea licking the back of her throat. This was the moment she dreamed of, sharing the news with everyone, especially the baby's father. If only she could be sure who he was ...

'I'm sorry I think I need some air,' she said, and ran out into the car park just in time to see Pierre's car pull in. Spotting her, he drove up to the entrance.

'Hi beautiful. Are you OK with the roof down?'

She nodded and slid into the passenger seat. Pierre slipped the car into first gear and the smooth suspension did nothing to quell her nausea. She hoped he wasn't in the mood for conversation, fearing that if she opened her mouth the vomit would grasp the opportunity and make a break for it. Unfortunately the late summer sunshine and the prospect of a party had put him in a sociable mood.

'It was kind of Sarah's mother to invite us to her engagement party. I've never been to a party on a paddle steamer before.'

Rachel nodded, wondering how she was going to cope with party food and the motion of a boat, even if it was only a gentle cruise up the Thames. They pulled up to a busy T-junction and while Pierre concentrated on the road, she closed her eyes, hoping that he would leave her in peace for the rest of the journey. Eventually a driver took pity on them and waved Pierre out. The traffic was stacked nose to tail, as if half of the South East had decided to come to Henley for a day out and with the air thick with exhaust fumes, Rachel knew it was only a matter of time before her stomach revolted. When it happened there was little warning and she threw up through the open window, leaving a trail of putrid yellow on the gleaming paintwork.

Pierre pulled the handbrake up hard. 'Rachel, what is going on? What did the doctor say? Are you ill?'

Rachel wiped the luminescent spittle from her chin. 'I'm not ill … I'm pregnant.'

'How? When?' he gasped.

Rachel smiled weakly, trying not to breathe vomit fumes in his face. 'Regatta weekend in my bed.' *At least that was the truth, or it could have been the kitchen table and not necessarily with him, but that seemed like a detail too far.*

The light at the end of the street changed to green and the traffic surged forward. Pierre released the hand brake and patted Rachel's knee. 'Our new family.'

Rachel bought his hand up to her cheek. 'I'm so lucky to have you,' she said. *If you knew what I'd done …* She leant back on the headrest and closed her eyes, exhausted by the nausea and the flashbacks to her drunken night with Andrew.

Chapter 38

On board the 'New Orleans' Sarah climbed the stairs to the upper deck, feeling guilty for pretending not to notice Rachel, who had arrived moments before with her gorgeous Frenchman in tow, but she needed a few moments alone. Preparing the Cafe for the grand opening and moving out of the family home into Rup's place, had left her physically and mentally exhausted.

Dwarfed by the boat's giant smoke stacks, she listened to the gentle swish of the paddle wheel and wished more than anything that her mother could have chosen a different venue for the party. When Jean announced that she had booked the nearest thing on the Thames to a Mississippi sternwheeler, she hadn't had the heart to say that the boat would be a painful reminder of Rhett and Scarlett on their honeymoon and the private joke she'd shared with Ted. After all, there were reminders of the Regatta, and therefore of Ted, all over town.

As the boat cast off, a deafening blast from the ship's horn made her jump and she turned to see Millie waving frantically from the bridge. Half-heartedly she waved back and turned once more to face the river. The good weather had drawn the crowds and the tow path was busy with people making the most of the late summer sunshine. Only Sarah didn't see them, her eyes were fixed on a single figure. Standing at the end of a pontoon, less than twenty feet away, was Ted. He raised his hand and smiled. Unable to move Sarah gripped the rail, as all sensation drained from her legs.

The boat continued upstream and Sarah forced her eyes shut, unable to bare the growing distance between them. Suddenly, she was hitching her dress over her hips and clambering onto the handrail, plunging into the water and with a few strokes, was quickly at the riverbank. She felt Ted pull her from the river, gently wiping her wet hair from her face and kissing the water from her eyelashes. They clung together, his clothes absorbing the water from her and she felt the warmth from his body coursing through her skin.

'Mum, Mum!' A small hand tugged hers from the

handrail. Reluctantly, she opened her eyes and looked around.

'Oh, Naomi, it's you.'

'What are you doing Mum? You were standing there with your eyes closed. Daddy says you're always daydreaming!'

'I wasn't daydreaming I was just ...' her voice tailed off, that was exactly what she'd been doing, 'anyway it doesn't matter what I was doing. What do you want?'

'I've got a splinter and it really hurts,' Naomi said and stuck out the offending hand for inspection. 'Can you get it out Mummy, please?'

Sarah squeezed her finger haphazardly. She was desperate to wave to Ted, to make some sort of contact with him before he was out of sight but she resisted the urge in front of Naomi who, with the bionic eyesight of a nine year old, would be bound to spot Ted and then bombard her with questions that she had no hope of answering.

'Ow! Mum you're not doing it properly, you're hurting me!' squealed Naomi, yanking her hand away.

'Sorry darling,' Sarah said, wiping trembling hands down the front of her dress. 'I just can't do it.'

What was she talking about exactly? The splinter, staying married to Dave or waving at Ted; all seemed impossible as she gripped the rail with one hand and brushed away hot tears with the other. Downriver she could see the blue motor boat and a large family group on the riverbank, which had stopped to admire it, but the pontoon was empty. Ted had gone. That's if he had been there at all - or was exhaustion making her hallucinate?

'What is it Mum? What's wrong?' asked Naomi, touching her arm.

Sarah pressed the heels of her hands into her eyes. 'Nothing darling, it's just a bit of hay fever that's all. Let's go and see if we can find a first aid box and sort out that finger.'

Taking Naomi's hand she walked towards the steps to the lower deck, when she heard a splash. Looking over the side she expected to see a Moorhen taking a dive, but there were no ducks and as an aching emptiness filled her chest, she wondered if in a final fit of pique, her heart had finally mutinied, jumping overboard.

Below deck the blue-rinse brigade were giving Jean a rapturous applause for her speech, on the joys of finding new love with George in her twilight years. Other speeches followed and when a tinkling of glass sounded from the corner of the room, Pierre stood up grinning from ear to ear.

'Jean, may I say a few words?' he asked, mesmerising her with his sexy accent. 'Congratulations to you and George and I wish you both bonne chance!' A further burst of applause rippled across the room and Pierre raised his hand. 'I also have some wonderful news to share with you all.'

Across the room, within dashing distance of the ladies toilets Rachel shook her head frantically, signalling for him to stop. Pierre only grinned and carried on regardless. 'Rachel and I are going to be parents. We are expecting a baby!' he beamed, raising his champagne glass in Rachel's direction. 'I must also raise a toast to the river. Rivers have always been symbols of fertility and the Thames is no exception, our baby was conceived during Regatta!'

Cheers of congratulations echoed around the room as guests hustled round Pierre to shake his hand. Everybody seemed to have something to say on the subject except Sarah, who despite enthusiastic prodding from Naomi, was lost for words (she was too busy doing the maths) and instantly she was torn. Who should she comfort first? Andrew, standing at the bar drowning the implications of Pierre's announcement in a pint of lager or Rachel, who'd made a dash for the Ladies as soon as the first glasses were raised? Her mother made the decision for her, hauling Andrew onto the dance floor for the first dance.

When Sarah pushed open the door to the cramped Ladies toilet, she could hear that someone was bringing up the contents of their breakfast. "Rachel, is that you?" she whispered through the lock. 'Are you OK?'

More retching followed while Sarah manned the door and re-directed half a dozen ladies towards the Gents. Finally there was the sound of the toilet flushing and the cubicle door opened.

'Here wipe your face with this,' Sarah said, handing Rachel a baby wipe.

Rachel leaned heavily against the wash basins. 'I think I want to die.'

Sarah knew she should be offering comfort and congratulations but she couldn't quite shape the words. Instead she said. 'The baby's father must be thrilled.'

Startled, Rachel looked up. The look on Sarah's face told her she knew about her drunken fumble with Andrew. 'So you know then?' she said, rubbing the back of her neck with the baby wipe.

Just then the door swung open and one of Jean's golf buddies made for the toilet cubicle. Simultaneously they turned and glared at the woman, sending her scuttling out the door like a frightened rabbit.

'What are you going to do? Presumably either man could be the father?' pressed Sarah.

Rachel nodded. 'Yes, it's possible. The thing is, I'm not even sure that anything happened with Andrew ... but then it might have. God what a mess ... I think I'm going to be sick again.'

Sarah took one of the kid's juice cartons from her handbag. 'Here, sip this slowly and take deep breaths.'

Rachel took a tentative sip, but the sweet juice made her gag. 'Sorry, nothing seems to stay down at the moment,' she said, wiping her mouth with the back of her hand. 'Pierre's the father. Anything else would be just too hideous.'

Sarah gripped the edge of the wash basin, she knew that the uncertainty was making Rachel insensitive but at that moment she wondered if she knew her at all, and if she really wanted to. 'Rachel, how could you!' she said, making for the door. 'You could be talking about my brother's child and you know how much he loves children.'

Rachel grabbed her arm. 'Don't go! I'm ruining everything aren't I? I didn't mean it like that, honestly Sarah, you know I didn't. It's just that I want this baby so much and it has to be Pierre's. Surely you can see that!'

Sarah shook her off. 'Are you trying to tell me that even if it's Andrew's child, you're planning on playing happy families with Pierre? You're prepared to live a lie?'

Rachel's body stiffened, as if expecting a blow and, defiant, she said, 'Yes, if you put it like that, I am.'

Sarah glared at her, trembling with rage. 'You make me sick with your lies. You'll lie about this baby the same way you lied to me about Dave, he told me about Gemma and the flight to New York - the one you claimed to know nothing about. You should have told me Rachel. It's what a real friend would have done, but why should I expect anything else from you? You're as fake as your *Prada*,' Sarah said, jabbing at Rachel's handbag with disgust.

Rachel rounded on her in an instant, eyes blazing like black coals. 'For fuck's sake get over yourself Miss Butter Wouldn't Melt Holier Than Thou! You think you've got the moral high ground, turning your nose up at Botox and designer rip-offs and getting your knickers in a twist about Dave. Tell me Sarah, what's your definition of infidelity - a meaningless fumble or falling in love with someone, even if you haven't got the courage to do anything about it?'

Sarah stared at her, open mouthed.

Determined Rachel continued. 'Well? That's what happened wasn't it, with Ted? Maybe you'll have to take a leaf out of my book for a change and bluff a little. After all, you've been dealt a good hand, almost a full deck – you've got your kids, your family, your café and you're living in a bloody mansion. Me? I'm a one trick pony. Without Pierre that's it, game over.'

They stared at each other in stunned silence, until at last Sarah nodded and, knowing the ties of their friendship were stretched to breaking point, turned to leave. Rachel let her go. She made a deal of looking for something in her handbag until she heard the door softly click to a close.

Still shaking, Sarah re-joined the party; standing on the edge of the dance floor she watched Dave, with Harry on his shoulders, twirling Naomi and Millie by the hands. He caught sight of her and beckoned her over and lifting Harry onto the floor, he said, 'Girls you can take care of Harry now. I want to dance with Mummy.'

Sarah stared at him in amazement; normally he would avoid dancing at all costs and she would end up doing a shuffle around her handbag with a group of women. This time Dave took the lead and taking her hands, pulled her close, and began to move in a way that was too slow for the music. At one time, she would have protested, embarrassed, but now she lay her head against his chest grateful for the comfort. She looked beyond the curve of Dave's arm, Andrew was busy propping up the bar and Rachel was standing at the opposite end of the boat, half leaning over the side trying to quell her nausea.

Maybe Rachel was right she told herself, as she let Dave sway her gently to the music - she could learn to bluff a little - but in the face of her biggest ever challenge, the real question was, could Rachel?

A waiter passed by with a tray and Dave reached for two glasses of champagne. Handing her one, he said. 'Great news about the pregnancy.'

Sarah nodded watching the riverside mansions slip past.

'Look there's Fotheringham-Allen's place, or should I say home?' laughed Dave.

Sarah looked towards the Edwardian villa, with its balconies and wide stone steps leading down to a sweep of immaculate lawn; it was a beautiful house and she was grateful to be living there, but it wasn't home. They rattled round inside and the children couldn't hear her when she called them down for tea - she had to pull on a lever in the kitchen which would sound a bell upstairs - she missed hearing the children's chatter.

She didn't suppose it would have been a problem for Rup and as his house disappeared from view, she wondered what had become of him. Nobody knew where he was and it seemed everyone was glad to see the back of him. Her own feelings were ambivalent; if he hadn't cleared off before sorting things out with Andrew, Andrew wouldn't have got drunk and slept with Rachel and if Rup hadn't persuaded Dave to host the crew, she wouldn't have had her head messed up by meeting Ted. And yet she had no regrets, and she suspected as she thought about how much Rachel wanted her baby, neither did she.

Dave wrapped his arm around her shoulders and she responded, tucking her arm around his waist.

'Penny for them?' he asked.

'I was thinking about Rup and if I was to meet him again, whether I would hit him or give him a great big hug.'

Chapter 39

Sarah parked her car next to Andrew's van and felt the same thrill she felt every morning, when she read the sign announcing to the world that she, Sarah Crouch, was the proprietor of Water Meadow's Café. She glanced at the dash board clock before grabbing her water bottle, 6.00am. Asking herself what time Andrew had arrived, she got out of the car and hearing a crunch of gravel behind her, swung round to see him carrying a crate of asparagus into the farm shop. 'Hey, don't I even get a good morning anymore?' she called after him.

Moments later his dishevelled head appeared around the door. 'Sorry Sarah, I was trying to remember how much asparagus Mirabel's restaurant had ordered. Miles away I'm afraid,' he said, rubbing the dark circles under his eyes.

'Andrew,' she asked, lifting a crate of cherry tomatoes off the floor and carrying it through to the shop, 'what time did you go home last night?'

He shrugged and busied himself unloading the crates.

Noticing his dirty clothes, she said, 'You didn't go home did you?'

'No, I prefer to keep busy, keep my mind off things ...'

As Rachel's due date got ever nearer, Sarah had been stealing herself for this moment and tentatively she said, 'I know... have you decided what to do, about the baby, I mean?'

He took the crate from her, banging it down on the counter top so the tomatoes bounced onto the floor like red bingo balls. 'What I always do I guess. I'm the kind, thoughtful one aren't I? Charging across the channel and into the maternity hospital to snatch a baby is hardly my style is it?'

Sarah bent down and began to pick up the fruit, checking each one for damage. 'So what is your style Andrew?' She asked quietly. 'This could be your son or daughter we're talking about.'

'Please Sarah. Believe me I've thought about nothing

else since the pregnancy was announced but the baby could just as easily be Pierre's. If I go in all guns blazing it'll destroy their relationship.'

Sarah tipped a handful of spoiled tomatoes into the bin, licking the juice from her fingers. 'So you're just going to give up without a fight, is that it?'

'For God's sake Sarah, think about it! Everything I own is tied up in the farm, I live here, Rachel's in France, and I'm gay for goodness sake. Pierre's a great guy, he's stinking rich and he loves Rachel,' he said, taking a cloth and wiping up the spilt tomato juice. 'I've decided it's better for everyone if I'm a favourite uncle.'

'And have you told Rachel?'

'Not yet, but I will, when I call her to congratulate her about the baby.'

'And you're really sure about this?'

'Completely,' he said, giving her a gentle shove, 'so you can get off my case and go for your run. I need you back here and nose to the grindstone by 7am sharp!' He set about tidying the display racks, signally that the conversation was over.

So, Sarah set off on her run, jogging along the footpath to the river and the sun was warm on her back, as she turned towards Henley. In the river meadows, she passed the bandstand, its silver octagon roof shaped like a giant mandarin hat, and the children's merry go-rounds silent and snoozing, wrapped in their thick tarpaulin night blankets. As she ran, she enjoyed the way her body responded to her demands. Dave had been true to his word, agreeing to manage the morning routine at home, so that she could make an early start at the café and squeeze a little 'me time' into the bargain. Several months of exercise had done her stamina the power of good and she knew that she wouldn't be out of breath again until she had crossed the bridge, and joined the tow path that ran parallel with the Regatta course. Even thinking about that part of her run made her shiver.

Impatiently, she jogged on the spot, waiting for a lull in the traffic and crossed the bridge to pass by the Leander

Rowing Club. The path led down to the river and on the launching docks, a crew of female rowers were lifting their boat into the water.

Further along the towpath she sent a gaggle of Canadian geese scattering into the water. Along the Regatta course, towards Temple Island, the horizon was shrouded in mist and she could pick out the faint silhouette of a pair of swans and breaking the water between them, a single oarsman.

She picked up speed, her breath coming in short bursts, her eyes riveted to the lettering on the oarsman's back, a single red 'B'. Pulling down her baseball cap to shield her face, she glanced at her watch, 6.45. Soon, Dave would be waking the kids, pouring cereal into three identical white bowls, searching for PE kit and school ties. Maybe tomorrow she would wave or shout hello, but for now... for today, it was enough.

Chapter 40

Leaving the bustle of Charles de Gaulle airport behind her, Rachel stepped off the chilly jet way into the soothing warmth of the first class cabin.

'Good afternoon Madam, welcome on board our flight to Mauritius. My name is Simone and I will be looking after you,' said a petite stewardess, so neat and perfect in her pin tucked uniform she reminded Rachel of a souvenir doll.

Ignoring the fact that Simone's gaze had shifted to her heavily pregnant abdomen Rachel said, 'I know you're supposed to show us to our seats but I need to visit the ladies room rather urgently.'

While Simone demonstrated the intricacies of the first class toilet, including how to flush, Rachel feigned polite interest, and when she was at last alone, peed barely enough to fill a teaspoon. It had been this way since the baby's head had engaged, an almost perpetual and urgent need to go, followed by a disproportionate end result. On her way out, a different stewardess offered to show her to her seat; one of four, crafted from leather and walnut as befitted first class, and as Goldilocks would have recognised, it was first and foremost a Daddy Bear's Chair. In Rachel's absence Simone had wasted no time in showing Pierre what buttons he should press, to turn his Daddy Bear's Chair into Daddy Bear's flat bed.

'Oh! Excuse me,' Rachel said, accidentally on purpose pushing her bump against Simone. It wasn't simply that the girl was flirting with Pierre that pissed her off, or even her size 8 waist; it was the girl's flawless complexion. Since the second tri-mester Rachel had developed a rash of freckles, giving her the appearance of someone, who only moments before had suffered a nasty encounter with an exploding caramel flavoured yogurt.

Oblivious to Rachel's icy glare, the young stewardess made a show of making her comfortable and disappearing to the galley, she returned after a few minutes with drinks and a plate of pre-flight snacks.

Pierre clinked his glass of champagne against Rachel's tumbler of mineral water. 'To you, and a wonderful holiday.'

'To *us*,' she grinned. 'I hope we're doing the right thing by staying at one of your hotels. Won't it be hard for the staff to treat you as a guest rather than the boss?'

Pierre grinned. 'Not at all. You've seen my new swimming trunks! The staff have never seen me in Hawaiian print before, I think they'll realise I'm on vacation.' He kissed her cheek and returned to his copy of *Le Monde*. Rachel amused herself watching Simone and her colleague buzzing back and forth, handing out hot towels, sleeper suits and enough reading material to fill a corner shop. When it was her turn, she declined the sleeper suit; her a-line maternity dress and stretch leggings with elasticated tummy pouch were comfortable enough but she gladly accepted a copy of *Vogue* and set about planning what she would buy as soon as she lost her baby weight.

Shortly after take-off, Simone reappeared with menus and wine lists and was at pains to emphasize that dining was a la carte; customers were invited to eat whatever and whenever they liked. It was every pregnant woman's dream and music to Rachel's ears; if she fancied a cheese and marmalade sandwich in the middle of the night, Simone wouldn't bat a Clarins Flash Balmed eyelid - she'd even cut the crusts off.

After a further round of drinks and canapés, Rachel settled back to watch *Pretty Woman* on her individual flat screen television and tried to ignore the dull ache that had suddenly appeared in her lower back.

When she awoke several hours later the film had ended and the screen was prompting her politely, to make her next selection from the extensive on-board film library. The dull back pain had developed into an insistent throbbing and indigestion was making her feel sick. She pressed the call bell and when Simone appeared, she asked for a glass of water and an extra pillow. Telling herself that the pains were nothing more than indigestion she sipped the water and, as she'd been taught in her ante-natal class, breathed deeply; it was simply her old wind problem come back to haunt her, nothing to worry about. She tried to squeeze out gas, nothing happened, she tried harder until a searing pain gripped her - front to back - holding her rigid in its grasp. Whatever this was, it wasn't indigestion. Should she tell Pierre what she suspected? He looked so peaceful sipping brandy, absorbed in a black and white art house movie in which very little appeared to be happening. She couldn't ask him for advice, he'd never been pregnant, but then, neither had she. She needed a woman, someone she could trust; someone with experience.

Rachel eyed the phone nestling in the wide armrest of her seat. Sarah was just a credit card swipe and a satellite link away, but other than exchanging Christmas cards, they hadn't spoken since the boat party. Sarah had made it crystal clear where her loyalties lay, but she would hardly hang up on her considering the circumstances, would she? Desperate to hear her voice, Rachel picked up the phone and dialled. Pressing it to her ear she could hear ringing at the other end and after what felt like an eternity it clicked and she heard a voice, heavy with sleep.

'Hello.'

'Sarah, it's Rachel. I know I'm not your favourite person right now and that you're not really talking to me but I'm in trouble. I think I'm in labour!'

Rachel heard Sarah yawn and she imagined her propping herself up on her elbows and peering at her bedside clock.

'Rachel, do you have any idea what time it is? You can't be in labour, it's too soon. I'm sure it's just Braxton Hicks, a practice contraction.'

A searing pain shot through Rachel's body and she gasped into the phone.

Sarah's voice became suddenly alert. 'That didn't sound like a Braxton Hicks. How often are these pains coming?'

'Every few minutes,' whispered Rachel, close to tears.

'OK, try to stay calm. Your baby has decided to arrive a little early that's all but it's nothing to worry about, Pierre will have you at the hospital in no time.'

'No, he won't.'

'Oh crickey, is he away on business? As soon as you put the phone down from me, call a taxi.'

'I can't.'

'Oh God, they're not on strike are they? The bloody French, they're always striking about something. You'll have to call an ambulance, please tell me they're not on strike too.'

There was a silence as Rachel rallied through another contraction.

'It wouldn't make any difference if they were. I'm on an aeroplane somewhere over the Indian ocean.'

Rachel heard Sarah's sharp intake of breath followed by a gulp.

'Bloody hell!'

'Exactly, what am I going to do? I'm definitely in labour, aren't I?' asked Rachel, gripping the arm rests as she was swamped by another wave of pain.

'Yes, I think you are,' said Sarah, 'and I'll tell you what you are going to do, you are going to get that plane diverted to the nearest hospital and you are going to have your baby and everything is going to be OK, OK?'

Rachel sniffed, trying hard not to cry. 'Yes, I am, and Sarah … I know you're cross with me but can we be friends again, I miss you so much?'

Rachel heard a smile in Sarah's voice.

'I miss you too … and of course we're still friends. You just concentrate on your baby … whoever's it is doesn't matter as long as you're both alright.'

Tearfully Rachel said goodbye and hung up. She couldn't decide what was more terrifying, the prospect of giving birth on an aeroplane or finally having the answer to the question that had plagued her since the doctor confirmed her dates. In her mind's eye she pictured Pierre and Andrew standing side by side; Pierre dark and brooding, and Andrew blonde and blue eyed. What should have been her greatest joy had turned into a game of Russian Roulette. If the odds were in her favour she could look forward to bringing up baby with Pierre, in the lavender scented vineyard Pierre had recently purchased, if not … a paternity test on daytime TV?

'Pierre,' she said, touching his arm with a trembling hand. 'The baby.'

'I know chérie,' he smiled and reaching over, placed his hand on her stomach. 'It won't be long now.'

He left his hand where it was and his gaze drifted back to his video screen. Rachel felt the beginning of another contraction and as her abdominal muscles tightened against Pierre's hand he turned to look at her, his eyes wide with alarm. 'Chérie?'

Rachel burst into tears. 'I'm in labour.'

'But you can't be, it's too early.'

'Try telling that to the baby,' said Rachel, her face glistening with perspiration. 'I think we should tell the crew.'

The colour drained from Pierre's face and he pressed the call bell. Simone appeared as if by magic and crouched down beside his chair to give him her undivided attention. Pierre spoke to her in rapid French and moments later she swiveled round on her heels to face Rachel. With her features twitching like frightened rabbit, she said, 'Madam, if you feel able, please could I ask you to come with me to the galley where we will have some privacy.'

Pierre was already on his feet and between them they helped Rachel take the few steps into the galley area, where Simone pulled down one of the crew seats.

'Thanks. I'd rather stand, it feels more comfortable,' Rachel said, gripping on to the edge of the galley worktop and swiveling her hips like the woman she'd seen on her 'Giving Birth the Natural Way' DVD. Simone nodded and picked up the phone to call the Cabin Service Director. Seconds later he appeared, visibly shaken and he explained that he would put out an immediate call for a 'health professional'. They stared awkwardly at each other while they waited for a response, as if at a party where no one had been properly introduced.

After a few minutes a crew member stepped through the curtain, followed by an attractive well dressed man in his late twenties. He shook Rachel's hand and introduced himself in broken English as Marc. Then he shook hands with Pierre and said something in French.

Unable to understand Rachel watched Pierre's face for clues. He seemed to be wrestling with his emotions, at first he had looked relieved but now he was looking worried. Marc had put himself forward as a health professional but what type? A Podiatrist? A Speech Therapist? Somewhere in between the two would be preferable thought Rachel grimly, and she released her grip on the work counter, giving Pierre's hand a squeeze of reassurance. 'Everything's going to be alright - at least we have a doctor.'

Pierre squeezed her hand in return and looked anxiously at Marc. 'Marc's not a doctor Rachel, he's a vet.'

Rachel's mouth opened and closed in disbelief.

'Please try not to worry; he says that he has delivered many times. He assisted with a birth only a week ago,' said Pierre, rubbing her back with his free hand.

'And what may I ask, was giving birth? A fucking poodle?' gasped Rachel, panting hard, gripped in another contraction.

Pierre pretended not to have heard and taking a cold towel from Simone's trembling hand, began to mop Rachel's brow. Meanwhile the Cabin Service Director had flipped open a medical manual and was showing it to Marc, who relayed questions to Pierre, who in turn translated for Rachel.

'Chérie, they need to know about your pregnancy and what you are experiencing now.'

Rachel rolled her eyes, only a man would describe labour as an experience. '34 weeks, normal pregnancy, first baby or should that be first litter, and what I'm experiencing now is agony … about once every five minutes.'

She said the last words to the galley floor as she hunched over with the pain. Pierre relayed the information to Marc and gripping the Cabin Service Director's arm he said, 'We must divert. She can not have the baby on a plane.'

'That is normal practice I assure you, sir,' said the CSD in English, for Rachel's benefit. 'The captain has been informed but I have to advise you that our nearest airport is now Mauritius, our scheduled destination.'

At which point Marc disappeared through the galley curtain and Rachel screamed. 'Where's he going? Pierre, bring him back! Vet or no vet, he's all I've got!'

'He's gone to wash his hands,' said Pierre, gently stroking back the damp hair sticking to her forehead. 'He will examine you when he gets back.'

Rachel buried her face in his chest, and tried not to think of the last place Marc had stuck his fingers. When he returned Marc snapped on a pair of surgical gloves and Simone spread a layer of newspapers on the galley floor and covered them with blankets and a first class duvet. Pierre and the cabin crew cleared the galley, leaving Rachel alone with the vet, and she didn't know whether to speak or moo. To her relief and in spite of the fact that his normal patients slept in baskets, Marc's bedside manner was gentle and reassuring and he explained with his thumb and forefinger that she was 6 centimetres dilated. Rachel took a slippery grip on his gloved hands and pleaded with him. 'I'm counting on you. You have to deliver my baby safely.'

It was a tall order. From her experience as Cabin Crew she knew what he would have available to him in the onboard medical kit; there were the usual suspects, needles, syringes and dressings, and for cases such as hers, a ventouse and forceps, but certainly nothing resembling pain relief. She would have to bite on something hard and hope for the best, even if it meant chewing on a dog biscuit.

Taking off his gloves Marc poked his head through the galley curtain to ask Pierre and Simone, now part of the midwifery team, to join them. As they mopped her brow and fed her sips of iced water, Rachel concentrated on mind over matter, imploring her cervix to open quickly; even with the best pilot in the world, landing with a passenger in the second stage of labour would be dangerous for mother, child and vets in attendance.

After an hour of mounting pain she felt a surge of liquid burst from between her legs. Marc announced that she was ready to push and she was vaguely aware that he was on his knees probing her bottom like an archeologist on a dig, and she had had enough.

'Stop fannying about and get this baby out,' she hollered, her face turning puce as another contraction ripped through her.

'You're doing a good job of that yourself,' encouraged Pierre, peering between her legs. 'I can see the baby's head.'

Rachel felt a new pain - a burning and splitting between her legs - as she pushed down. In spite of her agony she needed to know, was the baby blonde or brunette? Gasping for breath she screamed at Pierre. 'What colour is it?'

'What? The colour of what?' he asked, wincing as her nails pierced his skin.

'The baby's hair! What colour is the baby's hair?'

Pierre stuck his head between her thighs concentrating hard, as if he was changing a tyre. Rachel ignored the indignity; *Kwik-Fit*, the *AA* and the bloody *RAC* could look for all she cared. All she wanted to know was the colour of the baby's hair for Christ's sake! Why was that such a bloody challenge? Surely she was the one with the difficult job.

Pierre looked up through the gap in her thighs. 'I'm sorry Rachel. I really can't tell, it's covered in white stuff, like goat's cheese.'

Rachel groaned and bit down hard on a cushion. How could he be thinking of food at a time like this? She knew that there was only one thing to end agony, both physical and psychological, and that was to push the baby out, once and for all. With super human effort every cell in her body pushed down. Marc continued to murmur words of encouragement and Pierre suddenly remembered his role of translator.

'That's it, well done,' he soothed. 'The head is out, one more gentle push and we'll have your baby.'

Then, in one sudden wet, sliding, sinewy moment Rachel's body emptied itself and spent, she sank back into Pierre's arms. Exhaustion swamped her, more draining than the worst jet-lag and the space between her legs, felt cavernous and vulnerable.

'A son! Rachel, we have a son!' Pierre gasped. Tears rolled down his cheeks unchecked, but Rachel's eyes remained fixed on the baby's tiny puckered face. Tears welled in her eyes, bloodshot from the effort of labour. 'Why isn't he crying? Is he alright? Please, tell me he's alright.'

Marc answered, all his attention fixed on the baby, as he concentrated on clearing his tiny airways. Pierre translated, his voice choked with emotion. 'He's fine. He has some mucus in his nose and he needs oxygen to get his breathing underway. It's completely normal ... please don't worry.'

Suddenly, as if remembering his part of the bargain the baby's tiny chest shuddered and his spindly legs shot out, ramrod straight like tent pegs. Marc lifted the oxygen mask from the baby's face and wrapped him closely in a blanket, before lifting him onto Rachel's stomach. Instinctively she reached down to cradle him and with her free hand felt inside his tightly bound papoose, to touch his face.

Simone looked at her watch and announced in a hushed voice. 'Time of birth 3.30 a.m., local time.'

Rachel gasped as she felt a contraction followed by a sudden urge to push. She'd forgotten about the placenta and how delivering it could sometimes be as dangerous as giving birth to the baby. She pushed down hard, determined not to be beaten by this final obstacle and minutes later, felt its smooth mass slide between her thighs. Marc gathered it quickly into a biohazard bag, ready to be examined by the medical team when they reached hospital. Finally, he cut the umbilical cord and took the blanket Simone was holding in readiness, placing it gently over Rachel's lap.

Rachel held the baby close. Tightly bound in his blanket he reminded her of a chrysalis and she watched his eyes moving under their translucent lids; he was already dreaming. He jumped suddenly, as if startled and his eyes flew open making Rachel catch her breath. For a moment they stared at one another, each taking the measure of the other. And then, as if satisfied that she understood, some unspoken message, the baby sighed and closed his eyes, relieved his first journey was over at last.

With her fingertip Rachel traced a line from his chin to the soft down on the top of his ear, furled around itself like a flower bud. In his face she could see no part of herself; he was the image of his father.

Printed in the United Kingdom by
Lightning Source UK Ltd., Milton Keynes
2499UK00001B/176/P